# THE ALLEN HOUSE

OR,

TWENTY YEARS AGO AND NOW

T. S. ARTHUR

1st WORLD
LIBRARY
Literary Society

# The Allen House

## T. S. Arthur

© 1st World Library – Literary Society, 2005
PO Box 2211
Fairfield, IA 52556
www.1stworldlibrary.org
First Edition

LCCN: 2004195679

Softcover ISBN: 1-4218-0494-8
Hardcover ISBN: 1-4218-0394-1
eBook ISBN: 1-4218-0594-4

Purchase *"The Allen House"*
as a traditional bound book at:
www.1stWorldLibrary.org/purchase.asp?ISBN=1-4218-0494-8

1st World Library Literary Society is a nonprofit
organization dedicated to promoting literacy by:

- Creating a free internet library accessible from any
computer worldwide.
- Hosting writing competitions and offering book
publishing scholarships.

***The Allen House***
*contributed by Tim, Ed & Rodney*
*in support of*
*1st World Library Literary Society*

# PREFACE.

WE point to two ways in life, and if the young man and maiden, whose feet are lingering in soft green meadows and flowery walks, will consider these two ways in sober earnest, before moving onward, and choose the one that truth and reason tell them leads to honor, success, and happiness, our book will accomplish its right work for them. It is a sad thing, after the lapse of twenty years, to find ourselves amid ruined hopes; - to sit down with folded hands and say, "Thus far life has been a failure!" Yet, to how many is this the wretched summing up at the end of a single score of years from the time that reason takes the helm! Alas! that so few, who start wrong, ever succeed in finding the right way; life proving, even to its last burdened years, a miserable failure!

# CHAPTER I.

THE rain had poured in torrents all day, and now, for the third time since morning, I came home, wet, uncomfortable and weary. I half dreaded to look at the slate, lest some urgent call should stare me in the face.

"It must indeed be a case of life and death, that takes me out again to-night," said I, as my good wife met me in the entry, and with light hands, made active by love, assisted in the removal of my great coat and comforter.

"Now come into the sitting-room," she said, "your slippers are on the rug, and your dressing-gown warmed and waiting. Tea is ready, and will be on the table by the time you feel a little comfortable. What a dreadful day it has been!"

"Dreadful for those who have been compelled to face the storm," I remarked, as I drew off my boots, and proceeded to take advantage of all the pleasant arrangements my thoughtful wife had ready for my solace and delight.

It was on my lip to inquire if any one had called since I went out, but the ringing of the tea-bell sent my thought in a new direction; when, with my second self leaning on an arm, and my little Aggy holding tightly by my hand, I moved on to the dining-room, all the disagreeable things of the day forgotten.

"Has any one been here?" I asked, as I handed my cup for a third replenishing. Professional habit was too strong - the query would intrude itself.

"Mrs. Wallingford called to see you."

"Ah! Is anybody sick?"

"I believe so - but she evaded my inquiry, and said that she wished to speak a word with the Doctor."

"She don't want me to call over to-night, I hope. Did she leave any word?"

"No. She looked troubled in her mind, I thought."

"No other call?"

"Yes. Mary Jones sent word that something was the matter with the baby. It cried nearly all last night, her little boy said, and to-day has fever, and lies in a kind of stupor."

"That case must be seen to," I remarked, speaking to myself.

"You might let it go over until morning," suggested my wife. "At any rate, I would let them send again before going. The child may be better by this time."

"A call in time may save life here, Constance," I made answer; the sense of duty growing stronger as the inner and outer man felt the renovating effects of a good supper, and the brightness and warmth of my pleasant home. "And life, you know, is a precious thing - even a baby's life."

And I turned a meaning glance upon the calm, sweet face of our latest born, as she lay sleeping in her cradle. That was enough. I saw the tears spring instantly to the eyes of my wife.

"I have not a word to say. God forbid, that in the weakness of love and care for you, dear husband, I should draw you aside from duty. Yes - yes! The life of a baby is indeed a precious thing!"

And bending over the cradle, she left a kiss on the lips, and a tear on the pure brow of our darling. Now was I doubly strengthened for the night. There arose at this instant a wild storm-wail, that shrieked for a brief time amid the chimneys, and around the eaves of our dwelling, and then went moaning away, sadly, dying at last in the far distance. The rain beat heavily against the windows. But I did not waver, nor seek for reasons to warrant a neglect of duty. "I must see Mary Jones's baby, and that to-night." I said this to myself, resolutely, by way of answer to the intimidating storm.

Mrs. Jones was a widow, and poor. She lived full a quarter of a mile away. So in deciding to make the visit that night, I hardly think a very strong element of self-interest was included in the motives that governed me. But that is irrelevant.

"As there is no prospect of an abatement in the storm," said I, after returning to our cosy little sitting-room, "it may be as well for me to see the baby at once. The visit will be over, so far as I am concerned, and precious time may be gained for the patient."

"I will tell Joseph to bring around the horse," said my wife.

"No - I will walk. Poor beast! He has done enough for one day, and shall not be taken out again."

"Horse-flesh is not so precious as man-flesh," Constance smiled entreatingly, as she laid her hand upon my shoulder. "Let Tom be harnessed up; it won't hurt him."

"The merciful man is merciful to his beast," I made answer. "If horse-flesh is cheaper than man-flesh, like most cheap articles, it is less enduring. Tom must rest, if his master cannot."

"The decision is final, I suppose."

"I must say yes."

"I hardly think your great coat is dry yet," said my wife. "I had it hung before the kitchen fire. Let me see."

"You must wait for ten, or fifteen minutes longer," she remarked, on returning from the kitchen. "One sleeve was completely wetted through, and I have turned it in order to get the lining dry."

I sat down and took Agnes on my lap, and was just getting into a pleasant talk with her, when the door-bell rung. A shadow fell across my wife's face.

"People are thoughtless of Doctors," she remarked, a little fretfully, "and often choose the worst weather and the most untimely seasons to send for them."

T. S. Arthur

I did not answer, but listened as the boy went to the door. Some one was admitted, and shown into the office.

"Who is it?" I enquired, as Joseph came to the sitting-room.

"Mrs. Wallingford."

My wife and I exchanged glances. She looking grave and curious; but no remark was made.

"Good-evening, Mrs. Wallingford," said I, on entering my office. "This is a very bad night for a lady to come out. I hope no one is seriously ill."

"I wish you would come over and see our Henry, Doctor."

There was a choking tremor in her voice; and as I looked in her face, I saw that it was pale and distressed.

"What's the matter?" I inquired.

"I can't say what it is, Doctor. Something's wrong. I'm afraid - yes, I'm afraid he's going out of his senses."

And she wrung her hands together with a nervous uneasiness in singular contrast with her usual quiet exterior.

"How is he affected?"

"Well, Doctor, he came home last evening looking as white as a sheet. I almost screamed out when I saw the strange, suffering expression on his colorless face. My first thought was that he had fallen somewhere, and been hurt dreadfully. He tried to pass me without stopping; but I put both hands on him, and said - 'Oh, Henry! what does ail you?' 'Nothing of any account,' he answered, in a low, husky tone. 'I don't feel right well, and am going to my room to lie down.' And saying this, he brushed right past me, and went up stairs. I followed after him, but when I tried his door it was fastened on the inside. I called three times before he answered, and then he said - 'Mother, I'm not sick; but I feel bad and want to be alone. Please don't disturb me to-night.' I don't think I would have known the voice if it hadn't been just then and there. Knowing his disposition, anxious and troubled as I was, I felt that it would be best for the time being to let him alone. And I did so. For an hour or more all in his room was as still as death, and I began to grow very uneasy. Then I heard his feet upon the floor moving about. I heard him walk to his bureau - my ears served me for eyes - then to the mantlepiece, and then to the window. All was still again for some minutes. My heart beat like a hammer, as one vague suggestion after another floated through my mind. Then he crossed the room with a slow step; turned and went back again; and so kept on walking to and fro. I listened, waiting for the sound to cease; nut he walked on and on, backwards and forwards, backwards and forwards, tramp, tramp, tramp, until it seemed as if every jarring footfall was on my heart. Oh, Doctor! I never had anything to affect me so before in my whole life. An hour passed, and still he walked the floor of his room. I could bear it no longer, and went and called to him. But he seemed deaf, and made no reply. I rattled at the lock and called again and again. Then he came close to the door, and said, speaking a little impatiently for him -

T. S. Arthur

'Mother! Mother! For Heaven's sake don't trouble me! I don't feel just right, and you must let me alone for the present.'

"Well, he kept on walking for an hour longer, and then everything was still in his room for the night. This morning on trying his door it was unfastened. I went in. He was lying in bed wide awake. But, oh! such a change as I saw in his face. It was colorless as on the evening before; but less expressive of emotion. A dead calm seemed to have settled upon it. I took his hand; it was cold. I pressed his forehead; it was cold also. 'Henry, my son, how are you?' I asked. He did not reply; but looked in my face with a cold, steady gaze that chilled me. 'Are you sick, my son?' He merely shook his head slowly. 'Has anything happened? What has happened?' I pressed my question upon him; but it was of no use. He would not satisfy me. I then asked if he would not rise. 'Not yet,' he said. 'Shall I bring you some breakfast?' 'No - no - I cannot eat.' And he shook his head and shut his eyes, while there came into his face a look so sad and suffering that as I gazed on him I could not keep the tears back.

"And it has been no better with him all the day, Doctor," added Mrs. Wallingford, heaving a long sigh. "Oh, I am distressed to death about it. Won't you come and see him? I'm afraid if something isn't done that he will lose his senses."

"Have you no conjecture as to the cause of this strange condition of mind?" I asked.

"None," she replied. "Henry is a reserved young man, you know, Doctor; and keeps many things hidden in his mind even from me that should be outspoken."

"Has he no love affair on hand?"

"I think not."

"Hasn't he been paying attention to Squire Floyd's daughter?"

"Delia?"

"Yes."

"I believe not, Doctor."

"I've seen him at the Squire's."

"Nothing serious, or I should have known of it. Henry is rather shy about the girls."

"And you wish me to see him to-night?"

"Yes. Something ought to be done."

"What is his condition just now?" I inquired. "How did you leave him?"

"He's been in bed nearly all day, and hasn't touched a mouthful. To all my persuasions and entreaties he answers - 'Please, mother, let me alone. I will be better after a while.'"

"I think," said I, after musing on the case, "that, may be, the let-alone prescription will be the best one for the present. He is prostrated by some strong mental emotion - that seems clear; and time must be given for the mind to regain its equipoise. If I were to call, as you desire, it might annoy or irritate him, and so do

T. S. Arthur

more harm than good. No medicine that I can give is at all likely to reach his case."

Mrs. Wallingford looked disappointed, and demurred strongly to my conclusion.

I'm sure, Doctor, if you saw him you might suggest something. Or, may be, he would open his mind to you."

"I'll think it over," said I. "Mrs. Jones has sent for me to see her baby to-night. I was just about starting when you called. On my way back, if, on reflection, it seems to me advisable, I will drop in at your house."

"Call at any rate, Doctor," urged Mrs. Wallingford. "Even if you don't see Henry, you may be able to advise me as to what I had better do."

I gave my promise, and the troubled mother went back through storm and darkness to her home. By this time my overcoat was thoroughly dried. As Constance brought it forth warm from the fire, she looked into my face with an expression of inquiry. But I was not ready to speak in regard to Mrs. Wallingford, and, perceiving this at a glance, she kept silence on that subject.

As I opened the front door, the storm swept into my face; but I passed out quickly into the night, and shielding myself with an umbrella, as best I could, bent to the rushing wind, and took my solitary way in the direction of Mrs. Jones's humble dwelling, which lay quite upon the outskirts of our town. To reach my destination, I had to pass the Old Allen House, which stood within a high stone enclosure, surrounded by stately elms a century old, which spread their great arms above and around the decaying mansion, as if to ward off the encroachments of time. As I came opposite the gate opening upon the carriage way, I stopped suddenly in surprise, for light streamed out from both windows of the north-west chamber, which I knew had been closed ever since the death of Captain Allen, who passed to his account several years before.

This Allen House was one of the notable places in our town; and the stories in circulation touching the Allen family, now almost extinct, were so strongly tinctured with romance, that sober-minded people generally received them with a large measure of incredulity.

The spacious old two-story mansion, with its high-pitched roof and rows of dormer windows, was built by the father of Captain Allen, who had also followed the sea, and, it was said, obtained his large wealth through means not sanctioned by laws human or divine. Men and women of the past generation, and therefore contemporaries, did not hesitate to designate him an "old pirate," though always the opprobrious words were spoken in an undertone, for people were half afraid of the dark, reserved, evil-looking man, who had evidently passed a large portion of his life among scenes of peril and violence. There were more pleasing traditions of the beautiful wife he brought home to grace the luxurious dwelling he had fitted up in a style of almost princely splendor, compared with the plain abode of even the best off people in town. Who she was, or from whence she came, no one knew certainly. She was very young - almost a child - when the elder Captain Allen brought her to S -.

Very little intercourse, I believe, passed between the Allen family and the town's-people, except in a

T. S. Arthur

business way. The first regular entry made into the house beyond the formal drawing-room, was on the occasion of a birth, when the best nurse and gossip in town was summoned to attend the young mistress. A son was born. He was called John; though not under the sign of Christian baptism - John Allen; afterwards Captain Allen. The old sea-dog, his father, was absent at the time; but returned before the infant was four weeks old. The nurse described the meeting of husband and wife as very lover-like and tender on his part, but with scarcely a sign of feeling on hers. She did not repel him, nor turn from him; but received his caresses with the manner of one in whom all quick emotion had died. And so it continued between them - he thoughtful and assiduous, and she cold, and for the most part silent. But, to her babe, the young mother was passionate at times in her loving demonstrations. The pent up waters of feeling gave way in this direction, and poured themselves out, often, in a rushing flood. Towards all others she bore herself with a calm, sweet dignity of manner, that captivated the heart, and made it sigh for a better acquaintance with one around whom mystery had hung a veil that no hand but her own could push aside - and that hand was never lifted.

The next event in the Allen House, noted by the people, was the birth of a daughter. The same nurse was called in, who remained the usual time, and then retired; bearing with her a history of the period, which she related, very confidentially, at tea-tables, and in familiar gossip with choice spirits of her own.

Those who knew her best, were always something in doubt as to which of her stories contained truth and which romance. The latter element mingled largely, it is presumed, in all of them.

A great change had taken place in the Captain's manner. He no longer played the lover to a cold and distant mistress, but carried himself haughtily at times - captiously at times - and always with an air of indifference. All affection seemed transferred to his boy, who was growing self-willed, passionate, and daring. These qualities were never repressed by his father, but rather encouraged and strengthened. On learning that his next heir was a daughter, he expressed impatience, and muttered something about its being strangled at birth. The nurse said that he never deigned even to look at it while she was in the house.

The beautiful young wife showed signs of change, also. Much of the old sweetness had left her mouth, which was calmer and graver. Her manner towards Captain Allen, noted before, was of the same quiet, distant character, but more strongly marked. It was plain that she had no love for him. The great mystery was, how two so wholly unlike in all internal qualities, and external seeming, could ever have been constrained into the relationship, of man and wife. She was, evidently, an English woman. This was seen in her rich complexion, sweet blue eyes, fair hair, and quiet dignity of manner. Among the many probable and improbable rumors as to her first meeting with Captain Allen, this one had currency. A sailor, who had seen a good deal of service in the West Indies, told the following story:

An English vessel from Jamaica, richly freighted, had on board a merchant with his family, returning from a residence of a few years on the island, to the mother country.

They had been out only a day, when a pirate bore

T. S. Arthur

down upon them, and made an easy capture of the ship. The usual bloody scenes of that day followed. Death, in terrible forms, met the passengers and crew, and the vessel, after being robbed of its costliest treasures, was scuttled and sent down into the far depths of the ocean, from whence no sign could ever come.

But one living soul was spared - so the story went. An only child of the English merchant, a fair and beautiful young girl, whose years had compassed only the early spring-time of life, flung herself upon her knees before the pirate Captain and begged so piteously for life, that he spared her from the general slaughter he had himself decreed. Something in her pure, exquisitely beautiful face, touched his compassion. There were murmurs of discontent among his savage crew. But the strong-willed Captain had his way, and when he sailed back with his booty to their place of rendezvous, he bore with him the beautiful maiden. Here, it was said, he gave her honorable protection, and had her cared for as tenderly as was possible under the circumstances. And it was further related, that, when the maiden grew to ripe womanhood, he abandoned the trade of a buccaneer and made her his wife. The sailor told this story, shrugged his shoulders, looked knowing and mysterious, and left his auditors to draw what inference they pleased. As they had been talking of Captain Allen, the listeners made their own conclusion as to his identity with the buccaneer. True to human nature, in its inclination to believe always the worst of a man, nine out of ten credited the story as applied to the cut-throat looking captain, and so, after this, it was no unusual thing to hear him designated by the not very flattering sobriquet of the "old pirate."

Later events, still more inexplicable in their character, and yet unexplained, gave color to this story, and invested it with the elements of probability. As related, the old gossip's second intrusion upon the Aliens, in the capacity of nurse, furnished the town's-people with a few additional facts, as to the state of things inside of a dwelling, upon whose very walls seemed written mystery. In the beginning, Mrs. Allen had made a few acquaintances, who were charmed with her character, as far as she let herself be known. Visits were made and returned for a short season. But after the birth of her first child, she went abroad but rarely, and ceasing to return all visits, social intercourse came to an end. The old nurse insisted that this was not her fault, but wholly chargeable upon the Captain, who, she was certain, had forbidden his wife to have anything to do with the town's-people.

　　　　T. S. Arthur

# CHAPTER II.

One day, nearly two years after the birth of this second child, the quiet town of S - was aroused from its dreams by a strange and startling event. About a week before, a handsomely dressed man, with the air of a foreigner, alighted from the stage coach at the "White Swan," and asked if he could have a room. A traveler of such apparent distinction was a rare event in S -; and as he suggested the probable stay of a week or so, he became an object of immediate attention, as well as curiosity.

Night had closed in when he arrived, and as he was fatigued by his journey in the old lumbering stage coach that ran between the nearest sea-port town and S -, he did not show himself again that evening to the curious people who were to be found idling about the "White Swan." But he had a talk with the landlord. That functionary waited upon him to know his pleasure as to supper.

"The ride has given me a headache," the stranger said, "which a cup of tea will probably remove. Beyond that, I will take nothing to-night. Your name is -"

"Adams, sir. Adams is my name," replied the landlord.

"And mine is Willoughby - Col. Willoughby. "And the

Englishman bowed with a slight air of condescension.

"I am at your service, Col. Willoughby," said the landlord in his blunt way. "Just say what you want, and the thing is done."

"A cup of tea will serve me to-night, my friend. Let it be good and strong; for my head is a little unsettled with this throbbing pain. That stage coach of yours would be something better for a pair of new springs."

"It's seen service, and no mistake. But people in these parts don't calculate much on easy riding. Springs are no great account. We look to the main chance."

"What is that?"

"Getting over the ground."

The traveler smiled to himself in a quiet way, as if the landlord's answer had touched some memory or experience.

Nothing further being remarked, Mr. Adams retired to order a cup of tea for his guest. Something about the Englishman had stimulated his curiosity; and, so, instead of sending the cup of tea by his wife, who did most of the waiting, he carried it to the room himself.

"Sit down, Mr. Adams," said the traveler, after the tea had been put before him.

The landlord did not wait for a second invitation.

"I hope the tea is to your liking, sir."

"Excellent. I've not tasted better since I left London."

The traveler spoke blandly, as he held his cup a little way from his lips, and looked over the top of it at his host with something more than a casual glance. He was reading his face with an evident effort to gain from it, as an index, some clear impression of his character.

"My wife understands her business," replied the flattered landlord. "There is not her equal in all the country round."

"I can believe you, Mr. Adams. Already this delicious beverage has acted like a charmed potion. My headache has left me as if by magic."

He set his cup down; moved his chair a little way from the table at which he was sitting, and threw a pleasant look upon the landlord.

"How long have you been in this town, Mr. Adams?" The question seemed indifferently asked; but the landlord's ear did not fail to perceive in the tone in which it was given, a foreshadowing of much beyond.

"I was born here," he replied.

"Ah! Then you know all the people, I imagine?"

"I know all their faces, at least."

"And their histories and characters?"

"Perhaps."

Something in this "perhaps," and the tone in which it

was uttered, seemed not to strike the questioner agreeably. He bent his brows a little, and looked more narrowly at the landlord.

"I did not see much of your town as I came in this evening. How large is it?"

"Middling good size, sir, for an inland town," was the not very satisfactory answer.

"What is the population?"

"Well, I don't know - can't just say to a certainty."

"Two thousand?"

"Laws! no sir! Not over one, if that."

"About a thousand, then?"

"Maybe a thousand, and maybe not more than six or seven hundred."

"Call it seven hundred, then," said the traveler, evidently a little amused.

"And that will, in my view, be calling it enough."

There was a pause. The traveler seemed in doubt as to whether he should go on with his queries.

"Not much trade here, I presume?" He asked, at length.

"Not much to boast of," said Adams.

Another pause.

"Any well-to-do people? Gentlemen who live on their means?"

"Yes; there's Aaron Thompson. He's rich, I guess. But you can't measure a snake 'till he's dead, as they say."

"True," said the traveler, seeming to fall into the landlord's mood. "Executors often change the public estimate of a man as to this world's goods. So, Aaron Thompson is one of your rich men?"

"Yes, and there's Abel Reeder - a close-fisted old dog, but wealthy as a Jew, and no mistake. Then there is Captain Allen."

A flash of interest went over the stranger's face, which was turned at once from the light.

"Captain Allen! And what of him?" The voice was pitched to a lower tone; but there was no appearance of special curiosity.

"A great deal of him." The landlord put on a knowing look.

"Is he a sea captain?"

"Yes;" and lowering his voice, "something else besides, if we are to credit people who pretend to know."

"Ah! but you speak in riddles, Mr. Adams. What do you mean by something more?"

"Why, the fact is, Mr. Willoughby, they do say, that he got his money in a backhanded sort of fashion."

"By gambling?"

"No, sir! By piracy!"

Col. Willoughby gave a real or affected start.

"A grave charge that, sir." He looked steadily at the landlord. "And one that should not be lightly made."

"I only report the common talk."

"If such talk should reach the ears of Captain Allen?" suggested the stranger.

"No great likelihood of its doing so, for I reckon there's no man in S - bold enough to say 'pirate' to his face."

"What kind of a man is he?"

"A bad specimen in every way."

"He's no favorite of yours, I see?"

"I have no personal cause of dislike. We never had many words together," said the landlord. "But he's a man that you want to get as far away from as possible. There are men, you know, who kind of draw you towards them, as if they were made of loadstone; and others that seem to push you off. Captain Allen is one of the latter kind."

"What sort of a looking man is he?"

"Short; thick-set; heavily built, as to body. A full, coarse face; dark leathery skin; and eyes that are a match for the Evil One's. There is a deep scar across

T. S. Arthur

his left forehead, running past the outer corner of his eye, and ending against the cheek bone. The lower lid of this eye is drawn down, and the inside turned out, showing its deep red lining. There is another scar on his chin. Two fingers are gone from his left hand, and his right hand has suffered violence."

"He has evidently seen hard service," remarked the stranger, and in a voice that showed him to be suppressing, as best he could, all signs of interest in the landlord's communication.

"There's no mistake about that; and if you could only see him, my word for it, you would fall into the common belief that blood lies upon his conscience."

"I shall certainly put myself in the way of seeing him, after the spur you have just given to my curiosity," said Col. Willoughby, in a decided manner, as if he had an interest in the man beyond what the landlord's communication had excited.

"Then you will have to remain here something more than a week, I'm thinking," replied the landlord.

"Why so?"

"Captain Allen isn't at home."

There was a sudden change in the stranger's face that did not escape the landlord's notice. But whether it indicated pleasure or disappointment, he could not tell; for it was at best a very equivocal expression.

"Not at home!" His voice indicated surprise.

"No, sir."

"How long has he been absent?"

"About a month."

"And is expected to return soon, no doubt?"

"As to that, I can't say. Few people in this town I apprehend, can speak with certainty as to the going and coming of Captain Allen."

"Is he often away?"

"No, sir; but oftener of late than formerly."

"Is his absence usually of a prolonged character?"

"It is much longer than it used to be - never less than a month, and often extended to three times that period."

Colonel Willoughby sat without further remark for some time, his eyes bent down, his brows contracted by thought, and his lips firmly drawn together.

"Thank you, my friend," he said, at length, looking up, "for your patience in answering my idle questions. I will not detain you any longer."

The landlord arose, and, bowing to his guest, retired from the apartment.

T. S. Arthur

# CHAPTER III.

On the next morning Colonel Willoughby plied the landlord with a few more questions about Captain Allen, and then, inquiring the direction of his house, started out, as he said, to take a ramble through the town. He did not come back until near dinner time, and then he showed no disposition to encourage familiarity on the part of Mr. Adams. But that individual was not in the dark touching the morning whereabouts of his friend. A familiar of his, stimulated by certain good things which the landlord knew when and how to dispense, had tracked the stranger from the "White Swan" to Captain Allen's house. After walking around it, on the outside of the enclosure once or twice, and viewing it on all sides, he had ventured, at last, through the gate, and up to the front door of the stately mansion. A servant admitted him, and the landlord's familiar loitered around for nearly three hours before he came out. Mrs. Allen accompanied him to the door, and stood and talked with him earnestly for some time in the portico. They shook hands in parting, and Colonel Willoughby retired with a firm, slow step, and his eyes bent downwards as if his thoughts were sober, if not oppressive.

All this Mr. Adams knew; and of course, his curiosity was pitched to a high key. But, it was all in vain that he threw himself in the way of his guest, made leading remarks, and even asked if he had seen the splendid dwelling of Captain Allen. The handsome stranger held him firmly at a distance. And not only on that day and evening, but on the next day and the next. He was polite even to blandness, but suffered no approach beyond the simplest formal intercourse. Every morning he was seen going to Captain Allen's house, where he always stayed several hours. The afternoons he spent, for the most part, in his own room.

All this soon became noised throughout the town of S -, and there was a little world of excitement, and all manner of conjectures, as to who this Colonel Willoughby might be. The old nurse, of whom mention has been made, presuming upon her professional acquaintance with Mrs. Allen, took the liberty of calling in one afternoon, when, to her certain knowledge, the stranger was in the house. She was, however, disappointed in seeing him. The servant who admitted her showed her into a small reception-room, on the opposite side of the hall from the main parlor, and here Mrs. Allen met her. She was "very sweet to her" - to use her own words - sweet, and kind, and gentle as ever. But she looked paler than usual, and did not seem to be at ease.

The nurse reported that something was going wrong; but, as to its exact nature, she was in the dark. It certainly didn't look right for Mrs. Allen to be receiving daily the visits of an elegant looking stranger, and her husband away. There was only one opinion on this head.

And so it went on from day to day for nearly a week - Colonel Willoughby, as he had called himself, spending the greater part of every morning with Mrs.

T. S. Arthur

Allen, and hiding himself from curious eyes, during the afternoons, in his room at the "White Swan." Then came the denouement to this exciting little drama.

One day the stranger, after dining, asked Mr. Adams for his bill, which he paid in British gold. He then gave directions to have a small trunk, the only baggage he had with him, sent to the house of Captain Allen.

The landlord raised his eyebrows, of course; looked very much surprised, and even ventured a curious question. But the stranger repelled all inquisition touching his movements. And so he left the "White Swan," after sojourning there for nearly a week, and the landlord never saw him again.

The news which came on the following day, created no little sensation in S -. Jacob Perkins, who lived near Captain Allen's, and often worked for him, told the story. His relation was to this effect: About ten o'clock at night, Mrs. Allen sent for him, and he waited on her accordingly. He found her dressed as for a journey, but alone.

"Take a seat, Jacob," she said. "I wish to have some talk with you." The man noticed something unusual in her talk and manner.

"Jacob," she resumed, after a pause, bending towards Mr. Perkins, "can I trust you in a matter requiring both service and secrecy? I have done some kind things for you and yours; I now wish you to return the favor."

As she spoke, she drew out a purse, and let him see something of its golden contents.

"Say on, Mrs. Allen. You may trust me. If you ask anything short of a crime, it shall be done. Yes, you have been kind to me and mine, and now I will repay you, if in my power to do so."

Jacob Perkins was in earnest. But, whether gratitude, or that apparition of golden sovereigns, had most influence upon him, cannot at this remote period be said.

"Can you get a pair of horses and a carriage, or light wagon, to-night?"

"I can," replied Jacob.

"And so as not to excite undue curiosity?"

"I think so."

"Very well. Next, will you drive that team all night?"

And Mrs. Allen played with the purse of gold, and let the coins it contained strike each other with a musical chink, very pleasant to the ear of Jacob Perkins.

"You shall be paid handsomely for your trouble," added the lady, as she fixed her beautiful blue eyes upon Jacob with an earnest, almost pleading look.

"I hope there is nothing wrong," said Jacob, as some troublesome suspicions began turning themselves over in his mind.

"Nothing wrong, as God is my witness!" And Mrs. Allen lifted her pale face reverently upwards.

"Forgive me, madam; I might have known that," said Jacob. "And now, if you will give me your orders, they shall be obeyed to the letter."

"Thank you, my kind friend," returned Mrs. Allen. "The service you are now about to render me, cannot be estimated in the usual way. To me, it will be far beyond all price."

She was agitated, and paused to recover herself. Then she resumed, with her usual calmness of manner -

"Bring the carriage here - driving with as little noise as possible - in half an hour. Be very discreet. Don't mention the matter even to your wife. You can talk with her as freely as you choose on your return from Boston."

"From Boston? Why, that is thirty miles away, at least!"

"I know it, Jacob; but I must be in Boston early to-morrow morning. You know the road?"

"Every foot of it."

"So much the better. And now go for the carriage."

Jacob Perkins arose. As he was turning to go, Mrs. Allen placed her hand upon his shoulder, and said -

"I can trust you, Mr. Perkins?"

"Madam, you can," was his reply; and he passed from the quiet house into the darkness without. The night was moonless, but the stars shone down from an unclouded sky. When Jacob Perkins found himself alone, and began to look this adventure full in the face, some unpleasant doubts touching the part he was about to play, intruded themselves upon his thoughts. He had seen the handsome stranger going daily to visit Mrs. Allen, for now nearly a week, and had listened to the town talk touching the matter, until his own mind was filled with the common idea, that something was wrong. And now, to be called on to drive Mrs. Allen to Boston, secretly, and under cover of the night, seemed so much like becoming a party to some act of folly or crime, that he gave way to hesitation, and began to seek for reasons that would justify his playing the lady false. Then came up the image of her sweet, reverent face, as she said so earnestly, "Nothing wrong, as God is my witness!" And his first purpose was restored.

Punctually, at half-past ten o'clock, the team of Jacob Perkins drove noiselessly in through the gate, and up the carriage-way to the door of the Allen mansion. No lights were visible in any part of the house. Under the portico were two figures, a man and a woman - the man holding something in his arms, which, on a closer observation, Jacob saw to be a child. Two large trunks and a small one stood near.

"Put them on the carriage," said Mrs. Allen, in a low, steady voice; and Jacob obeyed in silence. When all was ready, she got in, and the man handed her the sleeping child, and then took his place beside her.

"To Boston, remember, Jacob; and make the time as short as possible."

No other words were spoken. Jacob led his horses down the carriage-way to the gate, which he closed carefully after passing through; and then mounting to his seat, drove off rapidly.

But little conversation took place between Mrs. Allen and her traveling companion; and that was in so low a tone of voice, that Jacob Perkins failed to catch a single word, though he bent his ear and listened with the closest attention whenever he heard a murmur of voices.

It was after daylight when they arrived in Boston, where Jacob Perkins left them, and returned home with all speed, to wake up the town of S - with a report of his strange adventure. Before parting with Mrs. Allen, she gave him a purse, which, on examination, was found to contain a hundred dollars in gold. She also placed in his hand a small gold locket, and said, impressively, while her almost colorless lips quivered, and her bosom struggled with its pent up feelings -

"Jacob, when my son - he is now absent with his father - reaches his tenth year, give him this, and say that it is a gift from his mother, and contains a lock of her hair. Can I trust you faithfully to perform this office of love?"

Tears filled her eyes; then her breast heaved with a great sob.

"As Heaven is my witness, madam," answered Jacob Perkins, "it shall be done."

"Remember," she said, "that you are only to give this to John, and not until his tenth year. Keep my gift sacred from the knowledge of every one until that time, and then let the communication be to him alone."

Jacob Perkins promised to do according to her wishes, and then left her looking so pale, sad, and miserable, that, to use his own words, "he never could recall her image as she stood looking, not at him, but past him, as if trying to explore the future, without thinking of some marble statue in a grave-yard."

She was never seen in S - again.

# CHAPTER IV.

The excitement in the little town of S -, when Jacob returned from Boston, and told his singular story, may well be imagined. The whole community was in a buzz.

It was found that Mrs. Allen had so arranged matters, as to get all the servants away from the house, on one pretence or another, for that night, except an old negro woman, famous for her good sleeping qualities; and she was in the land of forgetfulness long before the hour appointed for flight.

Many conjectures were made, and one or two rather philanthropic individuals proposed, as a common duty, an attempt to arrest the fugitives and bring them back. But there were none to second this, the general sentiment being, that Captain Allen was fully competent to look after his own affairs. And that he wood look after them, and promptly too, on his return, none doubted for an instant. As for Jacob Perkins, no one professed a willingness to stand in his shoes. The fire-eating Captain would most probably blow that gentleman's brains out in the heat of his first excitement. Poor Jacob, not a very courageous man, was almost beside himself with fear, when his view of the case was confidently asserted. One advised this course of conduct on the part of Jacob, and another advised that, while all agreed that it would on no account be safe for him to fall in the Captain's way immediately on his return. More than a dozen people, friends of Jacob, were on the alert, to give him the earliest intelligence of Captain Allen's arrival in S -, that he might hide himself until the first fearful outbreak of passion was over.

Well, in about two weeks the Captain returned with his little son. Expectation was on tip-toe. People's hearts beat in their mouths. There were some who would not have been surprised at any startling occurrence; an apparition of the scarred sea-dog, rushing along the streets, slashing his sword about like a madman, would have seemed to them nothing extraordinary, under the circumstances.

But expectation stood so long on tip-toe that it grew tired, and came down a few inches. Nothing occurred to arouse the quiet inhabitants. Captain Allen was seen to enter his dwelling about two o'clock in the afternoon, and although not less than twenty sharp pairs of eyes were turned in that direction, and never abated their vigilance until night drew down her curtains, no one got even a glimpse of his person.

Jacob Perkins left the town, and took refuge with a neighbor living two miles away, on the first intimation of the Captain's return.

The next day passed, but no one saw the Captain. On the third day a member of the inquisitorial committee, who had his house under constant observation, saw him drive out with his son, and take the road that went direct to the neighborhood where Jacob Perkins lay concealed in the house of a friend.

Poor Jacob! None doubted but the hour of retribution for him was at hand. That he might have timely warning, if possible, a lad was sent out on a fleet horse, who managed to go by Captain Allen's chaise on the road. Pale with affright, the unhappy fugitive hid himself under a hay rick, and remained there for an hour. But the Captain passed through without pause or inquiry, and in due course of time returned to his home, having committed no act in the least degree notable.

And so, as if nothing unusual had happened, he was seen, day after day, going about as of old, with not a sign of change in his deportment that any one could read. In a week, Jacob Perkins returned to his home, fully assured that no harm was likely to visit him.

No event touching Captain Allen or his family, worthy of record, transpired for several years. The only servants in the house were negro slaves, brought from a distance, and kept as much as possible away from others of their class in town. Among these, the boy, John, grew up. When he was ten years old, Jacob Perkins, though in some fear, performed the sacred duty promised to his mother on that memorable morning, when he looked upon her pale, statuesque countenance for the last time. A flush covered the boy's face, as he received the locket, and understood from whence it came. He stood for some minutes, wholly abstracted, as if under the spell of some vivid memory.

Tears at length filled his eyes, and glistened on the long fringed lashes. Then there was a single, half-repressed sob - and then, grasping the locket tightly in his hand, he turned from Jacob, and, without a word,

\walked hastily away.

When the boy was sixteen, Captain Allen took him to sea. From that period for n any years, both of them were absent for at least two-thirds of the time. At twenty-five, John took command of a large merchant-man, trading to the South American coast, and his father, now worn down by hard service, as well as by years, retired to his home in S -, to close up there, in such repose of mind as he could gain, the last days of his eventful life. He died soon after by apoplexy.

Prior to this event, his son, the younger Captain Allen, had brought home from Cuba a Spanish woman, who took the name of his wife. Of her family, or antecedents, no one in our town knew anything; and it was questioned by many whether any rite of marriage had ever been celebrated between them. Of this, however, nothing certain was known. None of the best people, so called, in S - paid her the hospitable compliment of a visit; and she showed no disposition to intrude herself upon them. And so they stood towards each other as strangers; and the Allen house remained, as from the beginning, to most people a terra incognita.

Neither Captain Allen nor his Spanish consort, to whom no children were born, as they advanced in years, "grew old gracefully." Both had repulsive features, which were strongly marked by passion and sensuality. During the last two years of his life I was frequently called to see him, and prescribe for his enemy, the gout, by which he was sorely afflicted. Mrs. Allen also required treatment. Her nervous system was disordered; and, on closer observation, I detected signs of a vagrant imagination, leading her

T. S. Arthur

away into states verging upon insanity. She was fretful and ill-tempered; and rarely spoke to the Captain except complainingly, or in anger. The visits I made to the Allen house, during the lifetime of Captain Allen, were among the most unsatisfactory of all my professional calls. I think, from signs which met my eyes, that something more than bitter words passed occasionally between the ill-matched couple.

Late in the day, nearly five years anterior to the time of which I am now writing, I was summoned in haste to visit Captain Allen. I found him lying on a bed in the north-west chamber, where he usually slept, in a state of insensibility. Mrs. Allen received me at the door of the chamber with a frightened countenance. On inquiry as to the cause of his condition, she informed me that he had gone to his own room about an hour before, a little the worse for a bottle of wine; and that she had heard nothing more from him, until she was startled by a loud, jarring noise in his chamber. On running up stairs, she found him lying upon the floor, insensible.

I looked at her steadily, as she gave me this relation, but could not hold her eyes in mine. She seemed more uneasy than troubled. There was a contused wound just below the right temple, which covered, with its livid stain, a portion of the cheek. A cursory examination satisfied me that, whatever might be the cause of his fall, congestion of the brain had occurred, and that but few chances for life remained. So I informed Mrs. Allen. At the words, I could see a shudder run through her frame, and an expression of something like terror sweep over her face.

"His father died of apoplexy," said she in a hoarse whisper, looking at me with a side-long, almost stealthy glance, not full and open-eyed.

"This is something more than apoplexy," I remarked; still observing her closely.

"The fall may have injured him," she suggested.

"The blow on his temple has done the fearful work," said I.

There was a perceptible start, and another look of fear-almost terror.

"For heaven's sake, doctor," she said, rousing herself, and speaking half imperatively, "do something! Don't stand speculating about the cause; but do something if you have any skill."

Thus prompted, I set myself to work, in good earnest, with my patient. The result was in no way flattering to my skill, for he passed to his account in less than an hour, dying without a sign.

I shall never forget the wild screams which rang awfully through the old mansion, when it was announced to Mrs. Allen that the Captain was dead. She flung herself upon his body, tore her hair, and committed other extravagances. All the slumbering passions of her undisciplined nature seemed quickened into sudden life, overmastering her in their strong excitement. So it would have seemed to a less suspicious observer; but I thought that I could detect the overacting of pretence. I may have done her wrong; but the impression still remains. At the funeral, this extravagant role of grief was re-enacted, and the impression was left on many minds that she was half mad with grief.

Occasionally, after this event, I was summoned to the Allen House to see its unhappy mistress. I say unhappy, for no human being ever had a face written all over with the characters you might read in hers, that was not miserable. I used to study it, sometimes, to see if I could get anything like a true revelation of her inner life. The sudden lighting up of her countenance at times, as you observed its rapidly varying expression, made you almost shudder, for the gleam which shot across it looked like a reflection from hell. I know no other word to express what I mean. Remorse, at times, I could plainly read.

One thing I soon noticed; the room in which Captain Allen died - the north-west chamber before mentioned - remained shut up; and an old servant told me, years afterwards, that Mrs. Allen had never been inside of it since the fatal day on which I attended him in his last moments.

At the time when this story opens the old lady was verging on to sixty. The five years which had passed since she was left alone had bent her form considerably, and the diseased state of mind which I noticed when first called in to visit the family as a physician, was now but a little way removed from insanity. She was haunted by many strange hallucinations; and the old servant above alluded to, informed me, that she was required to sleep in the room with her mistress, as she never would be alone after dark. Often, through the night, she would start up in terror, her diseased imagination building up terrible phantoms in the land of dreams, alarming the house with her cries.

I rarely visited her that I did not see new evidences of waning reason. In the beginning I was fearful that she might do some violence to herself or her servants, but her insanity began to assume a less excitable form; and at last she sank into a condition of torpor, both of mind and body, from which I saw little prospect of her ever rising.

"It is well," I said to myself. "Life had better wane slowly away than to go out in lurid gleams like the flashes of a dying volcano."

# CHAPTER V.

And now, reader, after this long digression, you can understand my surprise at seeing broad gleams of light reaching out into the darkness from the windows of that north-west chamber, as I breasted the storm on my way to visit the sick child of Mary Jones. No wonder that I stood still and looked up at those windows, though the rain beat into my face, half blinding me. The shutters were thrown open, and the curtains drawn partly aside. I plainly saw shadows on the ceiling and walls as of persons moving about the room. Did my eyes deceive me? Was not that the figure of a young girl that stood for a moment at the window trying to pierce with her eyes the thick veil of night? I was still in doubt when the figure turned away, and only gave me a shadow on the wall.

I lingered in front of the old house for some minutes, but gaining no intelligence of what was passing within, I kept on my way to the humbler dwelling of Mary Jones. I found her child quite ill, and needing attention. After doing what, in my judgment, the case required, I turned my steps towards the house of Mrs. Wallingford to look into the case of her son Henry, who, acording to her account, was in a very unhappy condition.

I went a little out of my way so as to go past the Allen House again. As I approached, my eyes were directed to the chamber windows at the north-west corner, and while yet some distance away, as the old elms tossed their great limbs about in struggling with the storm, I saw glancing out between them the same cheery light that met my astonished gaze a little while before. As then, I saw shadows moving on the walls, and once the same slender, graceful figure - evidently that of a young girl - came to the window and tried to look out into the deep darkness.

As there was nothing to be gained by standing there in the drenching storm, I moved onward, taking the way to Mrs. Wallingford's dwelling. I had scarcely touched the knocker when the door was opened, and by Mrs. Wallingford herself.

"Oh, Doctor, I'm so glad you've come!" she said in a low, troubled voice.

I stepped in out of the rain, gave her my dripping umbrella, and laid off my overcoat.

"How is Henry now?" I asked.

She put her finger to her lip, and said, in a whisper,

"Just the same, Doctor - just the same. Listen! Don't you hear him walking the floor overhead? I've tried to get him to take a cup of tea, but he won't touch any thing. All I can get out of him is - 'Mother - dear mother - leave me to myself. I shall come right again. Only leave me to myself now.' But, how can I let him go on in this way? Oh, Doctor, I am almost beside myself! What can it all mean? Something dreadful has happened."

I sat listening and reflecting for something like ten minutes. Steadily, from one side the room overhead to the other, went the noise of feet; now slowly, now with a quicker motion: and now with a sudden tramp, that sent the listener's blood with a start along its courses.

"Won't you see him, doctor?"

I did not answer at once, for I was in the dark as to what was best to be done. If I had known the origin of his trouble, I could have acted understandingly. As it was, any intrusion upon the young man might do harm rather than good.

"He has asked to be let alone," I replied, "and it may be best to let him alone. He says that he will come out right. Give him a little more time. Wait, at least, until to-morrow. Then, if there is no change, I will see him."

Still the mother urged. At last I said -

"Go to your son. Suggest to him a visit from me, and mark the effect."

I listened as she went up stairs. On entering his room, I noticed that he ceased walking. Soon came to my ears the murmur of voices, which rose to a sudden loudness on his part, and I distinctly heard the words:

"Mother! you will drive me mad! If you talk of that, I will go from the house. I *must* be left alone!"

Then all was silent. Soon Mrs. Wallingford came down. She looked even more distressed than when she left the room.

"I'm afraid it might do harm," she said doubtingly.

"So am I. It will, I am sure, be best to let him have his way for the present. Something has disturbed him fearfully; but he is struggling hard for the mastery over himself, and you may be sure, madam, that he will gain it. Your son is a young man of no light stamp of character; and he will come out of this ordeal, as gold from the crucible."

"You think so, Doctor?"

She looked at me with a hopeful light in her troubled countenance.

"I do, verily. So let your heart dwell in peace."

I was anxious to get back to my good Constance, and so, after a few more encouraging words for Mrs. Wallingford, I tried the storm again, and went through its shivering gusts, to my own home. There had been no calls in my absence, and so the prospect looked fair for a quiet evening - just what I wanted; for the strange condition of Henry Wallingford, and the singular circumstance connected with the old Allen House, were things to be conned over with that second self, towards whom all thought turned and all interest converged as to a centre.

After exchanging wet outer garments and boots, for dressing gown and slippers; and darkness and storm for a pleasant fireside; my thoughts turned to the north-west chamber of the Allen House, and I said -

"I have seen something to-night that puzzled me."

T. S. Arthur

"What is that?" inquired my wife, turning her mild eyes upon me.

"You know the room in which old Captain Allen died?"

"Yes."

"The chamber on the north-west corner, which, as far as we know, has been shut up ever since?"

"Yes, I remember your suspicion as to foul play on the part of Mrs. Alien, who, it is believed, has never visited the apartment since the Captain's death."

"Well, you will be surprised to hear that the shutters are unclosed, and lights burning in that chamber."

"Now!"

"Yes - or at least half an hour ago."

"That is remarkable."

My wife looked puzzled.

"And more remarkable still - I saw shadows moving on the walls, as of two or three persons in the room."

"Something unusual has happened," said my wife.

"Perhaps Mrs. Allen is dead."

This thought had not occurred to me. I turned it over for a few moments, and then remarked,

"Hardly probable - for, in that case, I would have been summoned. No; it strikes me that some strangers are in the house; for I am certain that I saw a young girl come to the window and press her face close up to one of the panes, as if trying to penetrate the darkness.

"Singular!" said my wife, as if speaking to herself. "Now, that explains, in part, something that I couldn't just make out yesterday. I was late in getting home from Aunt Elder's you know. Well, as I came in view of that old house, I thought I saw a girl standing by the gate. An appearance so unusual, caused me to strain my eyes to make out the figure, but the twilight had fallen too deeply. While I still looked, the form disappeared; but, through an opening in the shrubbery, I caught another glimpse of it, as it vanished in the portico. I was going to speak of the incident, but other matters pushed it, till now, from my thoughts when you were at home."

"Then my eyes did not deceive me," said I; "your story corroborates mine. There is a young lady in the Allen House. But who is she? That is the question."

As we could not get beyond this question, we left the riddle for time to solve, and turned next to the singular state of mind into which young Henry Wallingford had fallen.

"Well," said my wife, speaking with some emphasis, after I had told her of the case, "I never imagined that he cared so much for the girl!"

"What girl?" I inquired.

"Why, Delia Floyd - the silly fool! if I must speak

T. S. Arthur

so strongly."

"Then he is really in love with Squire Floyd's daughter?"

"It looks like it, if he's taking on as his mother says," answered my wife, with considerable feeling. "And Delia will rue the day she turned from as true a man as Henry Wallingford."

"Bless me, Constance! you've got deeper into this matter, than either his mother or me. Who has been initiating you into the love secrets of S -?"

"This affair," returned my wife, "has not passed into town talk, and will, I trust, be kept sacred by those who know the facts. I learned them from Mrs. Dean, the sister of Mrs. Floyd. The case stands thus: Henry is peculiar, shy, reserved, and rather silent. He goes but little into company, and has not the taking way with girls that renders some young men so popular. But his qualities are all of the sterling kind - such as wear well, and grow brighter with usage. For more than a year past, he has shown a decided preference for Delia Floyd, and she has encouraged his attentions. Indeed, so far as I can learn from Mrs. Dean, the heart of her niece was deeply interested. But a lover of higher pretensions came, dazzling her mind with a more brilliant future."

"Who?" I inquired.

"That dashing young fellow from New York, Judge Bigelow's nephew."

"Not Ralph Dewey?"

"Yes."

"Foolish girl, to throw away a man for such an effigy! It will be a dark day that sees her wedded to him. But I will not believe in the possibility of such an event."

"Well, to go on with my story," resumed Constance. "Last evening, seeing, I suppose, that a dangerous rival was intruding, Henry made suit for the hand of Delia, and was rejected."

"I understand the case better now," said I, speaking from a professional point of view.

"Poor young man! I did not suppose it was in him to love any woman after that fashion," remarked Constance.

"Your men of reserved exterior have often great depths of feeling," I remarked. "Usually women are not drawn towards them; because they are attracted most readily by what meets the eye. If they would look deeper, they would commit fewer mistakes, like that which Delia Floyd has just committed."

# CHAPTER VI.

Delia Floyd was a girl of more than ordinary attractions, and it is not surprising that young Wallingford was drawn, fascinated, within the charmed circle of her influence. She was, by no means, the weak, vain, beautiful young woman, that the brief allusion I have made to her might naturally lead the reader to infer. I had possessed good opportunities for observing her, for our families were intimate, and she was frequently at our house. Her father had given her a good education - not showy; but of the solid kind. She was fond of books, and better read, I think, in the literature of the day, than any other young lady in S -. Her conversational powers were of a high order. Good sense, I had always given her credit for possessing; and I believed her capable of reading character correctly. She was the last one I should have regarded as being in danger of losing a heart to Ralph Dewey.

In person, Delia was rather below than above the middle stature. Her hair was of a dark brown, and so were her eyes - the latter large and liquid. Her complexion was fresh, almost ruddy, and her countenance animated, and quick to register every play of feeling.

In manner, she was exceedingly agreeable, and had the happy art of putting even strangers at ease. It was no matter of wonder to me, as I said before, that Henry

Wallingford should fall in love with Delia Floyd. But I did wonder, most profoundly, when I became fully assured, that she had, for a mere flash man, such as Ralph Dewey seemed to me, turned herself away from Henry Wallingford.

But women are enigmas to most of us - I don't include you, dear Constance! - and every now and then puzzle us by acts so strangely out of keeping with all that we had predicated of them, as to leave no explanation within our reach, save that of evil fascination, or temporary loss of reason. We see their feet often turning aside into ways that we know lead to wretch-hedness, and onward they move persistently, heeding neither the voice of love, warning, nor reproach. They hope all things, believe all things, trust all things, and make shipwreck on the breakers that all eyes but their own see leaping and foaming in their course. Yes, woman is truly an enigma!

Squire Floyd was a plain, upright man, in moderately good circumstances. He owned a water power on the stream that ran near our town, and had built himself a cotton mill, which was yielding him a good annual income. But he was far from being rich, and had the good sense not to assume a style of living beyond his means.

Henry Wallingford was the son of an old friend of Squire Floyd's. The elder Mr. Wallingford was not a man of the Squire's caution and prudence. He was always making mistakes in matters of business, and never succeeded well in any thing. He died when his son was about eighteen years of age. Henry was at that time studying law with Judge Bigelow. As, in the settlement of his father's estate, it was found to be wholly insolvent, Henry, unwilling to be dependent on his mother, who had a small income in her own right, gave notice to the Judge that he was about to leave his office. Now, the Judge was a man of penetration, and had already discovered in the quiet, reserved young man, just the qualities needed to give success in the practice of law. He looked calmly at his student for some moments after receiving this announcement, conning over his face, which by no means gave indications of a happy state of mind.

"You think you can find a better preceptor?" said the Judge, at last, in his calm way.

"No, sir! no!" answered Henry, quickly. "Not in all this town, nor out of it, either. It is not that, Judge Bigelow."

"Then you don't fancy the law?"

"On the contrary, there is no other calling in life that presents to my mind any thing attractive," replied Henry, in a tone of despondency that did not escape the Judge.

"Well, if that is the case, why not keep on? You are getting along
bravely."

"I must support myself, sir - must do something besides sitting here and reading law books."

"Ah, yes, I see." The Judge spoke to himself, as if light had broken into his mind. "Well, Henry," he added, looking at the young man, "what do you propose doing?"

"I have hands and health," was the reply.

"Something more than hands and health are required in this world. What can you do?"

"I can work on a farm, if nothing better offers. Or, may be, I can get a place in some store."

"There's good stuff in the lad," said Judge Bigelow to himself. Then speaking aloud -

"I'll think this matter over for you, Henry. Let it rest for a day or two. The law is your proper calling, and you must not give it up, if you can be sustained in it."

On that very day, Judge Bigelow saw Squire Floyd, and talked the matter over with him. They had but one sentiment in the matter, and that was favorable to Henry's remaining where he was.

"Can he be of any service to you, in your office, Judge - such as copying deeds and papers, hunting up cases, and the like?" asked the Squire.

"Yes, he can be of service to me in that way; and is of service now."

"You can afford to pay him something?" suggested Squire Floyd.

"It is usual," replied the Judge, "to get this kind of service in return for instruction and office privileges."

"I know; but this case is peculiar. The death of Henry's father has left him without a support, and he is too independent to burden his mother. Unless he can earn something, therefore, he must abandon the law."

"I understand that, Squire, and have already decided to compensate him," said the Judge. "But what I can offer will not be enough."

"How much can you offer?"

"Not over a hundred dollars for the first year."

"Call it two hundred, Judge," was the ready answer.

The two men looked for a moment into each other's faces.

"His father and I were friends from boyhood," said Squire Floyd. "He was a warm-hearted man; but always making mistakes. He would have ruined me two or three times over, if I had been weak enough to enter into his plans, or to yield to his importunities in the way of risks and securities. It often went hard for me to refuse him; but duty to those dependent on me was stronger than friendship. But I can spare a hundred dollars for his son, and will do it cheerfully. Only, I must not be known in the matter; for it would lay on Henry's mind a weight of obligation, not pleasant for one of his sensitive disposition to bear."

"I see, Squire," answered Judge Bigelow to this; "but then it won't place me in the right position. I shall receive credit for your benevolence."

"Don't trouble yourself on that score," answered the Squire, laughing. "It may be that I shall want some law business done - though heaven forbid! In that case, I will call on you, and you can let Henry do the work.

Thus the equilibrium of benefits will be restored. Let the salary be two hundred."

And so this matter being settled, Henry Wallingford remained in the office of Judge Bigelow. The fact of being salaried by the Judge, stimulated him to new efforts, and made him forward to relieve his kind preceptor of all duties within the range of his ability. There came, during the next year, an unusually large amount of office practice - preparing deeds, making searches, and drawing up papers of various kinds. In doing this work, Henry was rapid and reliable. So, when Squire Floyd tendered his proportion of the young man's salary to his neighbor, the Judge declined receiving it. The Squire urged; but the Judge said -

"No; Henry has earned his salary, and I must pay it, in simple justice. I did not think there was so much in him. Business has increased, and without so valuable an assistant, I could not get along."

So the way had opened before Henry Wallingford, and he was on the road to a successful manhood. At the time of his introduction to the reader, he was in his twenty-third year. On attaining his majority, he had become so indispensable to Judge Bigelow, who had the largest practice in the county, that no course was left for him but to offer the young man a share in his business. It was accepted; and the name of Henry Wallingford was thenceforth displayed in gilt letters, in the office window of his preceptor.

From that time, his mind never rested with anything like care or anxiety on the future. His daily life consisted in an almost absorbed devotion to his professional duties, which grew steadily on his hands. His affection was in them, and so the balance of his mind was fully sustained. Ah, if we could all thus rest, without anxiety, on the right performance of our allotted work! If we would be content to wait patiently for that success which comes as the orderly result of well-doing in our business, trades, or professions, what a different adjustment would there be in our social condition and relations! There would not be all around us so many eager, care-worn faces - so many heads bowed with anxious thought - so many shoulders bent with burdens, destined, sooner or later, to prove too great for the strength which now sustains them. But how few, like Henry Wallingford, enter with anything like pleasure into their work! It is, in most cases, held as drudgery, and regarded only as the means to cherished ends in life wholly removed from the calling itself. Impatience comes as a natural result. The hand reaches forth to pluck the growing fruit ere it is half ripened. No wonder that its taste is bitter to so many thousands. No wonder that true success comes to so small a number - that to so many life proves but a miserable failure.

# CHAPTER VII.

The morning which broke after that night of storm was serene and beautiful. The air had a crystal clearness, and as you looked away up into the cloudless azure, it seemed as if the eye could penetrate to an immeasurable distance. The act of breathing was a luxury. You drew in draught after draught of the rich air, feeling, with every inhalation, that a new vitality was absorbed through the lungs, giving to the heart a nobler beat, and to the brain a fresh activity. With what a different feeling did I take up my round of duties for the day! Yesterday I went creeping forth like a reluctant school boy; to-day, with an uplifted countenance and a willing step.

Having a few near calls to make, I did not order my horse, as both health and inclination were better served by walking. Soon after breakfast I started out, and was going in the direction of Judge Bigelow's office, when, hearing a step behind me that had in it a familiar sound, I turned to find myself face to face with Henry Wallingford! He could hardly have failed to see the look of surprise in my face.

"Good morning, Henry," I said, giving him my hand, and trying to speak with that cheerful interest in the young man which I had always endeavored to show.

T. S. Arthur

He smiled in his usual quiet way as he took my hand and said in return,

"Good-morning, Doctor."

"You were not out, I believe, yesterday," I remarked, as we moved on together.

"I didn't feel very well," he answered, in a voice pitched to a lower key than usual; "and, the day being a stormy one, I shut myself up at home."

"Ah," said I, in a cheerful way, "you lawyers have the advantage of us knights of the pill box and lancet. Rain or shine, sick or well, we must travel round our parish."

"All have their share of the good as well as the evil things of life," he replied, a little soberly. "Doctors and lawyers included."

I did not observe any marked change in the young man, except that he was paler, and had a different look out of his eyes from any that I had hitherto noticed; a more matured look, which not only indicated deeper feeling, but gave signs of will and endurance. I carried that new expression away with me as we parted at the door of his office, and studied it as a new revelation of the man. It was very certain that profounder depths had been opened in his nature - opened to his own consciousness - than had ever seen the light before. That he was more a man than he had ever been, and more worthy to be mated with a true woman. Up to this time I had thought of him more as a boy than as a man, for the years had glided by so quietly that bore him onward with the rest, that he had not arisen in my thought to the full mental stature which the word manhood includes.

"Ah," said I, as I walked on, "what a mistake in Delia Floyd! She is just as capable of high development as a woman as he is as a man. How admirably would they have mated. In him, self-reliance, reason, judgment, and deep feeling would have found in her all the qualities they seek - taste, perception, tenderness and love. They would have grown upwards into higher ideas of life, not downwards into sensualism and mere worldliness, like the many. Alas! This mistake on her part may ruin them both; for a man of deep, reserved feelings, who suffers a disappointment in love, is often warped in his appreciation of the sex, and grows one-sided in his character as he advances through the cycles of life.

I had parted from Henry only a few minutes when I met his rival, Ralph Dewey. Let me describe him. In person he was taller than Wallingford, and had the easy, confident manner of one who had seen the world, as we say. His face was called handsome; but it was not a manly face - manly in that best sense which includes character and thought. The chin and mouth were feeble, and the forehead narrow, throwing the small orbs close together. But he had a fresh complexion, dark, sprightly eyes, and a winning smile. His voice was not very good, having in it a kind of unpleasant rattle; but he managed it rather skillfully in conversation, and you soon, ceased to notice the peculiarity.

Ralph lived in New York, where he had recently been advanced to the position of fourth partner in a dry goods jobbing house, with a small percentage on the

T. S. Arthur

net profits. Judging from the air with which he spoke of his firm's operations, and his relation to the business, you might have inferred that he was senior instead of junior partner, and that the whole weight of the concern rested on his shoulders.

Judge Bigelow, a solid man, and from professional habit skilled in reading character, was, singularly enough, quite carried away with his smart nephew, and really believed his report of himself. Prospectively, he saw him a merchant prince, surrounded by palatial splendors.

Our acquaintance was as yet but slight, so we only nodded in passing. As we were in the neighborhood of Squire Floyd's pleasant cottage, I was naturally curious, under the circumstances, to see whether the young man was going to make a visit at so early an hour; and I managed to keep long enough in sight to have this matter determined. Ralph called at the Squire's, and I saw him admitted. So I shook my head disapprovingly, and kept on my way.

Not until late in the afternoon did I find occasion to go into that part of the town where the old Allen house was located, though the image of its gleaming north-west windows was frequently in my thought. The surprise occasioned by that incident was in no way lessened on seeing a carriage drive in through the gateway, and two ladies alight therefrom and enter the house. Both were in mourning. I did not see their faces; but, judging from the dress and figure of each, it was evident that one was past the meridian of life, and the other young. Still more to my surprise, the carriage was not built after our New England fashion, but looked heavy, and of a somewhat ancient date. It was large and high, with a single seat for the driver perched away up in the air, and a footman's stand and hangings behind. There was, moreover, a footman in attendance, who sprung to his place after the ladies had alighted, and rode off to the stables.

"Am I dreaming?" said I to myself, as I kept on my way, after witnessing this new incident in the series of strange events that were half-bewildering me. But it was in vain that I rubbed my eyes; I could not wake up to a different reality.

It was late when I got home from my round of calls, and found tea awaiting my arrival.

"Any one been here?" I asked - my usual question.

"No one.' The answer pleased me for I had many things on my mind, and I wished to have a good long evening with my wife. Baby Mary and Louis were asleep: but we had the sweet, gentle face of Agnes, our first born, to brighten the meal-time. After she was in dream-land, guarded by the loving angels who watch with children in sleep, and Constance was through with her household cares for the evening, I came into the sitting-room from my office, and taking the large rocking-chair, leaned my head back, mind and body enjoying a sense of rest and comfort.

"You are not the only one," said my wife, looking up from the basket of work through which she had been searching for some article, "who noticed lights in the Allen House last evening."

"Who else saw them?" I asked.

"Mrs. Dean says she heard two or three people say that the house was lit up all over - a perfect illumination."

"Stories lose nothing in being re-told. The illumination was confined to the room in which Captain Allen died. I am witness to that. But I have something more for your ears. This afternoon, as I rode past, I saw an old-fashioned English coach, with a liveried driver and footman, turn into the gate. From this two ladies alighted and went into the house; when the coach was driven to the stables. Now, what do you think of that?"

"We are to have a romance enacted in our very midst, it would seem," replied my wife, in her unimpassioned way. "Other eyes have seen this also, and the strange fact is buzzing through the town. I was only waiting until we were alone to tell you that these two ladies whom you saw, arrived at the Allen House in their carriage near about daylight, on the day before yesterday. But no one knows who they are, or from whence they came. It is said that they made themselves as completely at home as if they were in their own house; selected the north-west chamber as their sleeping apartment; and ordered the old servants about with an air of authority that subdued them to obedience."

"But what of Mrs. Allen?" I asked, in astonishment at all this.

"The stories about her reception of the strangers do not agree. According to one, the old lady was all resistance and indignation at this intrusion; according to another, she gave way, passively, as if she were no longer sole mistress of the house."

Constance ceased speaking, for there came the usual interruption to our evening *tete-a-tete* - the ringing of my office bell.

"You are wanted up at the Allen House, Doctor, said my boy, coming in from the office a few moments afterwards.

"Who is sick?" I asked.

"The old lady."

"Any thing serious?"

"I don't know, sir. But I should think there was from the way old Aunty looked. She says, come up as quickly as you can."

"Is she in the office?"

"No, sir. She just said that, and then went out in a hurry."

"The plot thickens," said I, looking at Constance.

"Poor old lady!" There was a shade of pity in her tones.

"You have not seen her for many years?"

"No."

"Poor old witch of Endor! were better said."

"Oh!" answered my wife, smiling, "you know that the painter's idea of this celebrated individual has been reversed by some, who affirm that she was young and handsome instead of old and ugly like modern witches."

"I don't know how that may be, but if you could see Mrs. Allen, you would say that 'hag' were a better term for her than woman. If the good grow beautiful as they grow old, the loving spirit shining like a lamp through the wasted and failing walls of flesh, so do the evil grow ugly and repulsive. Ah, Constance, the lesson is for all of us. If we live true lives, our countenances will grow radiant from within, as we advance in years; if selfish, worldly, discontented lives, they will grow cold, hard, and repulsive."

I drew on my boots and coat, and started on my visit to the Allen House. The night was in perfect contrast with the previous one. There was no moon, but every star shone with its highest brilliancy, while the galaxy threw its white scarf gracefully across the sky, veiling millions of suns in their own excessive brightness. I paused several times in my walk, as broader expanses opened between the great elms that gave to our town a sylvan beauty, and repeated, with a rapt feeling of awe and admiration, the opening stanza of a familiar hymn: -

> "The spacious firmament on high,
> With all the blue ethereal sky,
> And spangled heavens, a shining frame,
> Their great Original proclaim."

How the beauty and grandeur of nature move the heart, as if it recognized something of its own in every changing aspect. The sun and moon and stars - the grand old mountains lifting themselves upwards into serene heights - the limitless expanse of ocean, girdling the whole earth - rivers, valleys, and plains - trees, flowers, the infinite forms of life - to all the soul gives some response, as if they were akin.

I half forgot my interest in old Mrs. Allen, as my heart beat responsive to the pulsings of nature, and my thoughts flew upwards and away as on the wings of eagles. But my faithful feet had borne me steadily onwards, and I was at the gate opening to the grounds of the Allen House, before I was conscious of having passed over half the distance that lay between that and my home. I looked up, and saw a light in the north-west chamber, but the curtains were down.

On entering the house, I was shown by the servant who admitted me, into the small office or reception room opening from the hall. I had scarcely seated myself, when a tall woman, dressed in black, came in, and said, with a graceful, but rather stately manner -

"The Doctor, I believe?"

How familiar the voice sounded! And yet I did not recognise it as the voice of any one whom I had known, but rather as a voice heard in dreams. Nor was the calm, dignified countenance on which my eyes rested, strange in every lineament. The lady was, to all appearance, somewhere in the neighborhood of sixty, and, for an elderly lady, handsome. I thought of my remark to Constance about the beauty and deformity of age, and said to myself, "Here is one who has not lived in vain."

I arose as she spoke, and answered in the affirmative.

"You have come too late," she said, with a touch of

T. S. Arthur

feeling in her voice.

"Not dead?" I ejaculated.

"Yes, dead. Will you walk up stairs and see her?"

I followed in silence, ascending to the chamber which had been occupied by Mrs. Allen since the old Captain's death. It was true as she had said; a ghastly corpse was before me. I use the word ghastly, for it fully expresses the ugliness of that lifeless face, withered, marred, almost shorn of every true aspect of humanity. I laid my hand upon her - the skin was cold. I felt for her pulse, but there was no sign of motion in the arteries.

"It is over," I said, lifting myself from my brief examination, "and may God have mercy upon her soul!" The last part of the sentence was involuntary.

"Amen!"

I felt that this response was no idle ejaculation.

"How was she affected?" I asked. "Has she been sick for any time? Or did life go out suddenly?"

"It went out suddenly," replied the lady - "as suddenly as a lamp in the wind."

"Was she excited from any cause?"

"She has been in an excited state ever since our arrival, although every thing that lay in our power has been done to quiet her mind and give it confidence and repose."

She spoke calmly, as one, who held a controlling position there, and of right. I looked into her serene face, almost classic in its outlines, with an expression of blended inquiry and surprise, that it was evident did not escape her observation, although she offered no explanation in regard to herself.

I turned again to the corpse, and examined it with some care. There was nothing in its appearance that gave me any clue to the cause which had produced this sudden extinguishment of life.

"In what way was she excited?" I asked, looking at the stranger as I stepped back from the couch on which the dead body was lying.

She returned my steady gaze, without answering, for some moments. Either my tone or manner affected her unpleasantly, for I saw her brows contract slightly, her full lips close upon themselves, and her eyes acquire an intenser look.

"You have been her physician, I believe?" There was no sign of feeling in the steady voice which made the inquiry.

"Yes."

"*I* need not, in that case, describe to you her unhappy state of mind. *I* need not tell you that an evil will had the mastery over her understanding, and that, in the fierce struggle of evil passion with evil passion, mind and body had lost their right adjustment."

"I know all this," said I. "Still, madam, in view of my professional duty, I must repeat my question, and urge

T. S. Arthur

upon you the propriety of an undisguised answer. In what way was she excited? and what was the cause leading to an excitement which has ended thus fatally?"

"I am not in the habit of putting on disguises," she answered, with a quiet dignity that really looked beautiful.

"I pray you, madam, not to misunderstand me," said I. "As a physician, I must report the cause of all deaths in the range of my practice. If I were not to do so in this case, a permit for burial would not be issued until a regular inquest was held by the Coroner."

"Ah, I see," she replied, yet with an air of indecision. "You are perfectly right, Doctor, and we must answer to your satisfaction. But let us retire from this chamber."

She led the way down stairs. As we passed the memorable north-west room, she pushed the door open, and said,

"Blanche, dear, I wish to see you. Come down to the parlor."

I heard faintly the answer, in a very musical voice. We had scarcely entered the parlor, when the lady said -

"My daughter, Doctor."

A vision of beauty and innocence met my gaze. A young girl, not over seventeen, tall like her mother, very fair, with a face just subdued into something of womanly seriousness, stood in the door, as I turned at mention of her presence.

A single lamp gave its feeble light to the room, only half subduing the shadows that went creeping into corners and recesses. Something of a weird aspect was on every thing; and I could not but gaze at the two strangers in that strange place to them, under such peculiar circumstances, and wonder to see them so calm, dignified, and self-possessed. We sat down by the table on which the lamp was standing, the elder of the two opposite, and the younger a little turned away, so that her features were nearly concealed.

"Blanche," said the former, "the Doctor wishes to know the particular incidents connected with the death of Mrs. Allen."

I thought there was an uneasy movement on the part of the girl. She did not reply. There was a pause.

"The facts are simply these, Doctor," and the mother looked me steadily in the face, which stood out clear, as the lamp shone full on every feature. "From the moment of our arrival, Mrs. Allen has seemed like one possessed of an evil Spirit. How she conducted herself before, is known to me only as reported by the servants. From the little they have communicated, I infer that for some time past she has not been ii her right mind. How is it? You must know as to her sanity or insanity."

"She has not, in my opinion, been a truly sane woman for years," was my answer.

"As I just said," she continued, "she has seemed like one possessed of an evil spirit. In no way could we soften or conciliate her. Her conduct resembled more nearly that of some fierce wild beast whose den was invaded, than that of a human being. She would hold no friendly intercourse with us, and if we met at any time, or in any part of the house, she would fix her keen black eyes upon us, with an expression that sent a shudder to the heart. My daughter scarcely dared venture from her room. She so dreaded to meet her. Twice, as she flew past me, in her restless wanderings over the house, muttering to herself, I heard her say, as she struck her clenched hand in the air, 'I can do it again, and I will!'"

A cold chill crept over me, for I remembered the death of Captain Allen; and this was like a confirmation of what I had feared as to foul play.

"There is no trusting one wholly or even partially insane. So we were always on our guard. Not once, but many times during the few nights we have spent here, have we heard the door of our chamber tried after midnight. It was plain to us that it was not safe to live in this way, and so we had come to the reluctant conclusion that personal restraint must be secured. The question as to how this could best be done we had not yet decided, when death unraveled the difficulty."

The speaker ceased at this part of her narrative, and lifting from the table a small bell, rung it. A maid entered. I had never seen her before.

"Tell Jackson that I want him."

The girl curtsied respectfully, and withdrew.

Nothing more was said, until a man, whom I

recognized at a glance to be a regularly trained English servant, presented himself.

"Jackson," said the lady, "I wish you to relate exactly, what occurred just previously to, and at the time of Mrs. Allen's death."

The man looked bewildered for a moment or two; but soon recovering himself, answered without hesitation.

"Hit 'appened just in this way, ma'am. I was a comin' hup stairs, when I met the hold lady a tearin' down like a mad cat. She looked kind o' awful. I never saw anybody out of an 'ospital look that way in all my life before. She 'eld an hiron poker in 'er 'and. As my young lady -" and he looked towards Blanche -" was in the 'all, I didn't think it safe for 'er if I let the hold woman go down. So I just stood in 'er way, and put my harms across the stairs so" - stretching his arms out. "My! but 'ow she did fire up! She stood almost a minute, and then sprung on me as if she was a tiger. But I was the strongest, and 'olding 'er in my harms like as I would a mad kitten, I carried 'er hup to 'er room, put 'er hin, and shut the door. My young lady saw it hall, for she followed right hup after me."

He looked towards Blanche.

"Just as it occurred," she said, in a low, sweet fluttering voice.

"I heard the strife," said her mother, "and ran up to see what was the matter. I reached the door of Mrs. Allen's room just as Jackson thrust her in. He did not use any more violence than was needed in a case of such sudden emergency. He is strong, and held her so

T. S. Arthur

tightly that she could not even struggle. One wild, fierce scream rent the air, as he shut the door, and then all was silent as death. I went in to her instantly. She was on the floor in a convulsion. You were sent for immediately; but it was too late for human intervention. Jackson, you can go."

The man bowed with an air of deferential respect, and retired.

"Now, sir," she added, turning to me, "you have the facts as they occurred. I have no wish to give them publicity, for they are family matters, and these are always in their degree, sacred. If, however, you think it your duty as a physician, to make the matter one of official investigation, I can have nothing to say."

I thought for some minutes before answering. The story, as related by the servant, I fully credited.

"Let me see the body again," said I, coming at length to a conclusion.

We went up stairs, all three together; but only two of us entered the chamber of death. As we neared the door, Blanche caught at her mother's arm, and I heard her say, in a whisper:

"Dear mamma! spare me that sight again. It is too horrible!"

"The presence of your daughter is not needed," said I, interposing. "Let her retire to her own room."

"Thank you!" There was a grateful expression in her voice, as she uttered these brief words, and then went back, while we passed in to the apartment where the dead woman was still lying.

As I looked upon her face again, it seemed even more ghastly than before; and I could hardly repress a shudder. My companion held a lamp; while I made as careful an examination as was possible under the circumstances. I did not expect to find any marks of violence, though I searched for them about her head, neck, and chest. But, under the circumstances, I felt it to be my duty to know, from actual search, that no such signs existed. In every aspect presented by the corpse, there was a corroboration of the story related by the serving man. It was plain, that in a fit of half insane, uncontrollable passion, the nice adjustment of physical forces had been lost.

"I am fully satisfied, madam," said I, at length, turning from my unpleasant task.

She let her calm, earnest eyes dwell on mine for a few moments, and then answered, with a softened tone, in which there was just a perceptible thrill of feeling -

"If I were a believer in omens, I should take this sad incident, following so quickly on our removal to a new country and a new home, as foreshadowing evil to me or mine. But I do not so read external events."

"Between a life like hers, and a life like yours, madam, there can be no possible nearness; nor any relation between your spiritual affinities and hers. The antipodes are not farther apart," said I, in return; "therefore, nothing that has befallen her can be ominous as to you."

T. S. Arthur

"I trust not," she gravely answered, as we left the room together.

To my inquiry if I could serve her in any way, in the present matter, she simply requested me to send a respectable undertaker, who would perform what was fitting in the last rites due to the dead.

I promised, and retired.

# CHAPTER VIII.

The appearance, manner, and bearing of the two strangers impressed me strongly. The elder had evidently moved in refined and cultivated society all her life. There was about her the air of "a lady, born and bred" - dignified, calm, easy, and courteous. The daughter was a lovely blossom on this stately stem - delicate, beautiful, sweet with the odors of innocence. I see her now as I saw her on that first night of our meeting - to my eyes a new born vision of loveliness.

I found Constance awaiting, with curious interest, my return. I was going right into the heart of this new wonder, and could not fail to bring back some revelation that would satisfy, in a measure, the excitement of mind produced by so singular an intrusion of strangers upon our quiet town. I answered her first look of inquiry by the words: -

"It is over. Another book of life is sealed up here to be opened in eternity."

"Dead! Not dead?"

"Yes, Constance, Mrs. Allen is dead. Her spirit had passed away before my arrival."

"How did she die? - from what cause?"

T. S. Arthur

"From what I can learn she died in a fit of passion." I then related all that I had seen and heard.

"But who can they be?" This query came as a natural sequence. "What right have they in the Allen House?"

"Whoever they may be," I replied, "they act, or, at least, the elder of the two ladies acts as if her right there was not even open to a question. And, perhaps, it is not."

"But what can they be to the Allens?"

"I will give you," said I, "the benefit of my guessing on the subject. You recollect the story told about Captain Allen's mother; how she went off a great many years ago with a stranger - an Englishman."

Constance remembered all about this family history, for it was the romance of our town.

"My conclusion is that this lady is the sister of Captain Allen - the child that his mother took with her when she fled from her husband's house. I am strengthened in this belief from the first impression of her voice, as if the tones had in them something familiar."

We talked this matter over, looking at it in every way, until we satisfied ourselves that my conjectures must be true. The quiet manner in which they had intruded themselves, and taken possession of the house - unheralded as far as we knew - could not but present itself to our minds as a matter of special wonder. The more we conned it over the more we were puzzled. Before coming home I had called at an undertaker's, and notified him that his services were wanted at the

Allen House. Early on the next day I took the liberty of calling there myself. I sent up my name, and awaited, with some interest, my reception. The visit might be regarded as an intrusion, and I was prepared to receive a message from the lady asking to be excused. Not so, however. I had been seated only a few moments, when I heard the rustle of her garments on the stairs. My first glance at her face assured me that I was no unwelcome visitor.

"Thank you, Doctor," she said, as she extended her hand, "for this early call. Our meeting last night for the first time can hardly be called a pleasant one - or the associations connected with it such as either of us might wish to recall."

"Our control over events is so slight," I made answer as I resumed my seat, "that we should separate unpleasant feelings as far as possible from any memories connected with them."

A faint, sad smile just lightened up her placid face as she said, in reply to the remark.

"Ah, Doctor, that may not be. Lives are too intimately blended here for any one to suffer or do wrong without leaving a burden of sadness on other memories."

"True; but the burden will be light or heavy according to our strength."

She looked at me without replying, for the remark was so palpable, that it seemed to involve nothing beyond a literal fact.

"Or rather," I said, "the burden will be heavy or light

T. S. Arthur

according to our state or quality."

There was a sign of awakening interest in her countenance as if my remark had touched some hidden spring of thought.

"If we are right with ourselves," I went on, "the disturbance produced by others' misconduct will not reach very far down. The pressure of sadness may lie upon us for a season; but cannot long remain; for the pure heart will lift itself into serene atmospheres."

"But, who is right with himself?" she said. "Whose heart is pure enough to dwell in these serene atmospheres? Not mine, alas!"

I looked into the suddenly illuminated face as she put these questions, in surprise at the quick change which had passed over it. But the tone in which she uttered the closing sentence was touched with tender sadness.

"Rather let me say," I made answer, "_in the degree_ that we are right with ourselves. None attain unto perfection here."

"Yet," said the lady, with a sweet calmness of manner that made her look beautiful, "is it not pleasant to imagine a state of perfection - or rather a state in which evil is quiescent, and the heart active with all good and loving impulses? How full of inspiration is such an ideal of life! But the way by which we must go, if we would rise into this state, is one of difficulty and perpetual warfare. The enemies of our peace are numbered by myriads; and they. seek with deadly hatred to do us harm."

"And yet are powerless," said I, "if we keep the outworks of our lives in order."

"Yes," she answered, "it is the very ultimate or last things of our lives where the power of repulsion resides. We can, in temptation, be it ever so strong, refuse to *act* in the wrong direction - refuse to do an evil thing, because it is sinful. And this is our bulwark; this is our tower of safety; for it is only in _wrong doing_ that our enemies gain the victory over us. They may assault us never so fiercely - may dazzle our eyes with the glitter of this world's most alluring things - may stir the latent envy, malice, pride, or dishonesty, that lurks in every heart; but if we stand still, hold back our hands and stay our feet - if we give our resolute 'No' to all enticements, and keep our *actions* free from evil, all hell cannot prevail against us. God will take care of the interior of our lives, and make them pure and heavenly, if we resist evil in the exterior. But, pardon me; I did not mean to read you a homily."

She smiled with a grave sort of smile, and then sat silent.

"I like your way of talking," said I. There was something about the lady that put me at ease with her, and I said this without reserve, as if I were speaking to a friend. "It looks to higher things in life than people usually regard as worthy of our chief consideration. To most of us, the outer world offers the highest attracttions; only the few turn inwardly to the more beautiful world of mind."

"Outward things fade - change - die; only spiritual things dwell in unfading beauty. We are in a world of mere effects as to our bodies; but the soul lives in the

T. S. Arthur

world of causes. Do we not spend a vain and unprofitable life, then, if we go on building, day after day, our tabernacle on the ever-shifting sands of time, instead of upon the immoveable Rock of Ages? But who is guiltless of this folly? Not I! not I!"

Again that calm, earnest voice fell to a lower key, and was veiled by a tender sadness.

"It is something gained," she added, with returning firmness of tone, "if, even after the sharp lessons of many years, we get glimpses of Truth, and are willing to follow, though it be at a far distance, the light she holds aloft. Yes, it is something gained - something gained!"

She spoke the last words as if merely thinking aloud, and not addressing an auditor.

"Can I aid you in anything, madam?" said I, breaking in upon a state of reverie into which her mind seemed to be falling. "The circumstances under which you find yourself are peculiar - I refer to the death of Mrs. Allen, following so quickly on your arrival among strangers - and you may stand in need of friendly service from one who knows the people and their ways. If so, do not hesitate to command me."

"I thank you sincerely," she answered, unbending still more from her almost stately manner. "Friendly consideration I shall need, of course - as who does not in this world? And I repeat my thanks, that you have so kindly and so promptly anticipated my needs So far as the remains of my unhappy kinswoman are concerned, I have referred all to the undertaker. He will carry out my wishes. To-morrow the interment will take place.

On the day following, if it it is altogether agreeable to yourself, I would esteem a call as a particular favor."

I arose, as she concluded the last sentence, saying as I did so,

"I will be sure to call, madam; and render any service in my power. You may regard me as a friend."

"Already you have extorted my confidence," she answered, faintly smiling.

I bowed low, and was retiring when she said -

"A moment, Doctor!"

I turned toward her again.

"Doctor, it may be well for you to see my daughter."

"Is she indisposed?" I asked.

"Not exactly that. But the excitement and alarm of the last two or three days have been, I fear, rather too much for her nerves. I say alarm, for the poor girl was really frightened at Mrs. Allen's wild conduct - and no wonder. Death following in so sad a way, shocked her painfully. She did not sleep well last night; and this morning she looks pale and drooping. In all probability, quiet of mind and body will soon adjust the balance of health; still, it may be safest for you to see her."

"A mere temporary disturbance, no doubt, which, as you suggest, quiet of mind and body will, in all probability, overcome. Yet it will do no harm for me to

T. S. Arthur

see her; and may save trouble."

"Excuse me a moment," she said, and left the room. In a little while she returned, and asked me to accompany her up stairs,

I found the daughter in a black and gray silk wrapper, seated on a lounge. She arose as I entered, a slight flush coming into her face, which subsided in a few moments, leaving it quite pale, and weary looking. After we were all seated, I took her hand, which was hot in the palm, but cold at the extremities. Her pulse was feeble, disturbed, and quick.

"How is your head?" I asked.

"It feels a little strangely," she replied, moving it two or three times, as if to get some well defined sensation.

"Any pain?"

"Yes; a dull kind of pain over my left eye, that seems to go deep into my head."

"What general bodily sensation have you? Any that you can speak of definitely?"

"None, except a sense of oppression and heaviness. When I raise my arm, it seems to fall like lead; if I move about, I am weary, and wish to be at rest."

"Rest is, by all means, the most desirable condition for you now," said I. Then addressing her mother, I added - "I think your daughter had better lie down. Let her room be shaded and kept quiet. She needs rest and sleep. Sleep is one of nature's great restorers."

"Will you make no prescription, Doctor?" the mother asked.

I reflected on the symptoms exhibited, for a few moments, and then said,

"Nothing beyond repose, now. I trust that nature, as the pressure is removed, will work all right again."

"You will call in again to-day."

"Yes; towards evening I will see your daughter, when I hope to find her improved in every way."

I spoke with a cheerfulness of manner that did not altogether express my feelings in the case; for, there were some indications, not yet clear enough for a diagnosis, that awakened slight concern. As I did not wish to go wrong in my first prescription, I deemed it better to wait a few hours, and see how nature would succeed in her efforts to repel the enemy. So I went away, with a promise to call again early in the afternoon.

T. S. Arthur

# CHAPTER IX.

It was between four and five o'clock in the afternoon, when I called again at the Allen House. An old colored servant, who had been in the family ever since my remembrance - she went by the name of "Aunty" - was standing by the gate as I alighted from my chaise.

"'Deed, massa, Ise glad you come," said she in a troubled way.

"Why so, Aunty? No body very sick, I hope."

"'Deed, an dar is den; else old Aunty don't know nothin'."

"Who?"

"Why dat blessed young lady what drapped in among us, as if she'd come right down from Heaven. I was jest a gwine to run down an' ax you to come and see her right away."

I did not linger to talk with "Aunty," but went forward to the house. The mother of Blanche met me at the door. She looked very anxious.

"How is your daughter now?" I asked.

"Not so well as when you saw her this morning," she answered. Her voice trembled.

"I would have called earlier, but have been visiting a patient several miles away."

"She has been lying in a kind of stupor ever since you were here. What can it mean, Doctor?"

The mother looked intently in my face, and paused for an answer, with her lips apart. But I knew as little as she what it meant. Ah! how often do anxious friends question us, and hearken eagerly for our replies, when the signs of disease are yet too indefinite for any clear diagnosis!

"I can tell better after seeing your daughter," said I. And we went up to the sick girl's chamber; that north-west room, at the window of which I had first seen the fair stranger, as I stood wondering in storm and darkness. I found her lying in apparent sleep, and breathing heavily. Her face was flushed; and I noticed the peculiar odor that usually accompanies an eruptive fever.

"How do you feel now?" I asked.

She had opened her eyes as I took her hand. She did not answer, but looked at me in a half bewildered way. Her skin was hot and the pulse small, but tense and corded.

"Does your head ache?"

I wished to arouse her to external consciousness.

"Oh, it's you, Doctor."

She recognized me and smiled faintly.

"How are you now?" I inquired.

"Not so well, I think, Doctor," she answered. "My head aches worse than it did; and I feel sick all over. I don't know what can ail me."

"Have you any uneasiness, or sense of oppression in the stomach?" I inquired.

"Oh, yes, Doctor." She laid her hand upon her chest; and drew in a long breath, as if trying to get relief.

"Have you felt as well as usual for a week, or ten days past?" I inquired.

"No, Doctor." It was the mother who answered my question. "And in order that you may understand the case clearly, let me say, that it is only a week since we arrived from England. We came over in a steamer, and were fifteen days in making the trip. From Boston, we came here in our own carriage. Before leaving home, Blanche went around to see a number of poor cottagers in our neighbourhood, and there was sickness at several of the places where she called. In one cottage, particularly, was a case of low fever. I was troubled when I learned that she had been there, but still hoped that her excellent state of health would repel anything like contagion. During the first part of our voyage, she suffered considerably from sea-sickness; but got along very well after that. If it hadn't been for the unhappy scenes of the last few days, with their painfully exciting consummation, I think she would have thrown off, wholly, any lurking tendency to disease."

I turned my face partly aside, so that its expression could not be seen. The facts stated, and the symptoms as now presented, left me in little doubt as to the nature of the malady against which I had to contend. Even while her mother talked, my patient fell away into the stupor from which I had aroused her.

My treatment of the case coincided with the practice of men eminent in the school of medicine to which I then belonged. I am not a disciple of that school now, having found a system of exacter science, and one compassing more certain results with smaller risk and less waste of physical energy.

In order to remove the uneasiness of which my patient complained, I gave an emetic. Its action was salutary, causing a determination towards the skin, and opening the pores, as well as relieving the oppression from which she suffered.

"How is your head now?" I asked, after she had been quiet for some minutes.

"Better. I feel scarcely any pain."

"So far, all is right," said I, cheerfully.

The mother looked at me with an anxious face. I arose, and we retired from the room together. Before leaving, I spoke encouragingly to my patient, and promised to see her early in the morning.

"My daughter is very sick, Doctor. What is the disease?" The mother spoke calmly and firmly. "I am

T. S. Arthur

not one towards whom any concealments need be practised; and it is meet that I should know the worst, that I may do the best."

"The disease, madam," I replied, "has not yet put on all of its distinctive signs. A fever - we call it the fever of incubation - is the forerunner of several very different ailments, and, at the beginning, the most accurate eye may fail to see what is beyond. In the present case, however, I think that typhoid fever is indicated."

I spoke as evenly as possible, and with as little apparent concern as possible. But I saw the blood go instantly back from the mother's face.

"Typhoid fever!" she ejaculated, in a low voice, clasping her hands together. I learned afterwards that she had cause to dread this exhausting and often fatal disease. "Oh, Doctor! do for her as if she were your own and only child."

She grasped my arm, like one catching at a fleeting hope.

"As if she were my own and only child!" I repeated her words in promise and assurance, adding -

"The first result of the medicine which I gave is just what I desired. I will leave something more to be taken at intervals of two hours, until midnight. In the morning, I hope to find a very encouraging change."

"But, Doctor," she replied, "if this is a case of typhoid fever, no hope of any quick change for the better can be entertained. I am no stranger to the fearful malady."

"Attacks of all diseases," I answered to this, "are more or less severe, according to the nature of the predisposing and exciting causes. So far as your daughter is concerned, I should think, from the very slight opportunity I have had of forming an opinion in regard to her, that she is not readily susceptible of morbific intrusions. Under an unusual exposure to exciting causes, the balance of health has been overcome. If my presumption is correct, we have the steady effort of nature, in co-operation with remedial agencies, working towards a cure."

"Do you think the attack light, or severe?" the mother asked, speaking more calmly.

"Neither light nor severe; but of a character, judging from the first impression made upon it, entirely controllable by medicines."

This opinion gave her confidence. As I had spoken without any apparent concealment, she evidently believed the case to stand exactly as I had stated it. After leaving medicine to be taken, every two hours, for the first part of the night, I went away.

In the morning, I found my patient in that comatose state, the usual attendant upon typhoid fever. She aroused herself on my entrance, and answered all questions clearly. She had no pain in the head, nor any distressing symptoms. Her skin was soft and moist. All things looked favorable. I gave, now, only gentle diaphoretics, and let the case progress, watching it with the closest attention. In this, I followed my usual course of treatment as to giving medicines. If I could produce a reaction, or remove some obstruction, and give nature a chance, I did not think it wise to keep on with drugs, which, from their general poisonous qualities, make even well people sick - regarding the struggle of life with disease as hazardous enough, without increasing the risk by adding a new cause of disturbance, unless the need of its presence were unmistakably indicated.

The course of this fever is always slow and exhausting. My patient sunk steadily, day by day, while I continued to watch the case with more than common anxiety. At the end of a week, she was feeble as an infant, and lay, for the most part, in a state of coma. I visited her two or three times every day, and had the thought of her almost constantly in my mind. Her mother, nerved for the occasion, was calm, patient, and untiring. The excitement which appeared on the occasion of my first visits, when there was doubt as to the character of the disease, passed away, and never showed itself again during her daughter's illness. I saw, daily, deeper into her character, which more and more impressed me with its simple grandeur, if I may use the word in this connection. There was nothing trifling, mean, or unwomanly about her. Her mind seemed to rest with a profoundly rational, and at the same time child-like trust, in Providence. Fear did not unnerve her, nor anxiety stay her hands in any thing. She met me, at every visit, with dignified self-possession, and received my report of the case, each time, without visible emotion. I had not attempted to deceive her in any thing from the beginning; she had seen this, and the fact gave her confidence in all my statements touching her daughter's condition.

At the end of a week, I commenced giving stimulants, selecting, as the chief article, sound old Maderia wine. The effect was soon apparent, in a firmer pulse and a quickened vitality. The lethargic condition in which she had lain for most of the time since the commencement of the attack, began to give way, and in a much shorter period than is usually the case, in this disease, we had the unmistakable signs of convalescence.

"Thank God, who, by means of your skill, has given me back my precious child!" said the mother to me, one day, after Blanche was able to sit up in bed. She took my hand and grasped it tightly. I saw that she was deeply moved. I merely answered:

"With Him are the issues of life."

"And I have tried to leave all with Him," she said. "To be willing to suffer even that loss, the bare thought of which makes me shudder. But I am not equal to the trial, and in mercy He has spared me."

"He is full of compassion, and gracious. He knows our strength, and will not test it beyond the limits of endurance."

"Doctor," she said, a light coming into her face, "I have much to say to you, but not now. I think you can understand me."

I merely bowed.

"There is one thing," she went on, "that I have liked in you from the beginning. I am to you a total stranger, and my presence in this house is a fact that must awaken many questions in your mind. Yet you have shown no restless curiosity, have plied me with no leading questions, have left me free to speak, or keep silence. There is a manly courtesy about this that accords with my feelings."

I bowed again, but did not venture upon mere words of compliment.

"I am not sure," said she, "that my name even is known to you."

"It is not," I answered. "You have seemed to avoid any allusion thereto, and delicacy forbade my asking."

"There has been no purposed concealment. My name is Montgomery; and I am sister to the late Captain Allen."

"I had already inferred this relationship." The remark evidently surprised her.

"On what ground could you base such an inference?" she asked, curiously.

"On traditional ground. The history of this old mansion is familiar to most persons in S -; and some of the incidents connected with the family have too strong a tinge of romance about them to easily pass into oblivion. It is well known to us that Captain Allen had an only sister."

"What is it said became of her?"

"When she was about two years of age her mother carried her off, sailing, as was believed, to England, of which country she was a native."

"Is the name of the child preserved in this tradition?"

"Yes. It was Flora."

"My own name," she said.

"And in person you are identical."

"Yes. My mother's early life embraced some dreadful experiences. Her father and mother, with two brothers and a younger sister, were all murdered by pirates. She alone was spared, and afterwards became the wife of a sea captain, who, I fear, was not a man innocent of blood. On this point, however, my mother was reserved, almost silent. In the course of time she grew so wretched, as the wife of this man, that she sent a letter to England, addressed to some remembered relative, imploring him to save her from a life that was worse than death. This letter fell into the right hands. A cousin was sent out from England, and she fled with him. No attempt, as far as we know, was ever made to follow and regain her She did not live many years afterwards. I grew up among my relatives, ignorant of her history. My memory of her is distinct, though she died when I was but eight years old.

"I married, at the age of twenty-six, an officer in the British army, one of the younger sons in a titled family, for whom no way in the world is opened, except through the church or the battle-field. General Montgomery chose the profession of a soldier, not from a love of its exciting and fearful concomitants, but because he had no fancy for the gown and cassock, and could not be a hypocrite in religion. He went quite early to British India, and distinguished himself there by many acts of bravery, as well as by his humane and honorable conduct. So highly was he regarded by the East India Company, that he was selected for most

T. S. Arthur

important services, and assigned to posts of great responsibility. He was past thirty years of age when I met him, on the occasion of one of his visits to England. The attraction was mutual; and when he returned to Calcutta, I went with him as his wife. Then came twenty years of a happy married life; - happy, I mean, so far as a perfect union of souls can make us happy in this world, but miserable, at times, through intense anxiety for the absent one exposed to fearful perils.

"We had three children." There was a tremor in the voice of Mrs. Montgomery as she referred to her children. "One only remains." She paused, as if to recover herself, and then went on.

"I lost my husband first. Ten years ago, he fell at the post of duty, and, while my heart lay crushed and bleeding under the terrible blow, it leaped with throbbings of pride, as his honored name went sounding from lip to lip, and from land to land. I had not the sad pleasure of being with him in that last time. For the sake of our children, I was residing in England.

"Troubles rarely come alone. Two years afterwards my oldest son died. My home was in the family of General Montgomery, where I was treated with great kindness; but as my income was not sufficient for an establishment of my own, I felt a sense of obligation that is always oppressive to one of my nature. This feeling grew upon me daily, and at last began to haunt me like a constantly re-appearing spectre. It is now about three years since, in looking over some old letters and papers, I came unexpectedly upon a document written by my mother - all the evidence as to this was clear - and addressed to myself. How it should have remained so long unobserved, and yet in my possession, is one of the mysterious things which I do not attempt to explain. There is a Providence in all things, even to the most minute, and I simply refer the fact to Providence, and leave it there. This document spoke briefly, but with no special particularity, of her marriage with a Captain Allen, and settlement in this town. It stated that she had two children, a son and a daughter, and that in leaving America for England, she had taken her daughter, but left the son behind. There was no suggestion as to the use to be made of these facts; but there was such a statement of them as left their verification, I thought, easy. I turned them over and over in my mind, and in the end resolved to gain all accessible information touching the present condition of things. To this end, I sent over about two years ago, a man of prudence and intelligence, versed in legal matters, with instructions to obtain all possible particulars in regard to my brother, his family and estate. He brought back word that my brother was dead; that he had left no children, and that his widow - if, indeed, she were ever his legal wife, which seemed to be doubted - was old, in poor health, and verging towards mental imbecility, if not insanity. That there was a large and valuable estate, to which I, as sister of Captain Allen, was undoubtedly the heir.

"I kept these things, for the time being, to myself, and pondered over them in some perplexity as to the best course to take. But from these thoughts, my mind was soon turned by the illness of my oldest daughter. After a lingering sickness of many weeks, she died. It seemed almost impossible to arouse myself from the stunning effects of this blow. It crushed me down more than any previous sorrow, for it fell upon a heart weakened by pain. It was many months before the discipline of this affliction awakened me to thoughts of a higher life. Then I began to rise into serener heights - to see as by an interior vision, to believe that even our saddest things may fall upon us in mercy.

"Finally, circumstances of which I need not speak, made me resolve to leave England, and under legal advice of the highest authority, take quiet possession of this estate, which is mine."

Mrs. Montgomery ceased speaking.

"Perhaps," she resumed, after a moment, "it may be as well, all things considered, that you do not speak of this for the present. I shall, as soon as my daughter's full recovery gives me time to enter into the subject, place my affairs in the hands of a safe legal agent, in order that they may assume due form and order. You can, no doubt, refer me to the right individual."

"I can," was my reply. "Judge Bigelow, of our town, is the man. I speak of him with the utmost confidence."

"Thank you, Doctor. You lay me under additional obligation," she said. "I will, at an early day consult him."

Thus closed this deeply interesting interview.

# CHAPTER X.

I attended Blanche Montgomery through her slow convalescence, and had many opportunities for observing her and her mother closely. The more intimately I knew them the higher did they rise in my estimation. A purer, sweeter, truer-hearted girl than Blanche I had never seen. There was an artlessness and innocence about her but rarely met with in young ladies of her age. Especially was she free from that worldliness and levity which so often mars young maidenhood. Her mind was well stored and cultivated, and she was beginning to use her mental treasures in a way that interested you, and made you listen with pleased attention when she spoke on even common-place subjects. Her manners had in them a grace and dignity that was very attractive. As she advanced towards health her deportment took on an easy, confiding air, as if she looked upon me as a true friend. Her smile, whenever I appeared, broke over her gentle face like a gleam of sunshine.

Mrs. Montgomery's manner towards me was distinguished by the same frankness that marked her daughter's deportment. The stately air that struck me in the beginning I no longer observed. If it existed, my eyes saw it differently. At her request, when her mind was sufficiently at ease about her daughter to busy itself with the common affairs of life, I brought Judge

T. S. Arthur

Bigelow to see her, and she placed her business matters in his hands. The judge was very much struck with her person and manner, and told me the day after his first meeting with her that she came nearer to his ideal of a lady than any woman he had ever met; and as for the daughter she seemed more like a picture he had once seen than a piece of real flesh and blood. I smiled at the Judge's enthusiasm, but did not wonder at the impression he had received.

Other characters in our story now claim attention, and we must turn to them. After Henry Wallingford had gained the mastery over himself: - the struggle was wild, but brief - he resumed his office duties as usual, and few noticed any change in him, except that he withdrew even more than ever into himself. I met him occasionally, and observed him closely. In my eyes there was a marked difference in the aspect of his face. It had an expression of patient suffering at times - and again I saw in it a most touching sadness.

The dashing nephew of Judge Bigelow offered himself to Squire Floyd's daughter in about a week after her rejection of Wallingford's suit, and was accepted. I became immediately cognizant of the fact through my wife, who had the news from Delia's aunt, Mrs. Dean. A day or two afterwards I met her in company with young Dewey, and observed her closely. Alas! In my eyes the work of moral retrocession had already begun. She was gay and chatty, and her countenance fresh and blooming. But I missed something - something the absence of which awakened a sigh of regret. Ralph was very lover-like in his deportment, fluttering about Delia, complimenting her, and showing her many obtrusive attentions. But eyes that were in the habit of looking below the surface of things, saw no heart in it all.

Squire Floyd was delighted with his daughter's fine prospects; and he and Judge Bigelow drew their heads together over the affair in a cosy and confidential way very pleasant to both of them. The Judge was eloquent touching his nephew's fine qualities and splendid prospects; and congratulated the Squire, time and again, on his daughter's fortunate matrimonial speculation. He used the word which was significative beyond any thing that entered his imagination.

A few days after the engagement Ralph Dewey returned to New York. The wedding-day had not been fixed; but the marriage, as understood by all parties, was to take place some time during the next winter.

From that time I noticed a change in Delia. She grew silent in company, and had an absent way about her that contrasted strongly with her former social disposition. Young people rallied her in the usual style about her heart being absent with the beloved one, but I read the signs differently. It could not but follow, that a soul, endowed like hers, would have misgivings in view of an alliance with one like Ralph Dewey. What was there in him to satisfy a true woman's yearnings for conjunction with a kindred nature? Nothing! He was all outside as to good. A mere selfish, superficial, speculating man of the world. While she had a heart capable of the deepest and truest affection. Would he make the fitting complement to her life? Alas! No! That were a thing impossible.

During the few months that preceded this marriage, I often heard its promise discussed by my wife and Mrs. Dean, neither of whom had any strong liking for the young New York merchant.

"It's my opinion," said Mrs. Dean, as she sat with my wife one evening, about two months after the engagement had taken place, "that Ralph has more froth than substance about him. He really talks, sometimes, as if he had the world in a sling and could toss it up among the stars. As far as my observation goes, such people flourish only for a season."

"If Delia were a child of mine," said my good Constance, in her earnest way, "I would a thousand times rather trust her with Henry Wallingford than with Ralph Dewey."

"Yes, and a thousand millions of times," responded Mrs. Dean. "He is a man. You know just what he is, and where he is. But, as for this splashing nephew of Judge Bigelow's - who knows what's below the surface? Delia's father is all taken up with him, and thinks the match a splendid one. Sister don't say much; but I can see that she has her misgivings. I can talk to you freely, you know."

"I don't think," said I, "that Delia has grown more cheerful since her engagement. Brides expectant ought to feel as happy as the day is long."

"More cheerful? Oh, dear, no! She isn't the same that she was at all; but mopes about more than half of her time. It's just my opinion - spoken between friends - that she cares, now, a great deal more for Henry than she does for Ralph."

"Do they ever meet?" I inquired.

"Not very often."

"They have met?"

"Yes, several times."

"Have you seen them together?"

"Oh, yes."

"How does she act towards him?"

"Not always the same. Sometimes she is talkative, and sometimes reserved - sometimes as gay as a lark, and sometimes sober enough; as if there were such a weight on her spirits, that she could not smile without an effort."

"Does the fact of his presence make any change in her?" I inquired. "What I mean is, if she were lively in spirits before he came in, would she grow serious - or if serious, grow excited?"

"Oh, yes, it always makes a change. I've known her, after being very quiet, and hardly having any thing to say, though in the midst of young company, grow all at once as merry as a cricket, and laugh and joke in a wild sort of way. And again, when she has been in one of her old, pleasant states of mind I have noticed that she all at once drew back into herself; I could trace the cause to only this - the presence of Henry Wallingford. But this doesn't often happen, for he rarely shows himself in company."

"Is there anything noticeable about Henry when they meet?" I asked.

"Not to an ordinary observer," replied Mrs. Dean. "But I look with sharper eyes than most people. Yes, there is something noticeable. He always puts himself in her way, but with a kind of forced, resolute manner, as if the act were a trial of strength, and involved a stern heart-discipline. And this I think, is just the real state of the case. He has deliberately and resolutely entered upon the work of unwinding from his heart the cord which love his thrown around it in so many intertwisted folds. So I read him. To break it by sudden force, would leave so many unwound portions behind, that the memory of her might sadden the whole of his after-life. And so he is learning to grow indifferent towards her. To search in her for such things as repel, instead of for those that charm the heart."

"A dangerous experiment," said my wife, "for one who has loved so deeply."

"It would be to most men," I remarked. "But there is stuff about Henry - the stuff that strong, persistent, successful men are made of. If he has begun this work, he will complete it certainly."

A few weeks afterwards, I had an opportunity of seeing them together, and I improved it to observe them closely. It was in a mixed company at the house of Judge Bigelow. Wallingford came in rather late. I was conversing with Delia when he entered the room, and we were at an interesting point in the subject under consideration. I noticed, all at once, a hesitation and confusion of thought, as her eyes rested, with a sudden interest, on some object in the room. Glancing around, I saw the young man. We went on with our conversation, Delia rallying herself, as I could see, with an effort. But she talked no longer from thought, only from memory - uttering mere truisms and common-places. She put on more animation, and affected a deeper interest; but I was not deceived.

We were still in conversation, when Wallingford joined us. I saw him fix his eyes, as they met, searchingly upon her face, and saw her eyes droop away from his. He was fully self-possessed; she not at ease. His mind was clear; hers in some confusion. I remained some time near them, listening to their conversation, and joining in occasionally. Never before had I seen him appear so well, nor her to such poor advantage. She tried to act a part - he was himself. I noticed, as he led the conversation, that he kept away from the esthetic, and held her thought in the region of moral causes; that he dwelt on the ends and purposes of life, as involving everything. Now and then she essayed a feeble argument, or met some of his propositions with light banter. But with a word he obliterated the sophism - and with a glance repressed the badinage. I think she could never before have so felt the superiority of this man, whose pure love - almost worship - she had put aside as a thing of light importance; and I think the interview helped him in the work upon which he had entered, that of obliterating from his heart all traces of her image.

After this interview, they did not draw together again during the evening. Delia tried to be gay and indifferent; but he acted himself out just as he was. I did not observe that he was more social than usual, or that he mingled more than was his wont with the young ladies present. For most of the time, he kept, as was usual with him, in company and in conversation with his own sex.

I could not but pity Delia Floyd. It was plain to me that she was waking up to the sad error she had committed - an error, the consequences of which would go with her through life. Very, very far was she from being indifferent to Wallingford - that I could plainly see.

During the winter, Ralph came up frequently from New York to visit his bride to be. As he was the nephew of Judge Bigelow, he and Wallingford were, as a thing of course, thrown often together during these visits. It can hardly excite wonder, that Wallingford maintained a reserved and distant demeanor towards the young man, steadily repelling all familiarity, yet always treating him with such politeness and respect that no cause of offence could appear. On the part of Dewey, it may be said that he saw little in the grave plodder among dusty law books and discolored parchments, that won upon his regard. He looked upon him as a young man good enough in his way - a very small way, in his estimation - good enough for S -, and small enough for a country town lawyer. He would have put on towards him a patronizing air, and tried to excite in his mind a nobler ambition than to move in our circumscribed sphere, if something in the young man's steady, penetrating, half-mysterious eye had not always held him back:

"I never can talk with that young associate or yours, uncle," he would say, now and then, to Judge Bigelow, "and I can't just make him out. Is he stupid, or queer?"

The Judge would smile, or laugh quietly to himself, or perhaps answer in this wise:

"I think Henry understands himself. Still waters, you know, run deep."

One day in February, on the occasion of a periodical visit to S -, young Dewey called in at Judge Bigelow's office, and finding Wallingford alone, sat down and entered into as familiar a talk with him as was possible, considering how little they had in common. Ralph had a purpose in view, and as soon as he saw, or thought he saw, Wallingford's mind in the right mood, said -

"I am going to ask a particular favor, and you must not refuse."

"If I can serve you in any thing, it will be my pleasure to do so," was the ready answer.

"You know that I am to be married next month?"

"So I have heard," replied Wallingford.

"You will stand my groomsman? Don't say no!"

He had seen an instant negative in the young man's face.

"Almost any thing else, but not that!" replied Henry, speaking with some feeling. He was thrown off his guard by so unexpected a request.

"Come now, my good friend, don't take the matter so much to heart!" said Dewey, in a light way. "Plenty of good fish in the sea yet - as good as ever were caught. You must forgive the girl for liking me the best."

"You jest on a grave subject," said Wallingford, his face growing pale, but his eyes, a little dilated, riveting his companion's where he stood.

T. S. Arthur

"No, I am in earnest," said Dewey, with something in his manner that was offensive.

"Jest or earnest, your familiarity is out of place with me," retorted Wallingford, with a sternness of manner, that quickened the flow of bad blood in Dewey's heart.

"Oh, you needn't take on airs!" replied the other with a sneer of contempt. Then muttering to himself, yet loud enough to be heard, - "I didn't suppose the puppy would growl at a familiar pat on the head."

This was too much for Wallingford. At another time, he might have borne it with a manly self-possession. But only an hour before he had met Miss Floyd in the street, and the look she then gave him had stirred his heart, and left a tinge of shadowy regret on his feelings. He was, therefore, in no mood to bear trifling, much less insult. Scarcely had the offensive words passed Dewey's lips, when a blow in the face staggered him back against the wall. Instantly recovering himself, he sprang towards Wallingford in blind rage, and struck at him with a savage energy; but the latter stepped aside, and let his assailant come, with stunning force, against the wall at the other side of the office, when he fell to the floor.

At this instant, Judge Bigelow came in.

"Henry! Ralph!" he exclaimed - " what is the meaning of this?"

"Your nephew insulted me, and in the heat of anger I struck him in the face. In attempting to return that blow, he missed his aim, and fell against the wall, as you see."

Wallingford spoke without excitement, but in a stern, resolute way. By this time, Dewey was on his feet again. The sight of his uncle, and the unflinching aspect of the person he had ventured to insult, had the effect to cool off his excitement many degrees.

"What is the meaning of this, young men?" sternly repeated Judge Bigelow, looking from one to the other.

"I have answered your question as far as I am concerned," replied Henry.

"Ralph! Speak! Did you offer him an insult?"

To this demand, the nephew replied, with no abatement of his originally offensive manner -

"If he chooses to consider my words as an insult, let him do so. I shall in no case take them back."

"What did you say?"

There was an imperative force in the Judge's manner.

Dewey was silent.

"What did he say," - Judge Bigelow turned to Wallingford, "that you should answer it with a blow?"

"If he is satisfied with the answer," replied the latter, "the case can rest where it is. If not, I am ready to meet him on any appeal. I He will find me no trifler."

The Judge turned again to his nephew.

"Ralph! I insist upon having this matter explained. I

T. S. Arthur

know Henry too well to believe that he would strike you, unless there had been strong provocation."

"Perhaps he regarded it as such; I did not," said Dewey.

"If he is satisfied with his chastisement, there is no occasion to press him farther, Judge." Wallingford was provoked to this by the young man's cool impertinence.

Dewey made a movement as if about to rush upon Wallingford, but the Judge interposed his body to keep them apart. The appearance of a fourth party at this juncture, in the person of Squire Floyd, the prospective father-in-law of one of the belligerents, changed materially the aspect of affairs.

"Good-morning, Squire," said Wallingford, with a quickly assumed cheerfulness of manner, smiling in his usual grave way.

Both the Judge and his nephew saw reason to imitate the example of Wallingford, and thus throw up a blind before the eyes of Squire Floyd, who thought he perceived something wrong as he came in, but was afterwards inclined to doubt the evidence of his senses.

Wallingford retired in a few moments. When he came back to the office an hour afterwards, he found a note of apology on his table, accompanied by a request that so unpleasant an incident as the one which had just occurred, might be suffered to pass into oblivion. No acknowledgment of this communication was made by the young lawyer. He felt the strongest kind of repugnance towards Dewey, and could not gain his own consent to have any intercourse with him. His position, as an associate with Judge Bigelow, occasionally brought him in contact with his nephew, who recognized him always in a respectful manner. But Wallingford held him ever coldly at a distance.

T. S. Arthur

# CHAPTER XI.

The marriage of Delia Floyd was an event in our quiet town. It was celebrated at the house of her father, in the presence of a large company, who were invited to witness the ceremony, and take part in the attendant festivities. The match was regarded generally as a most desirable one for the young lady; and there was more than one mother present who envied the good fortune which had given such a son-in-law to Mrs. Floyd. I heard many snatches of conversation, half aside, in which marvelous things were related, or suggested, touching the bridegroom's fortune and the splendid home he had prepared for his bride. He was looked upon as a prospective millionaire, and imagination pictured Delia as the jeweled mistress of a palace home. Few seemed to think of any thing beyond the promised worldly advantage.

"I am glad that your daughter has married so well."

"Let me congratulate you, Squire Floyd, on this splendid match."

"It is not often, Mrs. Floyd, that a mother sees her daughter go forth into the world with such brilliant prospects."

"You have all that your heart can desire, so far as Delia

is concerned, Mrs. Floyd."

"You are the envy of mothers."

And so I heard the changes rung on all sides of me, and from the lips of people who might have looked deeper if they had taken the trouble to use their eyes.

To me, the wedding was full of sad suggestions. It was one of those social self-sacrifices, as common now as then, in which the victim goes self-impelled to the altar, and lays upon its consuming fires the richest dower of womanhood.

I listened to the vows that were made on this occasion, and felt a low thrill of repulsion as words of such solemn import trembled on the air, for too well I knew that a union of souls in a true marriage, such as Delia Floyd might consummate, was impossible here. Could she be happy in this marriage? I gave to my own question an emphatic "No!" She might have a gay, brilliant, exciting life; but to that deep peace which is given to loving hearts, and which, in hours of isolation and loneliness, she would desire with an irrepressible longing, she must forever be a stranger.

I looked into her beautiful young face as she stood receiving the congratulations of friends, and felt as I had never felt before on such an occasion. Instinctively my thought ran questioning along the future. But no hopeful answer was returned. How was she to advance in that inner-life development through which the true woman is perfected? I pushed the question aside. It was too painful. Had she been one of the great company of almost soulless women - if I may use such strong language - who pass, yearly, through legal

T. S. Arthur

forms into the mere semblance of a marriage, I might have looked on with indifference, for then, the realization would, in all probability, be equal to the promise. But Delia Floyd was of a different spiritual organization. She had higher capabilities and nobler aspirations; and if the one found no true sphere of development, while the other was doomed to beat its wings vainly amid the lower atmospheres of life, was happiness in the case even a possibility?

Among the guests was Wallingford. It was six months, almost to a day, since the dearest hope in life he had ever cherished went suddenly out, and left him, for a season, in the darkness of despair. I did not expect to see him on this occasion; and there was another, I think, who as little anticipated his presence - I mean the bride. But he had shared in the invitations, and came up to witness the sacrifice. To see, what a few months before was to him the most precious thing in life, pass into the full possession of another. Had not the fine gold grown dim in his eyes? It had - dim with the tarnish that better natures receive when they consent to dwell with inferior spirits, and breathe in an atmosphere loaded with earthly exhalations. It would have been the highest delight of his life to have ascended with her into the pure regions, where thought builds tabernacles and establishes its dwelling-places. To have walked onward, side by side, in a dear life companionship, towards the goal of eternal spiritual oneness. But she had willed it otherwise; and now he had come, resolutely, to bear the pain of a final sundering of all bonds, that his soul might free itself from her soul completely and forever.

I first noticed him as the bridal party entered the room, and took their places in front of the clergyman who was to officiate on the occasion. He occupied a position that gave him a clear view of Delia's face, while he was removed from general observation. Almost from the commencement to the ending of the ceremony his gaze rested on her countenance. His head was thrown a little forward, his brows slightly contracted, his lips firmly set, and his eyes fixed as if the object upon which he was gazing held him by an irresistible fascination. I was so much interested in him that I scarcely looked at the bride during the ceremony. At last, the minister, in conclusion, announced the twain to be husband and wife. I saw Wallingford give a slight start as if a tensely strung chord of feeling had been jarred. A moment more and the spell was broken! Every lineament of his countenance showed this. The stern aspect gave way - light trembled over the softening features - the body stood more erect as if a great pressure had been removed.

I noticed that he did not hold back in the excitement of congratulation that followed the ceremony. I was near him when he took the hand of Delia, and heard him say - not - "I congratulate you" - but "May your life be a happy one." The tone was earnest and feeling, such as a brother might use to a beloved sister. I held that tone long afterwards in my memory, studying its signification. It had in it nothing of regret, or pain, or sadness, as if he were losing something, but simply expressed the regard and tender interest of a sincere well wisher. And so that great trial was at an end for him. He had struggled manfully with a great enemy to his peace, and this was his hour of triumph.

With the bride's state of mind, as read in external signs, I was far from being satisfied. Marriage, in any case, to one who thinks and feels, is a thing of serious import;

and even the habitually thoughtless can hardly take its solemn vows upon their lips without falling into a sober mood. We are, therefore, not surprised to see emotion put on signs of pain - like April showers that weep away into sunshine. But in Delia's face I saw something that went deeper than all this.

"There is no one here," said I, taking her hand, and holding it tightly in mine, "who wishes you well in the future more sincerely than I do."

"I know it, Doctor," she answered, returning the warm grasp I gave her. Her eyes rested steadily in mine, and saw a shadow in them.

"We are sorry to lose you from S -. Indeed we cannot afford to lose you."

"She is wanted," spoke up her young husband a little proudly, "to grace a wider and more brilliant sphere of life."

"It is not the brilliant sphere that is always the happiest," said I. "Life's truest pleasures come oftener to quiet home circles even among the lowly, than to gilded palaces where fortune's favorites reside."

"It is not to external condition," the bride remarked, "that we are to look for happiness." I thought her voice had in it a pensive tone, as if she were not wholly satisfied with the brilliant promise that lay before her. "You know, Doctor, we have talked that over more than once in our lives."

"Yes, Delia; and it is a truth which we ought never to forget - one that I trust you and your husband will lay up in your hearts."

I turned to the young man desiring my admonition to reach him also.

"Perhaps I might differ something from this sage conclusion," he answered a little flippantly. "As far as I can see, the external condition has a great deal to do with our happiness. I am very sure, that if I were situated as some people are whom I know, I would be miserable. So you see, Doctor, I have my doubts touching this theory of yours and Delia's."

"Time, I think, will demonstrate its truth," I said, in a graver tone, and turned from them to give place to those who could talk in a lighter strain than was possible for me on the occasion.

During the evening I saw Wallingford more than once in conversation with the bride; but only when she happened to be a little separated from her husband, towards whom his manner was coldly polite. The two young men, after the scene in Judge Bigelow's office, only kept up, for the sake of others, the shadow of acquaintanceship. Between them there was a strong mutual repulsion which neither sought to overcome.

As I remarked I saw Wallingford more than once in conversation with the bride. But nothing in his manner indicated any sentiment beyond that of friendship. He was polite, cheerful, and at his ease. But it was different with her. She was not at her ease in his company, and yet, I could see that his attention was grateful - even pleasant.

The augury was not good. As I read the signs, Delia

Floyd, when she passed from maidenhood to wifehood, departed from the path that led to happiness in this world. And I said to myself as I pondered her future - "May the disappointments and sorrows that are almost sure to come, turn her feet aside into the right way at last!"

# CHAPTER XII.

On the day following, the young husband bore his bride away to grace the prouder home that awaited her in New York; and affairs in our town settled themselves down into the old routine.

During the few months that have passed since the opening of our story, the only matter that has occurred, of any interest to the reader, at the Allen House, is the fact that Judge Bigelow has undertaken the management of Mrs. Montgomery's affairs, and the establishment of her claim to the possession, as only heir, of the whole of Captain Allen's property. Some legal difficulties, bearing upon her identification as his sister, were in the way; and in the effort to remove these, there had been considerable correspondence with persons in England.

The first fact to be clearly proved was the solemnization of a marriage between Mrs. Montgomery's mother and the elder Captain Allen. Next, the identity of Mrs. Montgomery as her child. No marriage certificate, nor any record of the fact, as to the exact time and place, were known to be in existence; and without them, or evidence of a very conclusive character, the title of Mrs. Montgomery could not be clearly established.

T. S. Arthur

This, Judge Bigelow stated to her in the beginning; but, up to this time, no such evidence had been found.

Mrs. Montgomery's health was not good, and as she required occasional medical aid, my visits to the Allen House were continued. The more intimately I came to know this lady, the higher did she rise in my esteem. She united strength of mind with clearness of perception: and decision of character with prudence and justice. She had, likewise, a depth and tenderness of feeling that often exhibited itself in beautiful incidents. The dignity of manner, which at first seemed touched with hauteur, now only gave grace to her fine proportions.

She had, from the beginning, spoken to me without reserve of her affairs, in which I naturally took deep interest. One day she said: -

"Doctor, I wish to get your opinion in regard to an individual whom Judge Bigelow proposes to send out to England for me on important business. He is a young man, associated with him, as I understand it, professionally.

"Mr. Wallingford, you mean?"

"Yes, that is the name, I believe. Do you know him?"

"Very well."

"Is he prudent, intelligent, and reliable?"

"I think so."

"You only think so, Doctor?"

"I can speak in stronger terms. As far as one can know another, I am ready to say that *he is* prudent, intelligent, and reliable. If I had important business to transact at a distant point, and needed a trusty agent, I would select him before any other man in S -."

I wish no better testimony, Doctor, and am glad to know that I can procure an agent so well qualified."

"Have you seen him?" I inquired.

"No. But Judge Bigelow is to bring him here today, in order that I may see and converse with him."

"You will find him," said I, a young man of few words and unobtrusive manners - but solid as a rock. I have seen him under circumstances calculated to test the character of any man."

"What are the circumstances, if you are free to speak of them?" asked Mrs. Montgomery. "We get always a truer estimate of a man, when we see him in some great battle of life; for then, his real qualities and resources become apparent."

I thought for a little while before answering. It did not seem just right to draw aside the veil that strangers' eyes might look upon a life-passage such as was written in Wallingford's Book of Memory. The brief but fierce struggle was over with him; and he was moving steadily onward, sadder, no doubt, for the experience, and wiser, no doubt. But the secret was his own, and I felt that no one ought to meddle therewith. Still, a relation of the fact, showing how deeply the man could feel, and how strong he was in self-mastery, could not but raise him in the estimation of Mrs.

Montgomery, and increase her confidence.

"It is hardly fair," said I, "to bring up the circumstances of a man's life over which he has drawn a veil; and which are sacred to himself alone. In this case, however, with the end of enabling you more fully to know the person you think of sending abroad on an important service, I will relate an occurrence that cannot fail to awaken in your mind an interest for the young man, such as we always feel for those who have passed through deep suffering."

Blanche was sitting by her mother. Indeed, the two were almost inseparable companions. It was a rare thing to find them apart. I saw her face kindle with an earnest curiosity.

"Judge Bigelow's nephew was married, recently," I said.

"So the Judge informed me. He spoke very warmly of his nephew, who is a merchant in New York, I think he said."

"He is a partner in a mercantile firm there. The bride was Squire Floyd's daughter; a very superior girl - lovely in character, attractive in person, and, mentally, well cultivated. I have always regarded her as the flower of our town."

"The young man had good taste, it seems," Mrs. Montgomery remarked.

"Better than the young lady showed in taking him for a husband," said I.

"Ah? Then your opinion of him is not so favorable."

"He was not worthy of her, if I possess any skill in reading character. But there was one worthy of her, and deeply attached to her at the same time."

"This young Wallingford, of whom we were speaking?"

"The same."

"But she didn't fancy him?"

"She did fancy him. But -"

"Was not able to resist the attractions of a New York merchant, when put in opposition to those of a humble country lawyer?"

"The truth lies about there. She took the showy effigy of a man, in place of the real man."

"A sad mistake. But it is made every day," said Mrs. Montgomery, "and will continue to be made. Alas for the blindness and folly that lead so many into paths that terminate in barren deserts, or wildernesses where the soul is lost! And so our young friend has been crossed in love."

"The experience is deeper than usual," said I. Then I related, with some particularity, the facts in the case, already known to the reader. Both the mother and daughter listened with deep attention. After I had finished my story, Mrs. Montgomery said,

"He possesses will and strength of character, that is

T. S. Arthur

plain; but I can't say that I just like the deliberate process of *un*loving, if I may use the word, which you have described. There is something too cold-blooded about it for me. Like the oak, bent under the pressure of a fierce storm, he comes up erect too soon."

I smiled at her view of the case, and answered,

"You look upon it as a woman, I as a man. To me, there is a certain oral grandeur in the way he has disenthralled himself from fetters hat could not remain, without a life-long disability."

"Oh, no doubt it was the wisest course," said Mrs. Montgomery.

"And may we not look among the wisest men, for the best and most reliable?" I queried.

"Among those who are truly wise," she said, her voice giving emphasis to the word *truly*.

"What is it to be truly wise?"

"All true wisdom," she answered, "as it appertains to the affairs of this life, has its foundation in a just regard for others; for, in the degree that we are just to others, are we just to ourselves."

"And is not the converse of your proposition true also? In the degree that we are just to ourselves, are we not just to others?"

"Undoubtedly. Each individual bears to common society, the same relation that a member, organ, or fibre, does to the human body, of which it makes a part. And as no member, organ, or fibre of the body, can injure itself without injuring the whole man; so no individual can do wrong to himself, without a conesquent wrong to others. Each has duties to perform for the good of common society, and any self-inflicted or self-permitted disabilities that hinder the right performance of these duties, involve a moral wrong."

"Then the case is very clear for my friend Wallingford," said I. "He is a wise man in your sense of the word - wise, in resolutely putting away from his mind the image of one who, if she had been worthy of him, would have taken her place proudly by his side; but, proving herself unworthy, could never afterward be to him more than a friend or stringer. He could not hold her image in his heart, and fondly regard it, without sin; for was she not to be the bride of another? Nor without suffering loss of mental power, and life-purpose, and thus injuring others trough neglect of duty. It was acting wisely, then, for him to come up, manfully, to the work of drawing back his misplaced affections, and getting them again fully into his own possession. And he has done the work, if I read the signs aright. All honor to his manhood!"

"He has, I see, a warm advocate in you, Doctor," said Mrs. Montgomery, again smiling. "Still, in an affair of the heart, where so much was involved, as seemed to be in his case, we can hardly fancy such a matter-of-fact, business-like proceeding as you have described. He might well have been forgiven, if he had shown more weakness of character, and acted even a little unreasonably. I will yield to no one in my regard for manly firmness and self-control, for bravery and endurance; and I have seen these qualities put to some of the severest tests. But in matters of the heart, I must own that I like to see a man show his weakness. Your Mr. Wallingford is too cool and calculating for me. But this is irrelevant to our consideration of his qualities as a business agent. For this purpose, I am satisfied that he is fitted in all things essential."

"And that is quite as far as we need go," said I.

"The business in hand," said Mrs. Montgomery, resuming the conversation after a pause, "is of great importance to me, and may require not only a visit to England, but also to the West Indies. Unless evidence of my mother's marriage can be found, there will be, as you know, considerable difficulty in establishing my full right to inherit my brother's property. And my identity as the sister of the late Captain Allen must also be proved. By the will of my father, which is on record, he left all of his property to my brother. He, as far as is known, died intestate. As next of kin, I am the legal heir; but the proof is yet wanting. My mother's cousin, a Colonel Willoughby, of whom we have before spoken, came over from England, on the strength of some vague rumors that reached the family from Jamaica, and was successful in discovering the only survivor of his uncle's family. She saw it best to abandon her husband, as you know. My purpose in sending an agent, versed in legal matters, and used to weighing evidence, is to have such papers of Colonel Willoughby's as the family possess and will submit for examination, carefully searched, in the hope that some record may be found in his hand-writing, sufficiently clear to establish the fact that my mother was the wife of the elder Captain Allen. So important an event as that of searching out my mother, and inducing her to flee from her husband, could hardly have taken place, it seems to me, without evidence of the fact being preserved. And my hope is, that this evidence, if it can be found, will prove of great value. So you see, Doctor, that I have good reasons for wishing to know well the agent who goes abroad with a matter so vital as this in his hands."

I admitted the importance of a thoroughly reliable man to go upon this mission, and repeated my faith in Wallingford.

# CHAPTER XIII.

I saw Mrs. Montgomery a few days afterwards, and inquired if she had seen the young associate of Judge Bigelow. She replied in the affirmative.

"How does he impress you?" I asked.

"Favorably, upon the whole; though," she added with one of her meaning smiles, "I can't help thinking all the time about the cool, calculating, resolute way in which he went about disentangling himself from an unfortunate love affair. I look at his calm face, over which you rarely see a ripple of feeling go, and ask myself, sometimes, if a heart really beats within his bosom."

"There does; a true, large, manly heart, full of deep feeling; you may be sure of this, madam," I answered, with some warmth.

"I will not gainsay your words, Doctor. I trust for his sake that it may be so."

"Leaving out the heart matter, and regarding him only as to his fitness for the work in hand, you are favorably impressed?"

"Quite so. I find him quick of apprehension, intelligent, and of sufficient gravity of deportment to ensure a respectful attention wherever he may go. He made one suggestion that ought to have occurred to me, and upon which I am acting. As no will has been found, it has been assumed that Captain Allen died intestate. Mr. Wallingford suggests that a will may have been executed; and that a thorough search be made in order to discover if one exists. In consequence of this suggestion, Blanche and I have been hard at work for two days, prying into drawers, examining old papers, and looking into all conceivable, and I had almost said inconceivable places."

"And if you were to find a will?" said I, looking into her earnest face.

"The question would be that much nearer to a solution."

"Is it at all probable that it would be in your favor?"

I saw her start at the query, while her brows closed slightly, as if from a sudden pain. She looked at me steadily for a few moments, without speaking; then, after a long inspiration, she said:

"Whether in my favor or not, any disposition that he has made of his property, in law and right, must, of course, stand good."

"You might contest such a will, if not in your favor."

She shook her head, compressed her lips firmly, and said:

"No. I should not contest the will. My belief was, when I came here, that he died without making a bequest of

T. S. Arthur

any kind, and that his property would go, in consequence, to the heir-at-law. This was the information that I received. If it should prove otherwise, I shall make no opposition."

"Do you intend, under this view, continuing the search for a will?"

Something in the tone of voice touched her unpleasantly. I saw the light in her eyes glow intenser, and her lips arch.

"Why not?" she asked, looking at me steadily. I could have given another meaning to my question from the one I intended to convey, had it so pleased me, and thus avoided a probable offence. But I wished to see a little deeper into the quality of her mind, and so used the probe that was in my hand.

"If you find a will, devising the property out of your line, all your present prospects are at an end," said I.

"I know it."

Her voice was firm as well as emphatic.

"Then why not take the other horn of this dilemma? Give up searching for a will that can hardly be in your favor, and go on to prove your title through consanguinity."

"And thus shut my eyes to the probable rights of others, in order to secure a personal advantage? Do you think I would do this, Doctor? If so, you have mistaken me."

There was a tone of regret in her voice.

"Pardon me," I replied. "The suggestion was natural under the circumstances, and I gave it utterance."

"Were you in my place, would you give up the search here?"

She fixed on me a penetrating look.

The probe had changed hands.

"It is difficult," I answered, "for us to say what we would do if we were to change places with another. In my experience, it is easy to see what is right for our neighbor, but very difficult to see the right way for ourselves, when under the allurement of some personal advantage."

"Would it be right in me to give up the search?"

"I think not."

My answer was without hesitation.

"And I will not," she said, firmly. "If my brother has devised his property, I have only to know the terms of his will. If it is against me, well. I shall not oppose its operation."

"It sometimes happens," I suggested, "that a testator is manifestly out of his right mind as to the direction given to his property, and bequeaths it in a manner so evidently unwise and improper, that both justice and humanity are served in the act of setting aside the will. And it might prove so in this case."

"I know not how that may be, "Mrs. Montgomery answered, soberly, yet firmly. "But this I do know" - she spoke resolutely - "God helping me, I will not stain my hands with gold that, in any legal right, belongs to another. What is clearly mine, I will take and use. as it is my right and duty. But I must be certain that it is mine. If there is no will, I am clear as to who is the owner of this estate; if there is a will, and I and mine are not included in its provisions, I will step aside. First, however, the obligation to search for a will is imperative; and I shall continue it until clearly satisfied that no such document exists."

What a womanly dignity there was in Mrs. Montgomery as she said this, drawing her tall form up to its full height in speaking - not proudly, but with conscious integrity!

"What is right is always best." I made the remark as well approvingly as in expression of an immutable truth.

"Always, always," she replied, with earnestness. "There is no blinder folly than that of grasping a present worldly good, at the expense of violated justice. Whoever does so, comes out that far wrong in the end. There is only one way that leads to peace of mind: the way of honor and right. All other ways, no matter into what rich harvest fields they may lead in the beginning, terminate in wretchedness. There never has been, and never will be, any exception to this rule. We see its operation daily, turn our eyes whatsoever way we choose. And God forbid that I should deliberately enter the way that leads to ultimate unhappiness! Self-denial in the present is better than gnawing regret in the future. The good things of this world prove to be curses instead of blessings, unless the mind be rightly adjusted for their enjoyment. And such a right adjustment is impossible where the very fact of their possession involves a moral wrong. I see this so clearly, Doctor, that I shudder inwardly at the bare imagination of committing such a wrong."

"It is by trial that God proves us," said I, "and may He bring you out of this one, should the trial come, as gold from the refiner's furnace!"

"Amen!" was her solemnly uttered response; "if it should come, may I be found strong enough to do the right!"

For over a week this search for a will was continued, until it was clear to all concerned that no such document was in existence. Then preparation was made for the visit to England, in search of evidence bearing upon the identity of Mrs. Montgomery as the sister of Captain Allen. Two or three months elapsed, however, before Mr. Wallingford could so arrange his business as to be absent for the length of time it might take to complete his mission. He sailed for England in June, between three and four months after the marriage of Delia Floyd. He called to see me on the day before leaving, and I had a brief but pleasant talk with him. He was in good health and good spirits, and anticipated a successful visit.

"I shall gain," he remarked, "in two ways by this trip. Professionally and intellectually. I have had many a dream of that land of our forefathers - England - now to be realized. I shall see London, walk its streets, and linger amid its historic places. Don't smile at this almost boyish enthusiasm, Doctor. London has always been the Mecca of my desires."

I had never seen him so animated. A higher life seemed flowing in his veins. His countenance had a brighter aspect than usual, and his head an erecter carriage. There was a depth of meaning in his eyes never observed before - a look as if some new born hope were lending its inspiration to his soul. Altogether manlier was his aspect and bearing than I had ever seen it.

"God speed your mission," said I, as I shook hands with him in parting.

"If it depends on human agency, directed with earnestness, patience, and will, my mission will have a prosperous result," he replied. "It is to be my first entirely self-reliant experience, and I think the discipline of mind it will involve must strengthen me for higher professional work than any in which I have yet been engaged. You are aware, Doctor, that my heart is in my profession."

"So I have seen from the beginning."

"I will not deny," he added, "that I have ambition. That I wish to be distinguished at the bar."

"An honorable ambition," said I.

"Nor that, sometimes - in moments of weakness, perhaps - my dreams have gone higher. But I am a very young man, and youth is ardent and imaginative," he added.

"And you have this great advantage," I replied, "that,

with every year added to your life, you may, if you will, grow wiser and stronger. You stand, as all young minds, at the bottom of a ladder. The height to which you climb will depend upon your strength and endurance."

"If we both live long enough, Doctor, you may see me on the topmost rundle, for I shall climb with unwearying effort."

He spoke with a fine enthusiasm, that lent a manly beauty to his face.

"Climb on," I answered, "and you will rise high above the great mass, who are aimless and indolent. But you will have competitors, few, but vigorous and tireless. In the contest for position that you must wage with these, all your powers will be taxed; and if you reach the topmost rundle to which you aspire, success will be, indeed, a proud achievement."

"I have the will, the ambition, the courage, and the endurance, Doctor," was his reply. "So, if I fail, the fault will lie here," and he touched, significantly, his forehead.

"For lack of brains?" said I, smiling.

"Yes. The defect will lie there," he answered, smiling in return.

"Brains are remarkable for latent capacity. If stimulated, they develop new powers, and this almost without limit. All they want is to be well supplied with the right kind of food, and well worked at the same time."

T. S. Arthur

"I believe that, Doctor, and find vast encouragement in the thought," and Wallingford laughed pleasantly.

Our parting words were growing voluminous. So we shook hands again, repeated our mutual good wishes, and separated. In the afternoon he started for Boston, from whence he sailed, on the next day, for England.

This was towards the latter end of June. He was to write to Mrs. Montgomery immediately on his arrival out, and again as soon as he had obtained an interview with the Willoughby family. Early in August, she received his first letter, which was brief, simply announcing his arrival at Liverpool.

About three weeks after the coming of this letter, I received a note from Mrs. Montgomery asking me to call. On meeting her, I noticed something in her manner that struck me as unusual. She did not smile, as was her wont, when we met, her countenance retaining its usual serious expression. I thought she looked paler, and just a little troubled.

"Thank you for calling so promptly, Doctor," she said. "I am afraid you will think me troublesome. But you have always shown a kindly interest in me, though a stranger; and have proved, in all cases, a sound adviser."

I bowed, and she continued:

"I have a second letter from Mr. Wallingford. He has, he writes, been well received by my relatives, who had placed in his hands, for examination, a large quantity of papers that belonged to Colonel Willoughby."

"If they contain any evidence in the right direction, he will be sure to find it," said I.

"No doubt of that. But" - I thought her voice faltered a little -" the question is solved, and he may return."

"Solved! How?" I asked quickly.

"I have found the will."

"What?"

"I have found the will," she repeated, in a steady tone, "and that solves the question."

"Is it in your favor?" I asked, and then held my breath for a reply. It came in a firmly uttered -

"No."

We looked steadily into each other's face for several moments.

"In whose favor?"

"In favor of Theresa Garcia his wife," she replied.

"But she is dead," I answered quickly.

"True - but I am not his heir."

She said this resolutely.

"She died childless," said I, "and will not the descent stop with her? - the property reverting to you, as next of kin to Captain Allen?"

"She may have relatives - a brother or sister," said Mrs. Montgomery.

"That is scarcely probable," I objected.

"It is possible; and in order to ascertain the fact, all right means ought to, and must be, taken."

"Where did you find the will?" I inquired.

"Blanche was examining a small drawer in an old secretary, when she accidentally pressed her hand against one side, which yielded. She pressed harder, lad it continued to yield, until it was pushed back several inches. On withdrawing this pressure, the side returned to its place. She then tried to see how far it could be forced in. As soon as it had passed a certain point, a secret drawer, set in vertically, sprung up, and from the side, which fell open, the will dropped out."

"It is singular," said I, "that it should come to light just at this time."

"It is Providential, no doubt," Mrs. Montgomery remarked.

"What course will you pursue?" I inquired.

"My first step will be to recall Mr. Wallingford."

"I must take the liberty of a friend, and object to that," said I.

"On what ground?"

"This will may be worth the paper on which it is

written, and no more. If the legatee have no relatives, you stand just where you stood before, and will require the evidence as to identity for which Mr. Wallingford is now in search. Oh, no, Mrs. Montgomery; he must not be recalled."

The lady mused for a little while, and then said -

"Perhaps you are right, Doctor."

"I am sure of it," I replied, speaking earnestly. "This will, if we find it, on examination, to be an instrument executed according to legal forms, puts your rights in jeopardy, though by no means sets them aside."

"You take the correct view, no doubt," was her reply to this. Her voice was not so firm as in the beginning. As the probabilities began to show themselves again in her favor, she lost a degree of self-possession.

"Let Mr. Wallingford complete his work," said I, "and find, if possible, the evidence you require, in case you prove to be the legal heir, as I trust you will. And until his return, the existence of this important document had better remain a secret."

"Shall I not submit it to Judge Bigelow?"

I reflected for some moments, and then replied -

"Yes. He is your legal adviser, and one in whom the highest confidence may be reposed. The will should be at once placed in his hands for examination."

"And go upon record?"

T. S. Arthur

"Better leave all to his superior legal judgment. But," as the thought occurred to me, "who are named as the executors of this will?"

"I did not examine as to that, being too much interested in the provisions of the writing," she replied.

"May I see the document?"

"Blanche, dear, you will find it in the right-hand drawer of the secretary, in our room;" and Mrs. Montgomery handed a key to her daughter, who left the apartment in which we were sitting. She came back in a few minutes, and handed me a paper, which, on examination, I found to be written throughout, and evidently by the hand of Captain Allen. It was dated San Juan de Porto Rico, January 10, 1820, and was witnessed by two signatures - the names Spanish. The executors were Judge Bigelow and Squire Floyd. There was an important sentence at the conclusion of the will. It was in these words: - "In case my wife, in dying, should leave no relatives, then every thing shall revert to my own right heirs, should any be living."

All this gave the affair, in my mind, a more serious aspect. Before mentioning the executors' names, I said -

"Do you know where Theresa Garcia resided, before her marriage with Captain Allen?"

"In Porto Rico, as I have learned from old 'Aunty,' and also from letters found in searching for the will."

"Which I find was executed at San Juan De Porto Rico, the principal town on the island. Judge Bigelow and

Squire Floyd are theexecutors."

I saw her start slightly, and grow a little pale as I said this.

"Judge Bigelow, and Squire Floyd! That is extraordinary!" She was more disturbed than I had yet seen her in reference to this matter.

"It is remarkable, certainly, that Judge Bigelow, your legal adviser, should be one of the executors of a will, which determines your brother's estate out of the line of consanguinity."

"He must, of course, cease to represent my interest in the case," remarked the lady.

"He cannot represent two diverse interests," said I.

"No; that is clear." She said this in a troubled way; and was, evidently, falling into a perplexed state of mind. "Well, Doctor, what is to be done?" She spoke with recovered self-possession, after a short period of silence, looking at me with her old calmness of expression.

I took some moments for reflection, and then said,

"My advice is, to keep your own counsel, and wait until Mr. Wallingford returns from England. Whenever you place this document in the hands of Judge Bigelow, he must go over to the adverse interest; when you will be compelled to seek another legal adviser. You are not just ready for this; nor will be until after your agent comes back with the result of his investigations. No wrong to any one can possibly occur

T. S. Arthur

from letting things remain just as they are for a few months."

"I think your view of the matter correct, Doctor," was her reply. "And yet, to keep this secret, even for an hour, when I have no right to its possession, touches my conscience. Is it just? This will is not in my favor. It does not even recognize my existence. It devises property, of large value, in another line; and there may be heirs ready to take possession, the moment its existence is made known to them. Am I not inter-meddling, unjustly, in the affairs of another?"

"But for you," I replied, "this will might never have seen the light. If heirs exist, they can, therefore, have no just reason for complaint at the brief delay to which, under the circumstances, you are, in common justice, entitled. Your conscience may be over sensitive, Mrs. Montgomery."

"I would rather it were over sensitive than obtuse," she said. "Worldly possessions are desirable. They give us many advantages. We all desire and cling to them. But they are dearly bought at the price of heavenly possessions. What will it profit a man if he gain the whole world and lose his own soul? Nothing! It were better for him to die like Lazarus. No, Doctor, I am resolved in this matter to be simply just. If, in justice and right, this estate comes into my hands, I will take the wealth thankfully and use it as wisely as I can. But I will not throw a single straw in the way of its passing to the legal heirs of my brother's wife, if any are in existence and can be found."

"But you will keep this secret until Mr. Wallingford's return?" I urged.

"I do not see that wrong to any one can follow such a delay," she answered. "Yes, I will keep the secret."

"And I will keep it also, even from my good Constance," said I, "until your agent's return. The matter lies sacred between us."

T. S. Arthur

# CHAPTER XIV.

"Mrs. Dewey is at her father's," said my wife to me, one evening in August, as we sat at the tea-table.

"Ah! have you seen her?" I was interested at once. Six months had elapsed since Delia's wedding, and this was her first visit home; though her mother had been twice down to New York, in company with the Squire, who had business with the firm to which Ralph belonged. In fact, since his marriage to Squire Floyd's daughter, young Dewey had prevailed upon his father-in-law to make the house of Floyd, Lawson, Lee & Co., agents for the entire product of his manufactory - an arrangement which the Squire regarded as greatly to his advantage.

My question was answered in the affirmative.

"How is she?"

"Looking very well."

There was no warmth or feeling in my wife's voice or manner, although Delia had been a favorite with her, and we had often talked about the pleasure we should have in meeting her again.

"Have you nothing more to say of our young friend?"

I asked.

"She is very much changed."

"For the better?"

"Some might think so. I do not." There was a disappointed manner about my wife.

"In what respect is she changed?"

"Some would say that she had grown handsome; and, in truth, her countenance strikes you, at first, as much improved. It is rounded to a fuller outline, and has a style about it, caught, I suppose, from city life and feeling. But she carries her head with a statelier air than is becoming Squire Floyd's daughter; and I am very sure, that, as the wife of Ralph Dewey, she has acquired no special consequence. Rich jewelry may be very well in city drawing-rooms, and public assemblages, where dress is made conspicuous. But to sport diamond ear-rings and breastpin, splendid enough for a countess, in her father's little parlor, and before the eyes of friends who loved her once for herself alone, savored so strongly of weak pride and vanity, that I could not look upon her with any of my old feelings. It was Delia Floyd no longer. Already, the pure, sweet, artless maiden, had changed into a woman of the world, dressed up for show. Ah, my husband! if this is the effect of city life, let me never breathe its tainted atmosphere."

And she dropped her eyes, with a sigh, and sat, lost in thought, for several moments.

"Your account of Delia pains me," said I. "Is the case

indeed so bad?"

"It is. Alas! the fine gold is dimmed. Our sweet young friend has strayed from the paths of nature, and will never, I fear, get back again."

"Had you any conversation with her?" I inquired.

"Yes: or, rather I listened to her, as she ran on about her city life; the grand people with whom, she had already become acquainted; and the splendor of balls, parties, soirees, and operas. I grew sober as she talked: for not one true womanly sentiment fell from her lips. She did not express interest in any of her new friends and acquaintances for the good qualities they possessed; but spoke of their wealth, style of living, social connections, and other attractions wholly external to the individual. She was even eloquent over star actresses and opera singers; one or two of whom she spoke of having met at the house of a fashionable friend."

"How true the old adage, that evil communications corrupt good manners!" said I.

"There must be some radical weakness in a case of such sudden deterioration as this," replied my wife. "Some latent vanity and love of the world. I cannot believe that one sensible young woman in ten would be spoiled to the degree that Delia is spoiled, if you passed her through like temptations."

I saw Delia myself, on the next day. She was dressed in New York, not in S -, style; and so, naturally, appeared to disadvantage in my eyes. I found her very bright and animated; and to my questions as to her new city life, she spoke warmly of its attractions. At times, in the intervals of exciting talk, her countenance would fall into its true expression, as nearly all countenances will when thought ceases to be active - that expression, in which you see, as in a mirror, the actual state of mind. It revealed far more than came into her consciousness at the time, else would she have covered it with one of the rippling smiles she had already learned to throw, like a spangled veil, over her face.

Mrs. Dewey spent nearly a month in S - and then went back with her husband to New York. I saw them several times together during this period. He had grown more pompous in manner, and talked in a larger way. Our little town was simply contemptible in his eyes, and he was at no pains to conceal his opinion. New York was everything; and a New York merchant of passable standing, able to put two or three towns like S - in his breeches pocket.

The only interest I felt in this conceited young man was as the husband of my young friend; and as touching their relation to each other, I observed both of them very closely. It did not take me long to discover that there was no true bond of love between them. The little fond attentions that we look for in a husband of only six months' standing; and the tender recipro-cations which are sure to follow, were all wanting here. Constance spoke of this, and I answered, lightly, to cover the regret the fact occasioned -

"It is not fashionable in good society, you know, for husband and wife to show any interest in each other."

She laid her hand suddenly upon my arm, and looked lovingly into my face.

T. S. Arthur

"May we never make a part of good society, then!"

I kissed her pure lips, and answered,

"There is no present prospect of it, my Constance. I am not ambitious of social distinction. Still, our trial in this direction may come, for you know that I am not without ambition professionally. A chair in one of the medical schools might tempt me to an Atlantic city."

Constance smiled, as she still rested her hand upon my arm. Then looking from my face to our little ones, two of whom were playing on the floor, while the third slept like a vision of innocence in the cradle, she said: -

"I shall not need the glitter of diamonds - these are my jewels."

Turn your eyes away, good society reader, lest they be offended at sight of a husband's kiss. Could I do less than breathe my tender love upon her lips again?

"And richer jewels were never worn in the diadem of a queen," said I. "As a mother, woman attains her highest glory."

"As wife and mother," Constance answered quickly. And now she leaned against me, and I drew my arm tenderly around her.

"And all this," she said, "a good society woman must give up; and for what? God help them in the time of life's bitter trials and painful experience, which all must endure in some degree!" She spoke with strong feeling. "On what arm can a woman lean, who has no husband in the true sense? Is she strong enough, standing alone, for life's great battles? What has she to sustain her, when all the external support, received from pride, is swept away? Alas! Alas! Is there a blinder folly than the pageantry of fashionable society? It is the stage on a grander scale, glittering, gorgeous, fascinating to the senses - but all a mere show, back from which the actors retire, each with an individual consciousness, and the sad words pressing to tremulous lips - 'The heart knoweth its own bitterness.'"

Like ourselves, most of Delia's best friends were disappointed, and when she returned to New York, no hearts followed her with tender interest, except those of her own family. She had carried herself with an air of too much self-consequence; or, if she came down to the level of old friends and companions, it was with too evident a feeling of condescension.

I happened to fall into the company of Squire Floyd and Judge Bigelow, not very long after the return of Delia and her husband to New York. The conversation turned upon business, and I learned that the Squire had thought of enlarging his mill, and introducing steam - the water power being only sufficient for its present productive capacity. Judge Bigelow was very much interested, I found, in the particular branch of manufacture in which his neighbor was engaged, and inclined to embark some capital with him in the proposed extension of the works. They frequently quoted the Judge's nephew, Mr. Ralph Dewey, as to the extent to which goods could be put into market by the house of Floyd, Lawson, Lee & Co., who possessed, it was conceded, almost unlimited facilities.

I listened to their conversation, which involved plans

of enlargement, statistics of trade, home and foreign production, capital, and the like, until I began to feel that I was moving in a narrow sphere, and destined, in comparison with them, to occupy a very small space on the world. And I will confess it, a shade of dissatisfaction crept over my heart.

A few months later I learned that my two neighbors were jointly interested in the mill, and that early in the ensuing spring steam-power would be introduced, and the capacity of the works increased to more than double their present range.

It was December when Wallingford returned from England. He brought back with him all the evidence required to prove the identity of Mrs. Montgomery. Up to this time only three persons knew of the existence of a will - Mrs. Montgomery, Blanche, and myself; and we formed a council on the question of what was now to be done. I gave it as my opinion, that, as Judge Bigelow was one of the executors, and must in consequence cease to act for Mrs. Montgomery, that we had better call in Mr. Wallingford, and get his view of the case before placing the will in Judge Bigelow's hands. The mother and daughter agreed with me. So a time of meeting was appointed, and a note sent to the young lawyer desiring his presence at the house of Mrs. Montgomery. He seemed very much gratified at the successful result of his visit to England, and referred to it with something of pardonable pride in his manner.

"We have every reason," said Mrs. Montgomery, in response to this, "to be satisfied with the manner in which you have executed an important mission. Since you left America, however, a document has come into my hands, which, had it reached me earlier, would have saved you a long and tedious search among mouldy and moth-eaten papers. It was nothing less than Captain Allen's will."

And she gave him the paper. He looked surprised, and for a moment or two bewildered. Then opening the will, he read it through rapidly. I saw the color leave his face as he progressed, and his hand move nervously. It was plain that his mind took in, at a grasp, the entire series of consequences which the appearance of this document involved.

"This is a serious matter," he said, looking up at Mrs. Montgomery.

"It is," she answered, calmly. "The will appears to be in legal form."

"Yes."

"And must go into the hands of those who are named as executors."

"And be by them entered in the office of probate," added Wallingford.

"I would have placed it in their hands immediately on its discovery, but have, acting under advice from my kind friend here, waited until your return from England. No interest has suffered, I presume, by this delay?"

"None."

Wallingford bent his eyes to the floor, and sat for some

T. S. Arthur

time as if half-confounded by the discovery.

"What step will the executors probably take?" I inquired.

"It will be their duty to assume possession of the estate, and hold it for the heirs of Mrs. Allen, if any are in existence," he replied.

"And it will be their duty to take all proper means for discovering these heirs?" said I.

"Yes. That follows, of course."

"And if none are found within a reasonable time?" I asked.

"The phrase, a reasonable time, is very indeterminate," said Wallingford. "It may include one, or ten years, according to the facts in the case, the views of the executors and the courts."

"But, finally?"

"Finally," he answered, "if no heirs come forward to claim the estate, it will revert to the old line of descent through the blood relations of Captain Allen."

"And come into the possession of Mrs. Montgomery?"

"Yes, if the courts are satisfied with the evidence which can be presented in her favor."

There followed a long silence, which Mrs. Montgomery was first to break.

"I believe," she said, firmly, "that I am prepared for the final issue of this matter, whatever it may be. I shall still require legal advice, Mr. Wallingford."

The young man bowed assent.

"And, as Judge Bigelow is one of the executors -"

"I do not think, madam," said Wallingford, interrupting her, "that the fact of his executorship will make him any the less a safe adviser for you. He is a man of the highest integrity of character, clear-seeing, and of impartial judgment."

"I believe in his judgment and integrity," she replied. "Still, I do not think it well to have these two interests represented by the same man. You are his associate, if I understand correctly the relation between you."

"I am, in a certain sense."

"Do you have a share in all of his business?"

"Not in all."

"So he can be independent of you in any special case if he deems it desirable."

"Yes."

"And this is also true as regards yourself?"

"Yes."

"Then, Mr. Wallingford, I shall consult you, individually, in future."

He bowed low in acquiescence.

"And let me say to you, once for all, that I want only my rights, if I have any, protected. I do not wish any impediments thrown in the way of a proper search for the heirs of Mrs. Allen; but desire to see the fullest notice given, and in channels by which it is most likely to reach them. At the same time, it is but just to me and mine that all right steps should be taken to protect my interests, in case no heirs should be found. And I have faith in you, Mr. Wallingford."

"You shall never have cause to regret your confidence, madam," he replied, in a tone so full of manly integrity, that I could not but gaze upon his fine countenance with a feeling of admiration.

"Will you place this will in the hands of Judge Bigelow?" asked Mrs. Montgomery.

"It will be best for you to do that yourself, madam," replied Wallingford.

"I will be guided by your judgment in the case, sir. This very day I will send him a note asking an interview."

"After that, madam," said Wallingford, rising, "I will be at your service."

We retired together.

# CHAPTER XV.

Both Judge Bigelow and Squire Floyd were discreet men, and did not, at the outset of their executorship, do more in the way of giving publicity to the fact, than probating the will, and entering into bonds for the faithful performance of the trust. For the present they decided to let Mrs. Montgomery remain in occupancy of the old mansion, and she accepted this concession in her favor.

The property left by Captain Allen was large. The grounds upon which the old house stood, embraced nearly twenty acres, and as the town had grown in that direction, its value might now be estimated by the foot, instead of the acre, as houses had grown up on all sides. Moreover, the stream of water upon which the mill of Squire Floyd stood, ran through these grounds, in a series of picturesque rapids, giving a fall of over twenty feet. The value of this property, including a mill site, was estimated at sixty thousand dollars. Then there were twenty thousand dollars in stock of the County Bank, the interest of which Mrs. Allen had drawn since the death of her husband, regularly, as administratrix of the estate. Besides this property, there were several pieces of unimproved land in and around the town, the value of which could not fall much below twenty thousand dollars. In addition to all this, was a coffee estate on the island of Porto Rico. But as to its extent, or value, no evidence appeared. It might now be richly productive, or a mere tropical wilderness. If productive, no evidence of any return since Captain Allen's death appeared.

The winter passed without any apparent movement on the part of the executors looking to the discovery of Mrs. Allen's heirs. Young Dewey came up from New York every few weeks, to hold business interviews with his uncle and Squire Floyd, touching the mill-extension which was fully determined upon; Judge Bigelow agreeing to invest twenty thousand dollars, and the nephew ten thousand. All these matters were talked of in the beginning, freely, before Wallingford, who still had his office with his old preceptor, and shared in his business. After a while, he noticed a growing reserve on the part of Judge Bigelow and Squire Floyd, when he was by, touching their private affairs; and then they ceased entirely all reference thereto.

Dewey came up as frequently as usual, but avoided any remark in relation to business while in the presence of Wallingford. During his stay in S - , the Judge spent but little time at the office; being, for the most part, at the mill with his nephew and the Squire.

In the spring, a large force of men was set to work on the extension of Squire Floyd's mill; and as Judge Bigelow had become largely interested in the new enterprise, he gave a great deal more attention to what was going on in that direction, than to the business of his office, the heaviest part of which devolved upon Mr. Wallingford. Still, no steps were taken to discover the heirs of Mrs. Allen. Once or twice Mr. Wallingford had approached the subject, but the Judge made no response. At last, he put the question direct, as to what had been done. The Judge seemed a little annoyed; but said, in a hurried way that was unusual with him,

"I must, and will attend to this matter immediately. I have had so much on my mind that it has been neglected."

But the spring months passed - summer glided by - and still there was no advertisement for heirs, nor any steps taken, so far as Wallingford could learn, to ascertain their existence.

Mrs. Montgomery still occupied the old mansion, waiting patiently the issue whatever it might be. Her health, I regretted to find, was not firm. She suffered a great deal from nervous debility; and I saw, plainly, that she had failed considerably during the past few months. Blanche, on the contrary, after recovering from the illness which followed immediately on her arrival in S -, had continued in excellent health; and was growing daily more matured and womanly both as to mental development and personal bearing.

The mill improvements went on all summer, exciting no little interest in our town, and occasioning no small amount of talk and speculation. It was some time in the fall of that year, that I was permitted to hear this brief conversation between a couple of townsmen. Mr. A - had made some query as to the source of all the money expended on the new mill of Squire Floyd, which was now standing forth, under roof, in most imposing proportions, compared with the old works. Mr. B - shrugged his shoulders, and replied,

"Floyd and the Judge are joint executors of old Allen's

estate, you know."

"What does that signify?" inquired Mr. A -.

"It may signify a great deal. They have trust funds in their possession to a large amount, I am told."

"They are both honorable men, and would not violate their trust," said A -.

"I will not gainsay that," answered Mr. B -. "Still, they may use these funds temporarily, and wrong no one."

Nothing more was said in my presence, but I turned their remarks over and over again, feeling less satisfied the more I pondered them. A day or two afterwards I met Mr. Wallingford, and said to him,

"How comes on the search for the heirs of the Allen estate?"

The question caused him to look grave.

"No progress has been made, so far as I can learn," he answered.

"Isn't this indifference on the part of the executors a little extraordinary?" I remarked.

"I must confess that I do not understand it," said the young lawyer.

"There is personal, as well as real estate?"

"Yes. Stocks worth twenty thousand dollars."

"I have heard it suggested, that trust funds in the case are going into Squire Floyd's mill."

Wallingford started at the suggestion, and looked for some moments intently in my face; then dropped his eyes, and stood lost in thought a good while.

"Where did you hear the suggestion?" he at length inquired.

I repeated the conversation just mentioned, and named the individuals with whom it had occurred.

"And now, Henry," said I, "put this hint, and the singular neglect of the executors to search for the heirs to the Allen property, together, and tell me how the matter shapes itself in your mind. We speak confidentially with each other, of course."

"I don't just like the appearance of it, that is all I can say, Doctor," he replied in a half absent manner.

"As you represent the interests of Mrs. Montgomery," said I, "is it not your duty to look a little closer into this matter?"

"It is; and I shall give it immediate attention."

He did so, and to his surprise, found that all the bank stock had been sold, and transferred. It was now plain to him where at least a part of the funds being so liberally expended on the mill property of Squire Floyd came from. On venturing to make some inquiries of Judge Bigelow bearing on the subject, that individual showed an unusual degree of irritation, and intimated, in terms not to be misunderstood, that he thought himself competent to manage any business he might undertake, and did not feel disposed to tolerate any intermeddling."

From that time, Wallingford saw that a separation from his old preceptor was inevitable; and he so shaped events, that in less than three months he made the separation easy and natural, and took an office to himself alone.

Still there was no movement on the part of the executors in regard to the valuable estate in their hands. Summer and fall passed, and Christmas saw the splendid improvements of Squire Floyd completed, and the new mill in operation, under the vigorous power of steam. The product thus secured was almost fabulous in the eyes of the half asleep and awake people of S -, many of whom could hardly imagine people enough in the country to consume the miles of cloth that came streaming out from the rattling looms. And yet, we were informed, that more than quadruple this product could be sold by the extensive house of Floyd, Lawson, Lee, & Co.; and that all that stood in the way of creating a magnificent fortune out of cotton bales, was the lack of productive facilities.

During this winter I saw more than usual of Mrs. Dewey. She came up from New York with her nurse and child, a babe not quite a year old, and spent over six weeks with her parents. She had lost, in the two years which had passed since her marriage, nearly all those beautiful traits of character which made her once so charming. Fashionable city life seemed to have spoiled her altogether. Her mind had not grown in the right direction. She had wholly abandoned that tasteful reading through which intellectual refinement comes;

and to all appearance, no longer cared for anything beyond the mere sensuous. Nothing in S - had any interest for her; and she scarcely took the pains to conceal her contempt for certain sincere and worthy people, who felt called upon, for the sake of her parents, to show her some attention. She was not happy, of course. When in repose; I noticed a discontented look on her face. Her eyes had lost that clear, innocent, almost child-like beauty of expression, that once made you gaze into them; and now had a cold, absent, or eagerly longing expression, as if her thought were straining itself forward towards some coveted good.

Her conversation was almost always within the range of New York fashionable themes; and barren of any food upon which the mind could grow. There was not even the pretence of affection between her and her husband. The fairest specimen of well bred indifference I had yet seen was exhibited in their conduct to each other. Their babe did not seem to be a matter of much account either. Delia took no personal care of it whatever - leaving all this to the nurse.

It happened one day that I was called in to see the child. I found it suffering from some of the ill effects of difficult dentition, and did what the case required. There was an old friend of Delia's at the house - a young lady who had been much attached to her, and who still retained a degree of her old friendship. They were talking together in a pleasant, familiar way, when I came down stairs from my visit to the sick child - the mother had not shown sufficient interest in the little sufferer to attend me to the nurse's room. A word or two of almost careless inquiry was made; - I had scarcely answered the mother's queries, when her friend said, in a laughing way, looking from the window at the same time,

"There, Delia! see what you escaped."

I turned my eyes in the same direction, and saw Mr. Wallingford walking past, on the opposite side of the street, with his head bent down. His step was slow, but firm, and his air and carriage manly.

Delia shrugged her shoulders, and drew up the corners of her lips. There was an expression very much like contempt on her face. - But she did not make any reply. I saw this expression gradually fade away, and her countenance grow sober. Her friend did not pursue the banter, and the subject dropped.

What she had escaped! It was a dark day in the calendar of her life, when she made that escape; and I think there must have been times when a consciousness of this fact pressed upon her soul like a suffocating nightmare.

# CHAPTER XVI.

Spring opened again, and the days glided swiftly on towards summer; and yet, so far as the movements of the executors could be traced, nothing had been done in the work of searching for the heirs. One day, early in June, Mrs. Montgomery sent for Mr. Wallingford. On attending her, she placed in his hands a communication which she had just received. It was from the executors, giving notice in a kind and respectful way, that, for the interest of the legal heirs, and their own security, it would be necessary for them to assume full possession of the mansion and grounds, unless she felt willing to pay a rental that was equivalent to the interest on their value.

"I have expected this," said the lady; "and, so far from considering myself aggrieved, feel grateful that a quiet residence here has been so long accorded me."

"You will remove?"

"There is no other course left. My income will not justify a rent of some three thousand dollars."

"As the property is unproductive, no such rent as that will be required."

"The letter says, 'a rental equivalent to the interest on

\their value.'"

"I will see Judge Bigelow this morning, and ascertain precisely what views are held in regard to this matter."

They were sitting near one of the parlor windows that looked out upon the portion of the grounds that sloped away towards the stream, that threw its white folds of water from one rocky ledge to another in graceful undulations. As Mr. Wallingford ceased speaking, Mrs. Montgomery turned her head quickly and looked out. The sound of voices had reached her ears. Three men had entered the grounds, and were passing the window at a short distance.

"Who are they?" asked Mr. Wallingford. Then, answering his own question, he said, "Oh, I see; Judge Bigelow, Squire Floyd, and Ralph Dewey, his son-in-law."

The three men, after going a few hundred rods in the direction of the stream, turned and stood for some minutes looking at the house, and talking earnestly. Dewey appeared to have the most to say, and gesticulated quite freely. Then they moved on to that portion of the stream where the water went gliding down the mimic rapids, and remained there for a considerable time. It was plain that some scheme was in their heads, for they took measurement by pacing off the grounds in various directions; drew together in close conference at times; then separated, each making some examination for himself; and again stood in close deliberation. At last, as if satisfied with their investigations, they returned by way of the mansion, and passed out without calling.

"Put that and that together, and there is a meaning in this procedure beyond the simple rental of the place," said Wallingford.

"What is your inference?" asked Mrs. Montgomery.

"I have made none as yet," he replied. "But I will see Judge Bigelow, and have some talk with him. Of course, I can have nothing to say, adverse to a requirement of rent. Executors are responsible for the right use of property in their hands, and must see that it produces an interest, if in a position to pay anything. You do not, of course, wish to occupy the whole of these grounds. It may be, that the use of the house, garden, lawn, and appurtenances, may be secured at a moderate rent. If so, do you wish to remain?"

"I would prefer remaining here, if the rent is within a certain sum."

"Say three hundred dollars?"

"Yes. If not beyond that sum, I will remain," replied Mrs. Montgomery.

The interview which Mr. Wallingford held with Judge Bigelow a few hours afterwards, was not satisfactory. The proposition to let Mrs. Montgomery and her daughter occupy the house, separate from the extensive grounds, would not be entertained. It finally came out, that an offer to purchase had been made by the firm of Floyd, Lawson, Lee, & Co., with a view to the erection of extensive mills, and that the executors were going to ask the Court for power to sell, as a handsome sum could now be obtained. It further came out, that in case this power was granted, Mr. Dewey was to reside in

S -, to superintend the erection of these mills, and afterwards to join Squire Floyd in the management of both establishments - a consolidation of interests between the mercantile and manufacturing branches being about to take place. The old mansion was to undergo a thorough revision, and become the domicile of the resident partner.

With these plans in view, the executors insisted upon the removal of Mrs. Montgomery; and notice as to time was given, which included three months. Formal application was made to the Court having power in the case, for authority to sell and re-invest. The reasons for so doing were set forth in detail, and involved plausible arguments in favor of the heirs whenever they should be found.

Mr. Wallingford had personal reasons for not wishing to oppose this application. The executors had been his friends from boyhood. Especially towards Judge Bigelow did he entertain sentiments of deep gratitude for his many favors and kindnesses. But his duty, as counsel to Mrs. Montgomery, left him no alternative. She was heir prospective to this property, and he did not believe that the plans in view were best for her interests, in case no other heir was found. So, he went before the Court, and opposed the prayer of the executors. In doing so, he gained their ill-will, but did not succeed in preventing a decree authorizing a sale of the property. Dewey was present, a deeply interested listener to the arguments that were advanced on both sides. After the decision, as Wallingford was passing from the court-room, Dewey, who stood near the door, talking with a gentleman, said, loud enough for the young lawyer to hear him.

"The hound! He got on the wrong scent that time!"

A feeling of indignation stirred in Wallingford's bosom; but he repressed the bitter feeling, and moved on without giving any intimation that the offensive remark had reached him.

As soon as this decree, authorizing a sale of the property, was made, Mrs. Montgomery began to make preparation for removal. At first she seemed inclined to favor a return to England; but after repeated conferences with Mr. Wallingford, she finally concluded to remain in this country.

Nearly three years had woven their many colored web of events, since Mrs. Montgomery had dropped down suddenly among us like a being from cloudland. The friendly relation established between us in the beginning, had continued, growing more and more intimate. My good Constance found in her a woman after her own heart.

"The days I spend at the Allen House," she would often say to me, "are days to be remembered. I meet with no one who lives in so pure and tranquil an atmosphere as Mrs. Montgomery. An hour with her lifts me above the petty cares and selfish struggles of this life, and fills my mind with longings after those higher things into which all must rise before that peace comes to the soul which passeth all understanding. I return home from these interviews, happier in mind, and stronger for life's duties. I do not know any term that so clearly expresses my idea of this lady, as Christian philosopher."

Occasionally Mrs. Montgomery would pay us a visit;

T. S. Arthur

and these also were times treasured up in my wife's remembrance. I always observed a certain elevation of feeling, a calmer spirit, and a more loving sphere about her after one of these pleasant seasons.

The daughter came very often. Our children loved her almost as much as they did their mother, and she seemed as happy with them, as if they were her own flesh and blood. Agnes, our oldest, now in her eighth year, almost lived at the Allen House. Blanche never came without taking her home with her, and often kept her for two or three days at a time.

Blanche had developed into a young woman of almost queenly beauty; yet her manners retained the easy grace and truthfulness of a child. She did not seem conscious of her remarkable personal attractions, nor of the admiration her presence always extorted. No one could meet her, as a stranger, without feeling that she stood removed from ordinary contact - a being of superior mould with whom familiarity was presumption.

The companion of such a mother, who had with tender solicitude, from childhood upwards, guarded all the avenues of her mind, lest false principles or false views of things should find entrance; and as carefully selected her mental food, in order that there might be health of mind as well as health of body - it was not surprising to find about her a solidity and strength of character, that showed itself beneath the sweet grace of her external life, whenever occasion for their exhibition arose. From her mother she had imbibed a deep religious sentiment; but this did not manifest itself so much in language, as in dutiful acts. I had often occasion to notice, how, almost instinctively, she referred all things to a superintending Providence; and looked into the future, veiled as it is to all eyes, with a confidence that every thing would come out right, beautiful to contemplate. What she meant by right, was something more than is usually included in the words; for she had learned from her wise teacher, that God's providence disposes the things of this world for every individual in a way that serves best his eternal interests; therefore, what was best in this sense, could not fail to be right.

To our deep regret, Mrs. Montgomery decided to change the place of her residence from S - to Boston. All the reasons that led her to this decision, I was not able to discover. Her life at the Allen House had been quite secluded. She had been courteous to all the people with whom she was brought into any degree of contact, and had reciprocated all friendly visits; but there was a certain distance between her and them, that it seemed impossible for either to pass over. One of my inferences was, that, in removing from the retired old mansion, and taking a modern house, she would stand out more prominently before all eyes than was agreeable to her. Be this as it may, she was in earnest about removing to Boston.

I happened to be present when the announcement of this purposed removal was made to Mr. Wallingford. He had called in, during one of my visits to Mrs. Montgomery, for the transaction of some business.

"To Boston?" he said, in a tone of surprise, and, I thought, disappointment. At the same time I saw his eyes turned towards Blanche.

"Yes; I think it will be best," she replied. "If I have any

interests here, I feel that they are safe in your hands, Mr. Wallingford."

She leaned a little towards him, and I thought her voice had in it a softer tone than usual. Her eyes looked steadily into his face.

"I will do all that is right, madam." He spoke a little lower than usual.

"And the right is always the best in any case, Mr. Wallingford," said she with feeling.

"How soon do you think of removing?" the young man inquired.

"In three or four weeks."

"So soon."

Again I noticed that his eyes wandered towards Blanche, who sat close to her mother, with her face bent down and turned partly away.

"There is no reason why we should linger in S -, after all things are ready for removal. It would have suited my feelings and habits of mind to have remained here; but as this cannot be, I prefer going to Boston on more than one account."

"You will leave behind you many sincere friends," said Wallingford.

There was more feeling in his voice than usually showed itself; and I again observed that Mrs. Montgomery, in responding to the remark, fixed her eyes upon him steadily, and with, I thought, a look of more than usual interest.

The few weeks of preparation glided swiftly away, and then we parted from friends who had won their way into our own hearts; and whose memory would ever be to us like the fragrance of holy incense. I learned from Mrs. Montgomery, before she left us, during a more confidential talk than usual, that her income was comparatively small, and that the chief part of this, a pension from Government in acknowledgment of her husband's services, would cease at her death. There was a momentary failure in her voice as she said this, and her eyes turned with the instinct of love towards Blanche.

At her desire, Mr. Wallingford attended them to Boston, and remained away for three or four days. He then returned to S -, bringing with him kind words from the absent ones. The old routine of life went on again, each of us taking up the daily duty; yet I think there was not one of the favored few who had known Mrs. Montgomery and her daughter intimately, that was not stronger to do right in every trial for the memory of these true-hearted strangers - no, friends!

# CHAPTER XVII.

It was in October when Mrs. Montgomery, after a residence of three years in the Allen House, went from among us. Old "Aunty," and another colored servant who had lived with Mrs. Allen, remained in charge of the mansion. There was, of course, no removal of furniture, as that belonged to the estate. Mrs. Montgomery had brought with her three servants from England, a coachman, footman, and maid. The footman was sent back after he had been a year in the country; but the coachman and maid still lived with her, and accompanied her to Boston.

The large schemes of men ambitious for gain, will not suffer them to linger by the way. Ralph Dewey had set his mind on getting possession, jointly with others, of the valuable Allen property; and as the Court had granted a decree of sale, he urged upon his father-in-law and uncle an early day for its consummation. They were in heart, honorable men, but they had embarked in grand enterprises with at least one dishonest compeer, and were carried forward by an impulse which they had not the courage or force of character to resist. They thought that spring would be the best time to offer the property for sale; but Dewey urged the fall as more consonant with their views, and so the sale was fixed for the first day of November. Notice was given in the country papers, and Dewey engaged to see that the proposed sale was duly advertised in Boston and New York. He managed, however, to omit that part of his duty.

On the day of sale, quite a company of curious people assembled at the Allen House, but when the property was offered, only a single bid was offered. That came from Dewey, as the representative of Floyd, Lawson, Lee & Co., and it was awarded to them for the sum of thirty-five thousand dollars, a little more than half its real value.

From that time until spring opened, all remained quiet. Then began the busy hum of preparation, and great things for our town foreshadowed themselves. A hundred men went to work on the site chosen for a new mill, digging, blasting, and hauling; while carpenters and masons were busy in and around the old mansion, with a view to its thorough renovation, as the future residence of Mr. Ralph Dewey. That gentleman was on the ground, moving about with a self-sufficient air, and giving his orders in a tone of authority that most of the work people felt to be offensive.

The antiquated furniture in the Allen House, rich though it was in style and finish, would not suit our prospective millionaire, and it was all sent to auction. From the auctioneers, it was scattered among the town's people, who obtained some rare bargains. An old French secretary came into my possession, at the cost of ten dollars - the original owner could not have paid less than a hundred. It was curiously inlaid with satin wood, and rich in quaint carvings. There seemed to be no end to the discoveries I was continually making among its intricate series of drawers, pigeon holes, slides, and hidden receptacles. But some one had

T. S. Arthur

preceded me in the examination, and had removed all the papers and documents it contained. It flashed across my mind, as I explored the mazes of this old piece of furniture, that it might contain, in some secret drawer, another will. This thought caused the blood to leap along my veins, my cheeks to burn, and my hands to tremble. I renewed the examination, at first hurriedly; then with order and deliberation, taking out each drawer, and feeling carefully all around the cavity left by its removal, in the hope of touching some hidden spring. But the search was fruitless. One drawer perplexed me considerably. I could not pull it clear out, nor get access above or below to see how closely the various partitions and compartments came up to its sides, top, and bottom. After working with it for some time, I gave up the search, and my enthusiasm in this direction soon died out. I smiled to myself many times afterwards, in thinking of the idle fancy which for a time possessed me.

In May, the furnishing of the renovated house began. This took nearly a month. Every thing was brought from New York. Car loads of enormous boxes, bales, and articles not made up into packages, were constantly arriving at the depot, and being conveyed to the Allen House - the designation which the property retains even to this day. The furniture was of the richest kind - the carpets, curtains, and mirrors, princely in elegance. When all was ready for the proud owners to come in and enjoy their splendid home, it was thrown open for examination and admiration. All S - went to see the show, and wander in dreamy amazement through parlors, halls, and chambers. I went with the rest. The change seemed like the work of magic. I could with difficulty make out the old landmarks. The spacious rooms, newly painted and decked out in rich, modern furniture, looked still more spacious. In place of the whitewashed ceilings and dingy papered walls, graceful frescoes spread their light figures, entrancing the eyes with their marvelous semblances. The great hall received you with a statelier formality than before; for it, too, had received also its gift of painting, and its golden broideries. As you passed from room to room, you said - "This is the palace of a prince - not the abode of a citizen."

The grounds around the mansion had been subject to as thorough a renovation as the mansion itself. The old gate had given place to one of larger proportions, and more imposing design. A new carriage-road swept away in a grander curve from the gate to the dwelling. Substantial stone-stabling had been torn down in order to erect a fanciful carriage-house, built in imitation of a Swiss cottage; which, from its singular want of harmony with the principal buildings, stood forth a perpetual commentary upon the false taste of the upstart owner.

I hardly think that either Mr. Dewey or his wife would have been much flattered by the general tone of remark that ran through the curious crowds that lingered in the elegant rooms, or inspected the improvements outside. Nobody liked him; and as for his wife, fashionable associations had so spoiled her, that not a single old friend retained either affection or respect. It was sad to think that three years of a false life could so entirely obliterate the good qualities that once blossomed in her soul with such a sweet promise of golden fruitage.

Early in June, the family of Mr. Dewey took possession of their new home, and the occasion was celebrated by a splendid entertainment, the cost of

T. S. Arthur

which, common rumor said, was over two thousand dollars. We - Constance and I - were among the invited guests. It was a festive scene, brilliant and extravagant beyond anything we had ever witnessed, and quite bewildering to minds like ours. Mrs. Dewey was dressed like a queen, and radiant in pearls and diamonds. I questioned her good taste in this, as hostess; and think she knew better - but the temptation to astonish the good people of S - was too strong to be resisted.

After the curtain fell on this brilliant spectacle, Mrs. Dewey assumed a stately air, showing, on all occasions, a conscious superiority that was offensive to our really best people. There are in all communities a class who toady to the rich; and we had a few of these in S -. They flattered the Deweys, and basked in the sunshine of their inflated grandeur.

I was not one towards whom Mrs. Dewey put on superior airs. My profession brought me into a kind of relation to her that set aside all pretence. Very soon after her removal to S -, my services were required in the family, one of her two children having been attacked with measles. On the occasion of my first call, I referred, naturally, to the fact of her removal from New York, and asked how she liked the change.

"I don't like it all, Doctor," she replied, in a dissatisfied tone.

"Could heart desire more of elegance and comfort than you possess?" I glanced around the richly decorated apartment in which we were seated.

"Gilded misery, Doctor!" She emphasized her words.

I looked at her without speaking. She understood my expression of surprise.

"I need not tell you, Doctor, that a fine house and fine furniture are not everything in this world."

I thought her waking up to a better state of mind, through the irrepressible yearnings of a soul that could find no sustenance amid the husks of this outer life.

"They go but a little way towards making up the aggregate of human happiness," said I.

"All well enough in their place. But, to my thinking, sadly out of place here. We must have society, Doctor."

"True." My voice was a little rough. I had mistaken her.

"But there is no society here!" And she tossed her head a little contemptuously.

"Not much fashionable society I will grant you, Delia."

She pursed up her lips and looked disagreeable.

"I shall die of ennui before six months. What am I to do with myself?"

"Act like a true woman," said I, firmly.

She lifted her eyes suddenly to my face as if I had presumed.

"Do your duty as a wife and mother," I added, "and

there will be no danger of your dying with ennui."

"You speak as if I were derelict in this matter."

She drew herself up with some dignity of manner.

"I merely prescribed a remedy for a disease from which you are suffering," said I, calmly. "Thousands of women scattered all over the land are martyrs to this disease; and there is only one remedy - that which I offer to you, Delia."

I think she saw, from my manner, that it would be useless to quarrel with me. I was so much in earnest that truth came to my lips in any attempt at utterance.

"What would you have me do, Doctor?" There was a petty fretfulness in her voice. "Turn cook or nursery-maid?"

"Yes, rather than sit idle, and let your restless mind fret itself for want of useful employment into unhappiness."

"I cannot take your prescription in that crude form," she replied, with more seriousness than I had expected.

"It is not requisite to a cure," said I. "Only let your thought and purpose fall into the sphere of home. Think of your husband as one to be made happier by your personal control of such household matters as touch his comfort; of your babes as tender, precious things, blessed by your sleepless care, or hurt by your neglect; of your domestics, as requiring orderly supervision, lest they bring discord into your home, or waste your substance. Every household, Delia, is a little government, and the governor must be as watchful over all its concerns as the governor of a state. Take, then, the reins of office firmly into your hands, dispose of everything according to the best of your judgment, and require orderly obedience from every subject. But act wisely and kindly. Do this, my young friend, and you will not be troubled with the fashionable complaint - ennui."

"That is, sink down into a mere housekeeper," she remarked; "weigh out the flour, count the eggs, fill the sugar bowls, and grow learned in cookery-books. I think I see myself wandering about from cellar to garret, jingling a great bunch of keys, prying into rubbish-corners, and scolding lazy cooks and idle chambermaids!"

She laughed a short, artificial laugh, and then added -

"Is that the picture of what you mean, Doctor?"

"It is the picture of a happier woman than you are, Delia," said I, seriously.

The suggestion seemed to startle her.

"You speak very confidently, Doctor."

"With the confidence of one who makes diseases and their cure his study. I know something of the human soul as well as the human body, and of the maladies to which both are subjected. A cure is hopeless in either case, unless the patient will accept the remedy. Pain of body is the indicator of disease, and gives warning that an enemy to life has found a lodgment; pain of mind is the same phenomenon, only showing itself in a higher sphere, and for the same purpose. If you are unhappy, surrounded by all this elegance, and with the means of gratifying every orderly wish, it shows that an enemy to your soul has entered through some unguarded gateway. You cannot get rid of this enemy by any change of place, or by any new associations. Society will not help you. The excitement of shows; gauds, glitter, pageants; the brief triumphs gained in fashionable tournaments, will not expel this foe of your higher and nobler life, but only veil, for brief seasons, his presence from your consciousness. When these are past, and you retire into yourself, then comes back the pain, the languor, the excessive weariness. Is it not so, Delia? Is not this your sad experience?"

I paused. Her eyes had fallen to the floor. She sat very still, like one who was thinking deeply.

"The plodding housekeeper, whose picture you drew just now - humble, even mean in your regard though she be - sinks to peaceful sleep when her tasks are done, and rises refreshed at coming dawn. If she is happier than your fine lady, whose dainty hands cannot bear the soil of these common things, why? Ponder this subject, Delia. It concerns you deeply. It is the happiest state in life that we all strive to gain; but you may lay it up in your heart as immutable truth, that happiness never comes to any one, except through a useful employment of all the powers which God has given to us. The idle are the most miserable - and none are more miserable in their ever-recurring ennuied hours, than your fashionable idlers. We see them only in their holiday attire, tricked out for show, and radiant in reflected smiles. Alas! If we could go back with them to their homes, and sit beside them, unseen, in their lonely hours, would not pity fill our hearts? My dear young friend! Turn your feet aside from this way - it is the path that leads to unutterable wretchedness."

The earnestness of my manner added force to what I said, and constrained at least a momentary conviction.

"You speak strongly, Doctor," she said, with the air of one who could not look aside from an unpleasant truth.

"Not too strongly, Delia. Is it not as I have said? Are not your mere society-ladies too often miserable at home?"

She sighed heavily, as if unpleasant images were forcing themselves upon her mind. I felt that I might follow up the impression I had made, and resumed:

There was a time, Delia - and it lies only three or four short years backward on your path of life - when I read in your opening mind a promise of higher things than have yet been attained - you must pardon the freedom of an old but true friend. A time when thought, taste, feeling were all building for themselves a habitation, the stones whereof were truths, and the decorations within and without pure and good affections. All this - "I glanced at the rich furniture, mirrors, and curtains - "is poor and mean to that dwelling place of the soul, the foundations for which you once commenced laying. Are you happier now than then? Have the half bewildering experiences through which you have passed satisfied you that you are in the right way? That life's highest blessings are to be found in these pageantries? Think, think, my dear young friend! Look inwards. Search into your heart, and try the quality of its motives. Examine the foundation upon which you are building, and if it is sand, in heaven's name stop, and look for solid earth on which to place the corner stone of your temple of happiness."

"You bewilder me, Doctor," she said, in reply to this. "I can't think, I can't look inwards. If I am building on a sandy foundation, God help me! - for I cannot turn back to search for the solid earth of which you speak."

"But -"

She raised her hand and said,

"Spare me, Doctor. I know you are truthful and sincere - a friend who may be trusted - but you cannot see as I see, nor know as I know. I have chosen my way, and must walk in it, even to the end, let it terminate as it will. I had once a dream of other things - a sweet, entrancing dream while it lasted - but to me it can never be more than a dream. There are quiet, secluded, peaceful ways in life, and happy are they who are content to walk in them. But they are not for my feet, and I do not envy those who hide themselves in tranquil valleys, or linger on the distant hill-slopes. The crowd, the hum, the shock of social life for me!"

"But this you cannot have in S -. And is it not the part of a wise woman -"

"Again, Doctor, let me beg of you to spare me." she said, lifting her hands, and turning her face partly away. "I only half comprehend you, and am hurt and disturbed by your well-meant suggestions. I am not a wise woman, in your sense of the word, and cannot take your admonitions to heart. Let us talk of something else."

And she changed the subject, as well as her whole manner and expression of countenance, with a promptness that surprised me; showing the existence of will and self-control that in a right direction would have given her large power for good.

It was the first and last time I ventured to speak with her so freely. Always afterwards, when we met, there was an impression of uneasiness on her part, as if she had an unpleasant remembrance, or feared that I would venture upon some disagreeable theme.

T. S. Arthur

# CHAPTER XVIII.

Steadily, under the busy hands of hundreds of workmen, the new buildings arose, stretching their far lengths along, and towering up, story after story. Steam, in addition to water power, was contemplated here also, for the looms and spindles to be driven were nearly twice the number contained in the other mill.

Disappointments and vexatious delays nearly always attend large building operations, and the present case formed no exception. The time within which everything was to be completed, and the mill to go into operation, was one year. Two years elapsed before the first bale of goods came through its ample doors, ready for market.

Of course there was a large expenditure of money in S -, and this was a great thing for our town. Property rose in value, houses were built, and the whole community felt that a new era had dawned - an era of growth and prosperity. Among other signs of advancement, was the establishment of a new Bank. The "Clinton Bank" it was called. The charter had been obtained through the influence of Judge Bigelow, who had several warm personal friends in the Legislature. There was not a great deal of loose money in S - to flow easily into bank stocks; but for all that the shares were soon taken, and all the provisions of the charter complied with. Judge Bigelow subscribed freely; so did Squire Floyd and Mr. Dewey. Other townsmen, to the number of twenty or thirty, put down their names for a few shares. It was from New York, however, that the largest subscriptions came; and it was New York shareholders, voting by proxy, who elected the Board of Directors, and determined the choice of officers. Judge Bigelow was elected President, and a Mr. Joshua King, from New York, Cashier. The tellers and book-keepers were selected from among our own people.

The Clinton Bank and the new mills went into operation about the same time. Years of prosperity followed. Money was plenty in our town, and every-body was growing better off. Dewey was still the manufacturing partner of the large house in New York, whose demand for goods it seemed impossible to satisfy. He was a great man in S -. People spoke of him as possessing vast mental as well as money resources; as having expansive views of trade and finance; as being a man of extraordinary ability. I listened to all these things as I passed around among our citizens, plodding along in my profession, and managing to grow just a little better off each year; and wondered within myself if I were really mistaken in the man - if there was a solid basis of right judgment below all this splendid seeming.

And what of our friend Wallingford, during those busy years? Like myself, he moved so quietly through his round of professional duties, as to attract little attention. But he had been growing in all this time - growing in mental stature; and growing in the confidence of all just men. Judge Bigelow's interest in the mills, and in the new Bank, drew his attention so much away from his law cases, that clients began to

T. S. Arthur

grow dissatisfied, and this threw a great deal of excellent business into the hands of Wallingford, who, if not always successful in his cases, so managed them as to retain the confidence and good will of all who employed him. He got the character in our town of a safe adviser. If a man had a difficulty with a neighbor, and talked of going to law with him, in all probability some one would say -

"Go to Mr. Wallingford; he will tell you, on the spot, if there is any chance for you in Court."

And he bore this character justly. A thorn in the side he had proved to the three great mill owners, Judge Bigelow, Squire Floyd, and Ralph Dewey. The two former failed entirely, in his view, as to the right steps for discovering the heirs to the large property in their hands, all of which had been changed from its original position; while the latter showed ill-feeling whenever Wallingford, as he continued to do, at stated intervals, filed interrogatories, and required answers as to the condition of the trust, and the prospects of finding heirs.

Ten years had elapsed since the discovery of Mr. Allen's will, and yet no heirs had presented themselves. And now Mr. Wallingford took formal issue in the case, and demanded the property for his client, Mrs. Montgomery, who was still living in Boston with her daughter, in a retired way. Nearly one-half of her income had been cut off, and her circumstances were, in consequence, greatly reduced. Her health was feeble, having steadily declined since her removal from S -. An occasional letter passed between her and my wife; and it was in this way that I learned of her health and condition. How free was all she wrote from repining or despondency - how full of Christian faith, hope, and patience! You could not read one of her letters without growing stronger for the right - without seeing the world as through a reversed telescope.

A time was fixed for hearing the case, which, now that it assumed this important shape, excited great interest among the people of S -. When the matter came fairly into court, Mr. Wallingford presented his clearly arranged documentary evidence, in proof of Mrs. Montgomery's identity as the sister of Captain Allen, and claimed the property as hers. He covered, in anticipation, every possible ground of objection; bringing forward, at the same time, such an array of precedents and decisions bearing upon the case, that it was clear to every one on which side the decision would lie.

At this important juncture a letter, post-marked in New York on the day before, was offered in court, and a demand, based on its contents, made for a stay of proceedings. It came from the Spanish Consul, and was addressed to Abel Bigelow and John Floyd, executors of the late Captain Allen, and notified them that he had just received letters from San Juan De Porto Rico, containing information as to the existence of an heir to the estate in the person of a boy named Leon Garcia, nephew to the late Mrs. Allen. The case was immediately laid over until the next term of court.

In the meantime, steps were promptly taken to ascertain the truth of this assumption. An agent was sent out to the island of Porto Rico, who brought back all the proofs needed to establish the claim, and also the lad himself, who was represented to be in his fourteenth year. He was a coarse, wicked-looking boy, who, it was plain, had not yet fully awakened to a realizing sense of the good fortune that awaited him.

A resolute opposition was made by Wallingford, but all the evidence adduced to prove Leon Garcia's relationship to Mrs. Allen was too clear, and so the court dismissed the case, and appointed Ralph Dewey as guardian to the boy, who was immediately placed at school in a neighboring town.

So ended this long season of suspense. Immediately on the decision of the case, Wallingford went to Boston to see Mrs. Montgomery, and remained absent nearly a week. I saw him soon after his return.

"How did she bear this final dashing of her hopes to the earth?" I asked.

"As any one who knew her well might have expected," he answered, with so little apparent feeling that I thought him indifferent.

"As a Christian philosopher," said I.

"You make use of exactly the right words," he remarked. "Yes, as a Christian philosopher. As one who thinks and reasons as well as feels. I have seen a great many so-called religious people in my time. People who had much to say about their-spiritual experiences and hopes of heaven. But never one who so made obedience to the strict law of right, in all its plain, common-sense interpretations, a matter of common duty. I do not believe that for anything this world could offer her, Mrs. Montgomery would swerve a hair's breadth from justice. I have been in the position to see her tempted; have, myself, been the tempter over and over again during the ten years in which I represented her claims to the Allen estate; but her principles were immovable as the hills. Once, I shall never forget the incident - I pressed her to adopt a certain course of procedure, involving a law quibble, in order to get possession of the property. She looked at me for a moment or two, with a flushing face. Then her countenance grew serene, almost heavenly, and she gave me this memorable reply - 'Mr. Wallingford, I have a richer estate than this in expectancy, and cannot mar the title.' And she has not marred it, Doctor."

"How did her daughter receive the news?" I inquired. I thought he turned his face a little away, as he answered.

"Not so well as her mother." I knew his voice was lower. "When I announced the fact that the claims of young Garcia had been admitted by the court, tears sprung to her eyes, and a shadow fell upon her countenance such as I have never seen there before."

"She is younger and less disciplined," said I.

"Few at her age," he answered, are so well disciplined"

"Will they still remain in Boston?" I asked.

"Yes, for the present," he answered, and we parted. A few months after this, my wife said to me one day,

"Did you hear that Mr. Wallingford had bought the pretty little cottage on Cedar Lane, where Jacob Homer lived?"

"Is that true?"

"It is said so. In fact, I heard it from Jane Homer, and that is pretty good authority."

"Is he going to live there with his mother?"

"Jane did not know. Her husband went behind hand the year he built the cottage, and never was able to get up even with the world. So they determined to sell their place, pay off their debts, and find contentment in a rented house. Mr. Homer said something to Mr. Wallingford on the subject, and he offered to buy the property at a fair price."

A few days afterwards, in passing along Cedar Lane, I noticed a carpenter at work in the pretty cottage above referred to; and also a gardener who was trimming the shrubbery.

Good morning, William, "I spoke to the gardener with whom I was well acquainted. This is a nice cozy place."

"Indeed and it is, Doctor. Mr. Homer took great pride in it."

"And showed much taste in gardening"

"You may well say that, Doctor. There isn't a finer shrubbery to any garden in S -."

"Is Mr. Wallingford going to live here, or does he intend renting the cottage?"

"That's more than I can answer, Doctor. Mr. Wallingford isn't the man, you know, to talk with everybody about his affairs."

"True enough, William," said I smiling and passed on.

"Did you know," said my wife, a few weeks later, "that Mr. Wallingford was furnishing the cottage on Cedar Lane?"

"Ah! Is that so?"

"Yes. Mrs. Dean told me that Jones the cabinet maker had the order, which was completed, and that the furniture was now going in. Everything, she says, is plain and neat, but good."

"Why, what can this mean, Constance? Is our young friend about to marry?"

"It has a look that way, I fancy."

"But who is the bride to be?" I asked.

"Mrs. Dean thinks it is Florence Williams."

"A fine girl; but hardly worthy of Henry Wallingford. Besides, he is ten year her senior," said I.

"What is the difference in our ages. dear?" Constance turned her fresh young face to mine - fresh and young still, though more than thirty-five years had thrown across it their lights and shadows, and laid her head fondly against my breast.

I kissed her tenderly, and she answered her own question.

"Ten years; and you are not so much my senior. I do not see any force in that objection. Still if I had been commissioned to select a wife for Mr. Wallingford, I would not have chosen Florence Williams."

"Her father is well off, and growing richer every day."

"Worth taking into the account, I suppose, as one of the reasons in favor of the choice," said my wife. "But I hardly think Wallingford is the man to let that consideration have much influence."

There was no mistake about the matter of furnishing Ivy Cottage, as the place was called. I saw carpets going in on the very next day. All the shrubbery had been trimmed, the grounds cleared up and put in order, and many choice flowers planted in borders already rich in floral treasures.

Curiosity now began to flutter its wings, lift up its head, and look around sharply. Many arrows had taken their flight towards the heart of our young bachelor lawyer, but, until now, there had been no evidence of a wound. What fair maiden had conquered at last? I met him not long after, walking in the street with Florence Williams. She looked smiling and happy; and his face was brighter than I had ever seen it. This confirmed to me the rumor.

Mrs. Wallingford was not to be approached on the subject. If she knew of an intended marriage, she feigned ignorance; and affected not to understand the hints, questions, and surmises of curious neighbors.

A week or two later, and I missed Wallingford from his office. The lad in attendance said that he was away from the town, but would return in a few days.

"I have a surprise for you," said my wife on that very afternoon. She had a letter in her hand just received by post. Her whole face was radiant with pleasure. Drawing a card from the envelope, she held it before my eyes. I read the names of *Henry Wallingford* and *Blanche Montgomery*, and the words, "At home Wednesday evening, June 15th. Ivy Cottage."

"Bravo!" I exclaimed, as soon as a momentary bewilderment passed, showing more than my wonted enthusiasm. "The best match since Hymen linked our fates together, Constance."

"May it prove as happy a one!" my wife answered, with a glance of tenderness.

"It will, Constance - it will. That is a marriage after my own heart; one that I have, now and then, dimly fore-shadowed in imagination, but never thought to see."

"It is over five years since we saw Blanche," remarked Constance. "I wonder how she looks! If life's sunshine and rain have produced a rich harvest in her soul, or only abraded the surface, and marred the sweet beauty that captivated us of old! I wonder how she has borne the shadowing of earthly prospects - the change from luxurious surroundings!"

"They have not dimmed the virgin gold; you may be sure of that, Constance," was my reply to this.

"At home, Wednesday evening, June fifteenth."

And this was Tuesday. Only a single day intervened. And yet it seemed like a week in anticipation, so eager did we grow for the promised re-union with friends whose memory was in our hearts as the sound of pleasant music.

It was eight o'clock, on Wednesday evening, when we entered Ivy Cottage, our hearts beating with quickened strokes under their burden of pleasant anticipation. What a queenly woman stood revealed to us, as we entered the little parlor! I would hardly have known her as the almost shrinking girl from whom we parted not many years before. How wonderfully she had developed! Figure, face, air, manner, attitude - all showed the woman of heart, mind, and purpose. Yet, nothing struck you as masculine; but rather as exquisitely feminine. It took but one glance at her serene face, to solve the query as to whether there had been a free gift of heart as well as hand. My eyes turned next to the pale, thin face of Mrs. Montgomery, who sat, or half reclined, in a large cushioned chair. She was looking at her daughter. That expression of blended love and pride, will it ever cease to be a sweet picture in my memory? All was right - I saw that in the first instant of time.

The reception was not a formal one. There was no display of orange blossoms, airy veils, and glittering jewels - but a simple welcoming of a few old friends, who had come to heart-congratulations. It was the happiest bridal reception - always excepting the one in which my Constance wore the orange wreath - that I had ever seen. Do you inquire of Wallingford, as to how he looked and seemed? Worthy of the splendid woman who stood by his side and leaned towards him with such a sweet assurance. How beautiful it was to see the proud look with which she turned her eyes upon him, whenever he spoke! It was plain, that to her, his words had deeper meanings in them, than came to other ears.

"It is all right, I see." I had drawn a chair close to the one in which Mrs. Montgomery sat, and was holding in mine the thin, almost shadowy hand which she had extended.

"Yes, it is all right, Doctor," she answered, as a smile lit up her pale face. "All right, and I am numbered among the happiest of mothers. He is not titled, nor rich, nor noble in the vulgar sense - but titled, and rich, and noble as God gives rank and wealth. I came to this land of promise ten years ago, in search of an estate for my child; and I have found it, at last. Ah, Doctor" - and site glanced upwards as she spoke - "His ways are not as our ways. And if we will only trust in Him, He will bring such things to pass, as never entered into the imagination of cur hearts. I did not dream of this man as the husband of my child, when I gave my business into his care. The remote suggestion of such a thing would have offended me; for my heart was full of false pride, though I knew it not. But there was a destiny for Blanche, foreshadowed for me then, but not seen."

"It is the quality of the man," I said, "that determines the quality of the marriage. She who weds best, weds the truest man. The rank and wealth are of the last consideration. To make them first, is the blindest folly of the blindest."

"Ah, if this were but rightly understood" - said Mrs. Montgomery - "what new lives would people begin to live in the world! How the shadows that dwell among so many households - even those of the fairest external seeming - would begin to lift themselves upward and roll away, letting in the sunlight and filling the

T. S. Arthur

chambers of discord with heavenly music! I have sometimes thought, that more than half the misery which curses the world springs from discordant marriages."

"The estimate is low," I answered. "If you had said two-thirds, you would have been, perhaps, nearer the truth."

Blanche crossed the room, and came and stood by her mother's chair, looking down into her face with a loving smile.

"I am afraid the journey has been too much for you," she said, with a shadow of concern in her face.

"You look paler than usual."

"Paler, because a little fatigued, dear. But a night's rest will bring me up even again," Mrs. Montgomery replied cheerfully.

"How is the pain in your side, now?" asked Blanche, still with a look of concern.

"Easier. I scarcely notice it now."

"Blanche is over anxious about my health, dear girl!" said Mrs. Montgomery, as the bride moved to another part of the room. She thinks me failing rapidly. And, without doubt, the foundations of this earthly house are giving way; but I trust, that ere it fall into ruin, a house not made with hands, eternal, in the heavens, will be ready for my reception."

There was no depressing solemnity in her tones, as she

thus alluded to that event which comes to all; but a smiling cheerfulness of manner that was contagious.

"You think of death as a Christian," said I.

"And how else should I think of it?" she replied. "Can I not trust Him in whom I have believed? What is it more than passing from a lower to a higher state of life - from the natural to the spiritual world? When the hour comes, I will lay me down in peace and sleep."

She remained silent for some moments, her thoughts apparently indrawn. The brief, closing sentence was spoken as if she were lapsing into reverie. I thought the subject hardly in place for a wedding occasion, and was about starting another theme, when she said -

"Do you not think, Doctor, that this dread of dying, which haunts most people like a fearful spectre - the good as well as the bad - is a very foolish thing? We are taught, from childhood, to look forward to death as the greatest of all calamities; as a change attended by indefinable terrors. Teachers and preachers ring in our ears the same dread chimes, thrilling the strongest nerves and appalling the stoutest hearts. Death is pictured to us as a grim monster; and we shudder as we look at the ghastly apparition. Now, all this comes from what is false. Death is not the crowning evil of our lives; but the door through which we pass, tranquilly, into that eternal world, which is our destined home. I hold in my thought a different picture of Death from that which affrighted me in childhood. The form is one of angelic beauty, and the countenance full of love. I know, that when I pass along the dark and narrow way that leads from this outer world of nature, to the inner world from which it has existence, that my hand will rest firmly in that of an angel, commissioned of God to guide my peaceful footsteps. Is not that a better faith?"

"Yes, a better and a truer," said I.

"It is not the death passage that we need fear. That has in it no intrinsic evil. It is the sleep of mortality, and the rest is sweet to all. If we give place to fear, let it be for that state beyond the bourne, which will be unhappy in the degree that we are lovers of self and the world - that is, lovers of evil instead of good. As the tree falls, so it lies, Doctor. As our quality is at death, so will it remain to all eternity. Here is the just occasion for dread."

She would have kept on, but her attention was drawn away by the remark of a lady who came up at the moment. I left her side and passed to another part of the room; but her words, tone, and impressive manner remained with me. I turned my eyes often during the evening upon her pale, pure face, which seemed like a transparent veil through which the spirit half revealed itself. How greatly she had changed in five years! There had been trial and discipline; and she had come up from them purer for the ordeal. The flesh had failed; but the spirit had taken on strength and beauty.

"How did Mrs. Montgomery impress you?" said I to my wife, as we sat down together on our return home.

"As one ready to be translated," she answered. "I was at a loss to determine which was the most beautiful, she or Blanche."

"You cannot make a comparison between them as to

beauty," I remarked.

"Not as to beauty in the same degree. The beauty of Blanche was queenly; that of her mother angelic. All things lovely in nature were collated, and expressed themselves in the younger as she stood blushing in the ripeness of her charms; while all things lovely in the soul beamed forth from the countenance of the elder. And so, as I have said, I was at a loss to determine which was most beautiful."

I was just rising from my early breakfast on the next morning when I received a hurried message from Ivy Cottage. The angel of Death had been there. Tenderly and lovingly had he taken the hand of Mrs. Montgomery, and led her through the gate that opens into the land of immortals. She received her daughter's kiss at eleven o'clock, held her for some moments, gazing into her face, and then said - "Good-night, my precious one! Good-night, and God bless you!" At seven in the morning she was found lying in bed with a smile on her face, but cold and lifeless as marble! There had been no strife with the heavenly messenger.

T. S. Arthur

# CHAPTER XIX.

No; - there had been no strife with the heavenly messenger. As a child falls asleep in its mother's arms, so fell Mrs. Montgomery asleep in the arms of an angel - tranquil, peaceful, happy. I say happy - for in lapsing away into that mortal sleep, of which our natural sleep is but an image, shall the world-weary who have in trial and suffering grown heavenly minded, sink into unconsciousness with less of tranquil delight than the babe pillowed against its mother's bosom? I think not.

As I gazed upon her dead face, where the parting soul had left its sign of peace, I prayed that, when I passed from my labors, there might be as few stains of earth upon my garments.

"Blessed are the dead who die in the Lord, Yea, saith the Spirit, for they rest from their labors, and their works do follow them."

I found myself repeating these holy words, as I stood looking at the white, shrunken features of the departed.

It was not until the next day that I saw Blanche. But Constance was with her immediately after the sad news jarred upon her sympathizing heart.

"How did you leave her?" was my anxious query, on

meeting my wife at home.

"Calm," was the brief answer.

How much the word included!

"Did you talk with her?"

"Not a great deal; she did not seem inclined to talk, like some who seek relief through expression. I found her alone in the room next to the one in which the body of her mother was lying. She was sitting by a table, with one hand pressed over her eyes, as I entered. 'Oh, my friend! my dear friend!' she said, in a tone of grief, rising and coming a step or two to meet me. I drew my arms around her, and she laid her head against me and sobbed three or four times, while the tears ran down and dropped upon the floor. 'It is well with her!' I said.

"'Oh, yes, my friend, it is well with her,' she answered, mournfully, 'well with her, but not with me. How shall I walk onward in life's difficult ways, without my mother's arm to lean upon? My steps already hesitate.'

"'You have another arm to lean upon,' I ventured to suggest.

"'Yes, a strong arm upon which I can lean in unfaltering trust. In this God has been good to me. But my wise, patient mother - how shall I live without her?'

"'She is only removed from you as to bodily presence,' said I. 'Love conjoins your souls as intimately as ever.'

"'Ah, yes, I know this must be. Too many times have I heard that comforting truth from her lips ever to forget

T. S. Arthur

it. But while we are in the body, the mind will not rest satisfied with any thing less than bodily presence.'

"I did not press the point, for I knew that in all sorrow the heart is its own best comforter, and gathers for itself themes of consolation that even the nearest friend would fail to suggest. We went in together to look at the frail tabernacle from which the pure spirit of her mother had departed forever! How sweetly the smile left upon the lips in the last kiss of parting, lingered there still, fixed in human marble with more than a sculptor's art! There was no passionate weeping, as we stood by the lifeless clay. Very calm and silent she was; but oh, what a look of intense love went out from her sad eyes! Not despairing but hopeful love. The curtain of death hid from her no land of shadows and mystery; but a world of spiritual realities. Her mother had not gone shrinking and trembling into regions of darkness and doubt; but in the blessed assurance of a peaceful reception in the house of her friends.

"How a true faith," said I, strongly impressed by the images which were presented to my mind, "strips from death its old terrors! When the Apostle exclaimed, 'Oh, grave, where is thy victory? oh, death, where is thy sting?' his mind looked deeper into the mystery of dying, and saw farther into the world beyond, than do our modern Christians, who frighten us with images of terror. 'I will lay me down in peace and sleep,' when the time of my departure comes, should be the heart-language of every one who takes upon himself the name of Him who said, 'In my Father's house are many mansions. I go to prepare a place for you, that where I am, ye may be also.'"

"Since I knew Mrs. Montgomery, and felt the sphere of

her quality," said Constance, "my perceptions of life and duty here, and their connection with life and happiness hereafter, have been elevated to a higher region. I see no longer as in a glass darkly, but in the light of reason, made clear by the more interior light of Revelation."

"And the same is true with me," I replied. "We may well say that it was good to have known her. She was so true, so just, so unconscious of self, that truth, justice, and unselfishness were always lovelier in your eyes for having seen them illustrated in her person. And there was no pious cant about her. No parade of her unworthiness; no solemn aspects, nor obtrusive writings of bitter things against herself. But always an effort to repress what was evil in her nature; and a state of quiet, religious trust, which said, 'I know in whom I have believed.'"

"Ah," said Constance, "if there was only more of such religion in the world!"

"It would be a happier world than it is," I answered.

"By the impress of a life like hers, what lasting good is done!" said my wife. "Such are the salt of the earth. Cities set upon hills. Lights in candlesticks. They live not in vain!'"

I did not see Blanche until the day of burial. Her beautiful face was calm, but very pale. It bore strongly the impress of sorrow, but not of that hopeless sorrow which we so often see on these mournful occasions. It was very plain that her thoughts were not lingering around the shrouded and coffined form of what was once her mother's body, but were following her into

T. S. Arthur

the world beyond our mortal vision, as we follow a dear friend who has gone from us on a long journey.

And thus it was that Blanche Montgomery entered upon her new life. Death's shadow fell upon the torch of Hymen. There was a rain of grief just as the sun of love poured forth his brightest beams, and the bow which spanned the horizon gave, in that hour of grief, sweet promise for the future.

These exciting events in the experience of our young friends had come upon us so suddenly, that our minds were half bewildered. A few weeks served, however, to bring all things into a right adjustment with our own daily life and thought, and Ivy Cottage became one of the places that grew dearer to us for the accumulating memories of pleasant hours spent there with true-hearted ones who were living for something more than the unreal things of this world.

How many times was the life that beat so feverishly in the Allen House, and that which moved to such even pulsings in Ivy Cottage, contrasted in my observation! Ten years of a marriage such as Delia Floyd so unwisely consummated, had not served for the development of her inner life to any right purpose. She had kept on in the wrong way taken by her feet in the beginning, growing purse proud, vain, ambitious of external pre-eminence, worldly-minded, and self-indulgent. She had four children, who were given up almost wholly to the care of hirelings. There was, consequent upon neglect, ignorance, and bad regimen, a great deal of sickness among them, and I was frequently called in to interpose my skill for their relief. Poor little suffering ones! how often I pitied them An occasional warning was thrown in, but it was scarcely heeded by the mother, who had put on towards me a reserved stateliness, that precluded all friendly remonstrance.

At least two months of every summer Mrs. Dewey was absent from S -, intermitting between Saratoga and Newport, where she abandoned herself to all the excitements of fashionable dissipation. Regularly each year we saw her name in the New York correspond-dence of the Herald, as the "fascinating Mrs. D -;" the "charming wife of Mr. D -;" or in some like style of reference. At last, coupled with one of these allusions, was an intimation that "it might be well if some discreet friend would whisper in the lady's ear that she was a little too intimate with men of doubtful reputation; particularly in the absence of her husband."

This paragraph was pointed out to me by one of my patients. I read it with a throb of pain. A little while afterwards I passed Mr. Floyd and Mr. Dewey in the street. They were walking rapidly, and conversing in an excited manner. I saw them take the direction of the depot.

"Here is trouble!" I said, sighing to myself. "Trouble that gold cannot gild, nor the sparkle of diamonds hide. Alas! alas! that a human soul, in which was so fair a promise, should get so far astray!"

I met Mr. Floyd half an hour later. His face was pale and troubled, and his eyes upon the ground. He did not see me - or care to see me - and so we passed without recognition.

Before night the little warning sentence, written by the Saratoga correspondent, was running from lip to lip all

T. S. Arthur

over S -. Some pitied, some blamed, and not a few were glad in their hearts of the disgrace; for Mrs. Dewey had so carried herself among us as to destroy all friendly feeling.

There was an expectant pause for several days. Then it was noised through the town that Mr. Dewey had returned, bringing his wife home with him. I met him in the street on the day after. There was a heavy cloud on his brow. Various rumors were afloat. One was - it came from a person just arrived from Saratoga - that Mr. Dewey surprised his wife in a moonlight walk with a young man for whom he had no particular fancy, and under such lover-like relations, that he took the liberty of caning the gentleman on the spot. Great excitement followed. The young man resisted - Mrs. Dewey screamed in terror - people flocked to the place - and mortifying exposure followed. This story was in part corroborated by the following paragraph in the Herald's Saratoga correspondence:

"We had a spicy scene, a little out of the regular performance, last evening; no less than the caning of a New York sprig of fashion, who made himself rather more agreeable to a certain married lady who dashes about here in a queenly way than was agreeable to her husband. The affair was hushed up. This morning I missed the lady from her usual place at the breakfast-table. Later in the day I learned that her husband had taken her home. If he'll accept my advice, he will keep her there."

"Poor Mrs. Floyd!" It was the mother's deep sorrow and humiliation that touched the heart of my Constance when this disgraceful exposure reached her. "She has worn to me a troubled look for this long while," she added. "The handsome new house which the Squire built, and into which they moved last year, has not, with all its elegant accompaniments, made her any more cheerful than she was before. Mrs. Dean told me that her sister was very much opposed to leaving her old home; but the Squire has grown rich so fast that he must have everything in the external to correspond with his improved circumstances. Ah me! If, with riches, troubles so deep must come, give me poverty as a blessing."

A week passed, and no one that I happened to meet knew, certainly, whether Mrs. Dewey was at home or not. Then she suddenly made her appearance riding about in her stylish carriage, and looking as self-assured as of old.

"That was a strange story about Mrs. Dewey," said I to a lady whom I was visiting professionally. I knew her to be of Mrs. Dewey's set. Don't smile, reader; we had risen to the dignity of having a fashionable "set," in S -, and Mrs. Dewey was the leader.

The lady shrugged her shoulders, drew up her eyebrows, and looked knowing and mysterious. I had expected this, for I knew my subject very well.

"You were at Saratoga," I added; "and must know whether rumor has exaggerated her conduct."

"Well, Doctor," said the lady, dropping her voice, and putting on the air of one who spoke in confidence. "I must say that our friend was not as discreet as she might have been. Nothing wrong - that is, criminal - of course. But the truth is, she is too fond of admiration, and encourages the attentions of young men a great

　　　　　　　T. S. Arthur

deal more than is discreet for any married woman."

"There was an actual rencontre between Mr. Dewey and a person he thought too familiar with his wife?" said I.

"Oh, yes. Why, it was in the newspapers!"

"How was it made up between the parties?"

"It isn't made up at all, I believe; There's been some talk of a duel."

"A sad affair," said I. "How could Mrs. Dewey have been so thoughtless?"

"She isn't prudent, by any means," answered this intimate friend. "I often look at the way she conducts herself at public places, and wonder at her folly."

"Folly, indeed, if her conduct strikes at the root of domestic happiness."

The lady shook her head in a quiet, meaning way.

I waited for her to put her thoughts into words, which she did in a few moments after this fashion:

"There's not much domestic happiness to spoil, Doctor, so far as I can see. I don't think she cares a farthing for her husband; and he seems to have his mind so full of grand business schemes as to have no place left for the image of his wife. At least, so I read him."

"How has this matter affected their relation one to the other?"

"I have not seen them together since her return, and therefore cannot speak from actual observation," she replied.

There was nothing very definite in all this, yet it revealed such an utter abandonment of life's best hopes - such a desolation of love's pleasant land - such a dark future for one who might have been so nobly blest in a true marriage union, that I turned from the theme with a sad heart.

T. S. Arthur

## CHAPTER XX.

Almost daily, while the pleasant fall weather lasted, did I meet the handsome carriage of Mrs. Dewey; but I noticed that she went less through the town, and oftener out into the country. And I also noticed that she rode alone more frequently than she had been accustomed to do. Formerly, one fashionable friend or another, who felt it to be an honor to sit in the carriage of Mrs. Dewey, was generally to be seen in her company when she went abroad. Now, the cases were exceptional. I also noticed a gathering shade of trouble on her face.

The fact was, opinion had commenced setting against her. The unhappy affair at Saratoga was not allowed to sleep in the public mind of S -. It was conned over, magnified, distorted, and added to, until it assumed most discreditable proportions; and ladies who respected themselves began to question whether it was altogether reputable to be known as her intimate friends. The less scrupulous felt the force of example as set by these, and began receding also. In a large city, like New York, the defection would only have been partial; for there, one can be included in many fashionable circles, while only a few of them may be penetrated by a defaming rumor. But in a small town like S -, the case is different.

I was surprised when I comprehended the meaning of this apparent isolation of herself by Mrs. Dewey, and saw, in progress, the ban of social ostracism. While I pitied the victim, I was glad that we had virtue enough, even among our weak-minded votaries of fashion, to stamp with disapproval the conduct of which she had been guilty.

"I saw Mrs. Dewey this morning," said my wife, one day, late in November. "She was in at Howard's making some purchases."

"Did you speak to her?"

"Yes, we passed a few words. How much she has changed!"

"For the worse?"

"Yes. She appears five years older than she did last summer, and has such a sad, disappointed look, that I could not help pitying her from my heart."

"There are few who need your pity more, Constance. I think she must be wretched almost beyond endurance. So young, and the goblet which held the shine of her life broken, and all its precious contents spilled in the thirsty sand at her feet. Every one seems to have receded from her."

"The common sentiment is against her; and yet, I am of those who never believed her any thing worse than indiscreet."

"Her indiscretion was in itself a heinous offence against good morals," said I; "and while she has my compassion, I have no wish to see a different course of treatment pursued towards her."

"I haven't much faith in the soundness of this common sentiment against her," replied Constance. "There is in it some self-righteousness, a good deal of pretended horror at her conduct, but very little real virtuous indignation. It is my opinion that eight out of ten of her old fashionable friends would be just as intimate with her as ever, though they knew all about the affair at Saratoga, if they only were in the secret. It is in order to stand well with the world that they lift their hands in pretended holy horror."

"We cannot expect people to act from any higher principles than they possess," said I; "and it is some-thing gained to good morals, when even those who are corrupt in heart affect to be shocked at departures from virtue in their friends."

"Yes, I can see that. Still, when I look beneath the surface, I feel that, so far as the motives are concerned, a wrong has been done; and my soul stirs with a feeling of pity towards Mrs. Dewey, and indignation against her heartless friends. Do you know, dear, that since I met her this morning, I have had serious thoughts of calling upon her?"

"You!"

Constance gave me one of her placid smiles in answer to my surprised ejaculation.

"Yes; why not?"

"What will people say?"

"I can tell you what they will not say," she replied,

"Well?"

"They will not say, as they do of her, that of all men, I care least for my husband."

"I am not afraid of their saying that; but -"

I was a little bewildered by this unexpected thought on the part of my wife, and did not at first see the matter clear.

"She has held herself very high, and quite aloof from many of her old friends," Constance resumed. "While this was the case, I have not cared to intrude upon her; although she has been kind and polite to me whenever we happened to meet. Now, when the summer friends who courted her are dropping away like autumn leaves, a true friend may draw near and help her in the trial through which she is passing."

"Right, Constance! right!" said I, warmly. "Your clearer eyes have gone down below, the surface. Oh, yes; call upon her, and be her true friend, if she will permit you to come near enough. There can be no loss to you; there may be great gain to her. Was there any thing in her manner that encouraged you to approach?"

"I think so. It was this, no doubt, that stirred the suggestion in my mind."

Constance waited a day or two, pondering the matter, and then made a call at the Allen House.

"How were you received?" I asked, on meeting her.

T. S. Arthur

"Kindly," she said.

"But with indifference?"

"No. Mrs. Dewey was surprised, I thought, but evidently pleased."

"How long did you stay?"

"Only for a short time."

"What did you talk about?"

"Scarcely any thing beyond the common-place topics that come up on formal visits. But I penetrated deep enough into her mind to discover the 'aching void' there, which she has been so vainly endeavoring to fill. I do not think she meant to let me see this abyss of wretchedness; but her efforts to hide it were in vain. Unhappy one! She has been seeking to quench an immortal thirst at broken cisterns which can hold no water."

"Can you do her any good, Constance?" I asked.

"If we would do good, we must put ourselves in the way," she replied. "Nothing is gained by standing afar off."

"Then you mean to call upon her again?"

"She held my hand at parting, with such an earnest pressure, and looked at me so kindly when she said, 'Your visit has been very pleasant,' that I saw the way plain before me."

"You will wait until she returns your call?"

"I cannot say. It will depend upon the way things shape themselves in my mind. If I can do her good, I shall not stand upon etiquette."

As I came in sight of my modest little home a few days afterwards, I saw the stylish carriage of Mrs. Dewey dash away from my door, taking a direction opposite to that by which I was approaching.

"How are the mighty fallen!" It was hardly a good spirit by whom this thought was quickened, for I was conscious of something like a feeling of triumph. With an effort I repressed the ungenerous state of mind.

"So your call has been returned," said I, on entering our sitting room.

"Yes. How did you know?" Constance looked up, smiling, but curious.

"I saw Mrs. Dewey's carriage leave our door as I turned into the street. Did she come in, or only leave her card?"

"She came in, and sat for half an hour."

"And made herself very agreeable, - was patronizing, and all that?"

"No - nothing of the kind suggested by your words." And Constance looked at me reproachfully. "She was, on the contrary, quiet, subdued, and womanly. I called to see her, with the manner of one who had about her no consciousness of inferiority; and she returned the call, without a sign that I could regard as offensive."

"It is well," I answered, coming back into my better state. "If true friends can take the place of false friends, who left her the moment a shadow fell upon her good name, then the occasion of blame may pave the way to life instead of ruin. There must be remains of early and better states covered up and hidden away in her soul, but not lost; and by means of these she may be saved - yet, I fear, that only through deep suffering will the overlying accretions of folly be broken away."

"She is in the hands of one to whom all spirits are precious," said Constance, meekly; "and if we can aid in His good work of restoration and salvation, our reward shall be great."

After the lapse of a week, Constance called again upon Mrs. Dewey. She found her in a very unhappy state of mind, and failed, almost entirely, in her efforts to throw a few sunbeams across the shadow by which she was environed. Her reception was neither cold nor cordial.

"I think," she said, "that my visit was untimely. Some recent occurrence had, probably, disturbed her mind so deeply; that she was not able to rise above the depression that followed. I noticed a bitterness of feeling about her that was not apparent on the occasion of my first call; and a hardness of manner and senti-ment, that indicated a condition of mental suffering having its origin in a sense of wrong. Mr. Dewey passed through the hall, and went out a few minutes after I entered the house, and before his wife joined me in the parlor. It may have been fancy; but I thought, while I sat there awaiting her appearance, that I heard angry words in the room above. The heavy tread of a man's foot was there; but the sound ceased all at once - so did the voices. A little while afterwards Mr. Dewey came down stairs, and went out, as I have said. Some minutes passed before I heard the rustle of Mrs. Dewey's garments. There was the air of one disturbed and ill at ease about her, when she entered; and though she made an effort to seem pleased, all was forced work. Poor woman! The path she selected to walk in through the world has proved rough and thorny, I fear, beyond any thing dreamed of in her young imagination."

T. S. Arthur

# CHAPTER XXI.

Weeks passed after this second visit to the Allen House, but the call was not returned by Mrs. Dewey. We talked the matter over, occasionally, and concluded that, for some reason best known to herself, the friendly overtures of Constance were not agreeable to the lady. She was not often seen abroad, and when she did appear, the closed windows of her carriage usually hid her face from careful observation.

Of late, Mr. Dewey was away from S - more than usual, business connected with the firm of which he was a member requiring his frequent presence in New York. He did not remain absent over two or three days at a time.

Nearly opposite to where I resided lived Mr. Joshua Kling, the Cashier of the new Clinton Bank. He and Mr. Dewey seemed to be on particularly friendly terms. Often I noticed the visits of Mr. Dewey to the Cashier's house after bank hours, and many times in paying evening calls would I meet the two gentlemen, arm in arm, engaged in close conversation.

It was pretty generally understood in S - that the Clinton Bank was in the hands or parties in New York, and that a large proportion of the discounts made were of paper bearing the endorsement of Floyd, Lawson,

Lee, & Co., which was passed by the directors as the legitimate business paper received by that house in its extensive business operations; or of paper drawn to the order of John Floyd & Co., given in payment of goods manufactured at the mills in S - . It was also generally conceded that as, through their partner, Mr. Dewey, this firm of Floyd, Lawson, Lee, & Co., had invested a large amount of capital in S - , and by their liberality and enterprise greatly benefited the town, they were entitled to all the favors it was in the power of the bank to give; more particularly as the firm was one of great wealth - "solid as gold" - and the interests of the stockholders would, therefore, be best served by keeping the line of discount mainly in so safe a channel.

Now and then a disappointed storekeeper, whose small offerings were thrown out, would inveigh bitterly against the directors, calling hard names, and prophesying "a grand explosion one of these days;" but these invectives and predictions hardly ever found a repetition beyond the narrow limits of his place of business.

And so the splendid schemes of Ralph Dewey and Company went on prospering, while he grew daily in self-importance, and in offensive superciliousness toward men from whom he had nothing to expect. In my own case I had little to complain of, as my contact with him was generally professional, and under circumstances that caused a natural deference to my skill as a physician.

Nothing out of the ordinary range of things transpired until towards Christmas, when my wife received a note from Mrs. Dewey, asking her as a special favor to call at the Allen House. She was there in half an hour after the note came to hand.

I was at home when she returned, and saw the moment I looked into her face that she had been the witness of something that had moved her deeply.

"Is anything wrong with Mrs. Dewey?" I asked.

"Yes." Her countenance took on a more serious aspect.

"In what respect?"

"The story cannot be told in a sentence. I received a note from her as you are aware. Its earnest brevity forewarned me that the call involved something of serious import; and I was not mistaken in this conclusion. On calling, and asking for Mrs. Dewey, I noticed an air of irresolution about the servant. 'Mrs. Dewey is not well,' she said, 'and I hardly think can see company to-day.'

"'She is not ill, I hope?' said I.

"'No, ma'am; not ill exactly, but - ' and she hesitated and looked embarrassed.

"'She will see me,' I spoke confidently. 'Take her my name, and I will wait here in the parlor.'

"In a few minutes the girl returned and asked me to walk up stairs. I followed her to Mrs. Dewey's room. She tapped lightly on the door, which was opened. I passed in, and found myself alone with Delia. She grasped my arm tightly as she shut the door and locked it, saying as she did so, in a voice so altered from her usual tone, that it sounded strangely in my ears -

"'Thank you, my friend, for coming so soon. I am in deep trouble, and need a counselor as well as a comforter. I can trust you for both.'

"I drew my arm around her, so that by act I could give more than the assurance of words, and walked from the door with her to a lounge between the windows, where we sat down. Her face had a shrunken aspect, like the face of one who had been sick; and it showed also the marks of great suffering.

"'You may trust me as your own sister, Delia,' said I, 'and if in my power to counsel or to comfort, both will be freely accorded.'

"I called her Delia, instead of Mrs. Dewey; not from design, but because the old name by which I had known her was first on my lips.

"I thought there was a sudden lifting of her eyes as I pronounced this name. The effect, if any followed, was not to repel, but to draw her closer.

"'I am standing,' she said, speaking slowly and solemnly, 'at the edge of a deep abyss, my way hedged up on both sides, and enemies coming on behind. I have not strength to spring over; and to fall is destruction. In my weakness and despair, I turn to you for help. If there is help in any mortal arm, something tells me it is in yours.'

"She did not weep, nor show strong emotion. But her face was almost colorless, and presented an image of woe such as never met my eyes, except in pictures.

"'You have heard, no doubt,' she went on, 'some of the

stories to my discredit which have been circulated in S -. That I was gay and imprudent at Saratoga, cannot be denied - gay and imprudent as are too many fashionable women, under the exciting allurements of the place. Little fond flirtations with gentlemen made up a part of our pastime there. But as for sin - it was not in my thoughts!' She said this with an emphasis that assured me of its truth. 'A mere life of fashionable pleasure is a great exhauster of resources. One tires of this excitement and of that, pushing them aside, as a child does an old or broken toy, to grasp after something new. It is not surprising, therefore, that mere pleasure-seeking women forget at times the just proprieties of life, and, before they are aware of danger, find themselves in very equivocal positions. This was simply my case. Nothing more - nothing less.'

"She paused and looked earnestly into my face, to see if I credited this assertion.

"'I have never believed any thing else,' said I.

"A faint, sad smile flitted across her wan face.

"'The consequences of this error on my part,' she went on, 'threaten to be of the most disastrous kind. My husband has ever since conducted himself towards me as if I were a guilty and disgraced thing. We occupy separate apartments; and though we sit together at the same table, words rarely pass between us. Occasionally he comes home under the influence of wine, and then his abuse of me is fearful to think of. If any thing could waken a thoughtless creature sleeping on enchanted ground, it was this.'

"'There has never been anything more than the semblance of love between us,' she continued. 'The more intimately I came to know him, after our marriage, the more did my soul separate itself from him, until the antipodes were not farther apart than we. So we lived on; I seeking a poor compensation in fashionable emulations and social triumphs; and he in grand business enterprises - castles in the air perhaps. Living thus, we have come to this point in our journey; and now the crisis has arrived!'

"She paused.

"' What crisis?' I asked.

"'He demands a separation.' Her voice choked - 'a divorce -'

"'On what ground?'

"'On legal ground.' She bent down, covered her face, and uttered a groan so full of mental anguish, that I almost shuddered as the sound penetrated my ears.

"'I am to remain passive,' she resumed, while he charges me before the proper court, with infidelity, and gains a divorce through failure on my part to stand forth and defend myself. This, or a public trial of the case, at which he pledges himself to have witnesses who will prove me criminal, is my dreadful alternative. If he gains a divorce quietly on the charge of infidelity, I am wronged and disgraced; and if successful in a public trial, through perjured witnesses, the wrong and disgrace will be more terrible. Oh, my friend! pity and counsel me.'

T. S. Arthur

"'There is one,' said I, 'better able to stand your friend in a crisis like this than I am.'

"'Who?' She looked up anxiously.

"'Your father.'

"A shadow fell over her face, and she answered mournfully,

"'Even he is against me. How it is I cannot tell; but my husband seems to have my father completely under his influence.'

"'Your mother?' I suggested.

"'Can only weep with me. I have no adviser, and my heart beats so wildly all the time, that thought confuses itself whenever it makes an effort to see the right direction. Fear of a public trial suggests passive endurance of wrong on my part; but an innate sense of justice cries out against this course, and urges me to resistance.'

"'If you are innocent,' said I, firmly, 'in the name and strength of innocence defend yourself! All that a woman holds dearest is at stake. If they drive you to this great extremity, do not shrink from the trial.'

"'But what hope have I in such a trial if false witnesses come up against me?'

"'God and justice are stronger than all the powers of evil,' said I.

"'They might be, in your case,' she answered,

mournfully; 'for you have made God your friend, and justice your strong tower. But I - what have I to hope for in God? He has not been in all my thoughts; and now will He not mock at my calamity?'

"'No - no, my unhappy friend!' I answered. 'He never turns from any; it is we who turn from Him. His tender mercy is over all His works. All human souls are alike precious in His eyes. If you trust in Him, you need not fear your bitterest enemies.'

"'How shall I trust in him?'

"She bent towards me eagerly.

"'In the simple work of doing right,' said I.

"'Doing right?'

"She did not clearly understand me.

"Do you think it would be right to let a charge of crime lie, unrepelled, against you; a great crime, such as is alleged - destroying your good name, and throwing a shadow of disgrace over your children!'

"'No,' was her unhesitating reply.

"'Then it would be wrong for you to suffer a divorce to issue on the ground of infidelity, without a defence of yourself by every legal means in your power. Do right, then, in so defending yourself, and trust in God for the result.'

"I shudder at the bare thought of a public trial,' she answered.

"'Don't think of anything but right action, said I. If you would have the Hosts of Heaven on your side, give them power by doing the right; and they will surely achieve for you the victory over all your enemies. Have any steps been taken by Mr. Dewey?'

"'I fear so.'

"'How long is it since your husband entertained this purpose?'

"'I think it has been growing in his mind ever since that unhappy affair at Saratoga.'

"As she said this, her thoughts seemed to turn aside upon something else, and she sat looking down upon the floor in a state of deep abstraction. At last, taking a long breath, she looked up, and said with trembling lips and a husky voice,

"'I have something more to tell you. There is another aspect to this miserable affair.'

"And she drew forth a crumpled letter.

"'I found this, sealed, and directed, lying on the floor of my husband's room, two days ago. It is in his hand writing; addressed to a lady in New York, and signed R. D. I will read you its contents.' And she unfolded the letter, and read:

"'My dearest Caroline,' it began; and then went on for a few paragraphs, in a lover-like strain; after which, the divorce from the writer's wife was referred to as a thing of speedy attainment, there being little fear of opposition on her part, as he had given her to understand that he had witnesses ready to prove her criminal conduct; if she dared to resist his will in the matter. 'A few months of patient waiting, dearest Caroline,' was the concluding sentence, 'and then for that happy consummation we have so long desired.'

"'What do you think of that?' asked poor Delia, looking almost wildly into my face.

"'I think,' said I, 'that you hold in your hands the means of safety. Your husband will not dare to force you into a defensive position, when he learns that you have this document in your possession. It would tell strongly against him and his perjured witnesses if produced in court. Then take heart, my friend. This worst evil that you dreaded will not come to pass. If a divorce is granted, it will have to be on some different allegation.'

"She grasped my hand, and said, 'Oh, do you think so? Do you think so?'"

"'I am sure of it,' was my confident answer. 'Sure of it. Why the man would only damage his cause, and disgrace himself, by venturing into a trial with a witness like this against him.'"

"'Oh, bless you for such confidently assuring words!' and the poor creature threw herself forward, and laid her face upon my bosom. For the first time she wept, and for a season, oh how wildly! You will not wonder that my tears fell almost as fast as hers.

"'I turned in my despair to you,' she said, on growing calm, 'you whom I loved, and almost revered, in the earlier and better days of my life, and my heart tells me that I have not turned in vain. Into the darkness that surrounded me like the pall of death, a little light has already penetrated.'"

"May it shine unto the perfect day!" I answered fervently.

"And, dear husband! it will shine," said Constance, a glow of enthusiasm lighting up her face, and giving it a new beauty, "even unto the perfect day! Not the perfect day of earthly bliss - for I think the sun of that day has gone down never to rise again for her - but the perfect day of that higher life, which to many comes not, except through the gates of tribulation."

# CHAPTER XXII.

I was shocked and distressed by the painful revelation which Mrs. Dewey had made to Constance. A sadder history in real life I had never heard.

A few days after this memorable visit to the Allen House, a note was received by my wife, containing this single word, "*Come*," and signed *Delia*.

"Any change in the aspect of affairs?" I inquired of Constance on her return.

"Yes. Mrs. Dewey has received notice, in due form, of her husband's application for a divorce."

"What has she done?"

"Nothing yet. It was to ask my advice as to her best course that she sent for me."

"And what advice did you give her?"

"I gave none. First, I must consult you."

I shook my head and replied,

"It will not do for me to be mixed up in this affair, Constance."

T. S. Arthur

Worldly prudence spoke there.

My wife laid her hand upon my arm, and looking calmly in my face, said,

"The right way is always a safe way."

"Granted."

"It will be right for you to give such advice as your judgment dictates, and therefore safe. I do not know much about law matters, but it occurs to me that her first step should be the employment of counsel."

"Is her father going to stand wholly aloof?" I inquired.

"Yes, if she be resolved to defend herself in open court. He will not sanction a course that involves so much disgrace of herself and family."

"Has she shown him the letter you saw?"

"No."

"Why?"

"I think she is afraid to let it go out of her hands."

"She might trust it with her father, surely," said I.

"Her father has been very hard with her; and seems to take the worst for granted. He evidently believes that it is in the power of Dewey to prove her guilty; and that if she makes any opposition to his application for a divorce, he will hold her up disgraced before the world."

"This letter might open his eyes."

"The letter is no defence of her; only a witness against him. It does not prove her innocence. If it did, then it would turn toward her a father's averted face. In court its effect will be to throw doubt upon the sincerity of her husband's motives, and to show that he had a reason, back of alleged infidelity, for wishing to be divorced from his wife."

"I declare, Constance!" said I, looking at my wife in surprise, "you have taken upon yourself a new character. I think the case is safe in your hands, and that Mrs. Dewey wants no more judicious friend. If you were a man, you might conduct the defence for her to a successful issue."

"I am not a man, and, therefore, I come to a man," she replied, "and ask the aid of his judgment. I go by a very straight road to conclusions; but I want the light of your reason upon these conclusions."

"I am not a lawyer as you are aware, Constance - only a doctor."

"You are a man with a heart and common sense," she answered, with just a little shade of rebuke in her tones, "and as God has put in your way a wretched human soul that may be lost, unless you stretch forth a saving hand, is there any room for question as to duty? There is none, my husband! Squire Floyd believes his daughter guilty; and while he rests in this conclusion, he will not aid her in anything that points to exposure and disgrace. She must, therefore, if a vigorous defence is undertaken, look elsewhere for aid and comfort."

I began to see the matter a little clearer.

"Mr. Wallingford is the best man I know."

"Mr. Wallingford!" I thought Constance would have looked me through.

"Mr. Wallingford!" she repeated, still gazing steadily into my face. "Are you jesting?"

"No," I replied calmly. "In a case that involves so much, she wants a wise and good defender; and I do not know of any man upon whom she could so thoroughly rely."

Constance dropped her eyes to the floor.

"It would not do," she said, after some moments.

"Why?"

"Their former relation to each other precludes its possibility."

"But, you must remember, Constance, that Delia never knew how deeply he was once attached to her."

"She knows that he offered himself."

"And that, in a very short time afterwards, he met her with as much apparent indifference as if she had never been to him more than a pleasant acquaintance. Of the struggle through which he passed, in the work of obliterating her image from his mind, she knows nothing."

"But he knows it," objected Constance.

"And what does that signify? Will he defend her less skillfully on this account? Rather will he not feel a stronger interest in the case?"

"I do not think that she will employ him to defend her," said Constance. "I would not, were the case mine."

"Womanly pride spoke there, Constance."

"Or rather say a manly lack of perception in your case."

"Perception of what?"

"Of the fitness of things," she answered.

"That is just what I do see," I returned. "There is no man in S - better fitted for conducting this case than Mr. Wallingford."

"She will never place it in his hands; you may take a woman's word for that," said my wife confidently. "Of all living men he is the last one to whom she could talk of the humiliating particulars involved in a case like this."

"Suppose you suggest his name to her. Twelve years of such a life as she has led may have almost obliterated the memory of that passage in her life."

"Don't believe it. A woman never forgets a passage like that; particularly when the events of every passing day but serve to remind her of the error she once committed."

"I don't know what else to advise," said I. "She ought to have a good and discreet man to represent her, or all may be lost."

"Would you have any objection to confer with Mr. Wallingford on the subject in a private, confidential way?"

"None in the world," I replied.

"Will you see him at once?" The interest of Constance was too strongly excited to brook delay.

"Yes, immediately."

And putting on my overcoat I went to the office of Mr. Wallingford. I found him alone, and at once laid the whole case before him - relating, with particularity, all that had occurred between my wife and Mrs. Dewey. He listened with deep and pitying attention; and when I was through, expressed his opinion of Dewey in very strong language.

"And now what is to be done?" I asked, going at once to the vital question.

"Your wife is right," he answered. "I can hardly become her advocate. It would involve humiliation on her part too deep to be borne. But my aid she shall have to the fullest extent; and it will be strange if I do not thwart his wicked scheme."

"How will you aid her?"

"Through her right attorney, if my advice as to the choice be followed. You know James Orton?"

"Yes."

"He is a young man to be relied upon. Let Mrs. Dewey put the case in his hands. If she does so, it will be, virtually, in mine."

"Enough, Mr. Wallingford," said I. "It looks more hopeful for our poor unhappy friend, against whom even her own flesh and blood have turned."

When I gave Constance the result of my interview with Mr. Wallingford, she was quite elated at the prospect of securing his most valuable aid for Mrs. Dewey. Orton was young, and had been practising at the bar for only a couple of years. Up to this time he had not appeared in any case of leading importance; and had, therefore, no established reputation. Our fear was that Mrs. Dewey might not be willing to place her case in such inexperienced hands. In order to have the matter settled with as little delay as possible, Constance paid an early visit to the Allen House, and suggested Mr. Orton as counsel. Mrs. Dewey had not even heard his name; but, after being assured that I had the fullest confidence in him, and particularly advised his employment, she consented to accept of his services.

Their first interview was arranged to take place at my house, and in the presence of my wife, when the notice Mrs. Dewey had received on the institution of proceedings, was placed in the young lawyer's hands, and some conversation had as to the basis and tenor of an answer. A second interview took place on the day following, at which Mrs. Dewey gave a full statement of the affair at Saratoga, and asserted her innocence in the most solemn and impressive manner. The letter from her husband to the lady in New York, was produced, and at the request of Mr. Orton, given into his possession.

The answer to Mr. Dewey's application for a divorce was drawn up by Mr. Wallingford, who entered with great earnestness into the matter. It was filed in court within a week after notice of the application was received. This was altogether unexpected by the husband, who, on becoming aware of the fact, lost all decent control of himself, and ordered his wretched wife to leave his house. This, however, she refused to do. Then she had her father's angry opposition to brave. But she remained firm.

"He will cover you with infamy, if you dare to persevere in this mad opposition," he said. And she answered -

"The infamy may recoil upon his own head. I am innocent - I will not be such a traitor to virtue as to let silence declare me guilty."

There was a pause, now, for a few weeks. The unhappy state of affairs at the Allen House made it hardly proper for my wife to continue her visits there, and Mrs. Dewey did not venture to call upon her. The trial of the case would not come up for some two or three months, and both parties were waiting, in stern resolution, for the approaching contest.

One day I received a message from Mrs. Dewey, desiring me to call and see two of her children who were sick. On visiting them - the two youngest - I found them seriously ill, with symptoms so like scarletina, that I had little question in my mind as to the character of the disease from which they were suffering. My second visit confirmed these fears.

"It is scarlet fever?" said Mrs. Dewey, looking at me calmly, as I moved from the bed-side after a careful examination of the two little ones.

I merely answered -

"Yes."

There was no change in her countenance.

"They are both very ill."

She spoke with a slow deliberateness, that was unusual to her.

"They are sick children," said I.

"Sick, it may be, unto death."

There was no emotion in her voice.

I looked at her without replying.

"I can see them die, Doctor, if that must be."

Oh, that icy coldness of manner, how it chilled me!

"No hand but mine shall tend them now, Doctor. They have been long enough in the care of others - neglected - almost forgotten - by their unworthy mother. But in this painful extremity I will be near them. I come back to the post of duty, even at this late hour, and all that is left for me, that will I do."

I was deeply touched by her words and manner.

The latter softened a little as she uttered the closing sentence.

"You look at the darkest side," I answered. "With God are the issues of life. He calls us, our children, or our friends, in His own good time. We cannot tell how any sickness will terminate; and hope for the best is always our truest state."

"I hope for the best," she replied; but with something equivocal in her voice.

"The best is life," I said, scarcely reflecting upon my words.

"Not always," she returned, still speaking calmly. "Death is often the highest blessing that God can give. It will be so in the present case."

"Madam!"

My tone of surprise did not move her.

"It is simply true, Doctor," she made answer. "As things are now, and as they promise to be in the future, the safest place for these helpless innocents is in Heaven; and I feel that their best Friend is about to remove them there through the door of sickness."

I could not bear to hear her talk in this way. It sent cold chills through me. So I changed the subject.

On the next day, all the symptoms were unfavorable. Mrs. Dewey was calm as when I last saw her; but it was plain from her appearance, that she had taken little if any rest. Her manner towards the sick babes was full of tenderness; but there was no betrayal of weakness or distress in view of a fatal termination. She made no anxious inquiries, such as are pressed on physicians in cases of dangerous illness; but received my directions, and promised to give them a careful observance, with a self-possession that showed not a sign of wavering strength.

I was touched by all this. How intense must have been the suffering that could so benumb the heart! - that could prepare a mother to sit by the couch of her sick babes, and be willing to see them die! I have witnessed many sad scenes in professional experience; but none so sad as this.

Steadily did the destroyer keep on with his work. There were none of those flattering changes that sometimes cheat us into hopes of recovery, but a regular daily accumulation of the most unfavorable symptoms. At the end of a week, I gave up all hope of saving the children, and made no more vain attempts to control a disease that had gone on from tie beginning, steadily breaking away the foundations of life. To diminish the suffering of my little patients, and make their passage from earth to Heaven as easy as possible, was now my only care.

On the mother's part, there was no sign of wavering. Patiently, tenderly, faithfully did she minister to her little ones, night and day. No lassitude or weariness appeared, though her face, which grew paler and thinner every day, told the story of exhausting nature.

T. S. Arthur

She continued in the same state of mind I have described; never for an instant, as far as I could see, receding from a full consent to their removal.

One morning, in making my usually early call at the Allen House, I saw, what I was not unprepared to see, a dark death sign on the door.

"All over?" I said to the servant who admitted me.

"Yes, sir, all is over," she replied.

"Both gone?"

"Yes, sir, both."

Tears were in her eyes.

"When did they die?"

"About midnight."

"At the same time?"

"Yes, sir. Dear little souls! They went together."

"I will go up to see them," said I.

And the girl showed me to the room in which they were laid. The door was closed. I opened it, and stepped in softly. The room was darkened; but light came in through a small opening in the curtains at the top of the window, and fell in a narrow circle around the spot where the bodies, already in their snowy grave clothes, were laid. In a chair beside them sat the mother. She was alone with her dead. I felt that I was an intruder upon a sorrow too deep for tears or words; but it was too late to recede. So I moved forward and stood by the bedside, looking down upon the two white little faces, from which had passed every line of suffering.

Mrs. Dewey neither stirred nor spoke, nor in any way gave token that she was aware of my presence in the room. I stood for over a minute looking upon the sweet images before me - for in them, death had put on forms of beauty - and still there was no movement on the part of Mrs. Dewey. Then, feeling that she was with One who could speak to her heart by an inner way, better than I could speak through the natural ear, I quietly receded and left the apartment. As my eyes rested on her a moment, in closing the door, I saw that her form remained as still as a statue.

# CHAPTER XXIII.

An hour later, when Constance went to see Mrs. Dewey, she found her in a state of unconsciousness, nature having at last given way. Not long after I left the house, her mother, on entering the room where the children were laid out, found her insensible, lying across the bed, with her dead babes clasped in her arms.

Mrs. Floyd sent word for me to come and see her daughter, as she continued in a lethargic state. I found her like one in a deep sleep, only her breathing was light, and her pulse very feeble, but regular. She was out of the reach of my skill, and in the hands of the Great Physician. I could only trust the cure to Him. No medicine for the body would be of any avail here. I called again in the afternoon; but found no change. How little was there in the pale, pinched face that lay among the white pillows, to remind me of the handsome, dashing Mrs. Dewey, of a year gone by!

"What do you think of her, Doctor?"

Mrs. Floyd put the question. The tone had in it something that made me look narrowly into the speaker's face. My ears had not deceived me.

There was the wish in her heart that Delia might die!

I was not surprised at this. And yet the revelation of such a state of feeling, in so good and true a woman, as I had reason to know Mrs. Floyd to be, made my heart bound with a throb of pain.

Alas! alas! Into what unnatural conditions may not the mind fall, through suffering that shuts out human hope!

"Nature," said I, in answer to the question of Mrs. Floyd, "may be only gathering up her powers after a long period of exhaustion. The strife through which your daughter has passed - calmly passed to all external seeming - has not been without a wasting of internal life. How she kept on so evenly to the end, passes my comprehension. There is not one woman in a thousand who could have so borne herself through to the final act. It is meet that she should rest now."

"If she were sleeping with her babes, happy would it be for her!"

Tears fell over the face of Mrs. Floyd.

"God knows what is best," I remarked.

"She has nothing to live for in this world." A sob broke from its repression, and heaved the mother's bosom. "O Doctor, if I saw the death dews on her brow, I would not weep!"

"Leave her, my dear friend," said I, "in the hands of Him who sees deeper into the heart than it is possible for our eyes to penetrate. Her feet have left the soft, flowery ways they trod for a time, and turned into rough paths, where every footfall is upon sharp stones; but it may be that a blessed land is smiling beyond, he has been astray in the world, and God may only be leading her homeward by the way of sorrow."

Mrs. Floyd wept freely as I talked.

"His will be done," she said, sobbing.

"Your daughter," said I, taking the occasion to bear my testimony on the favorable side, "has been wronged without question. She was doubtless imprudent, but not sinful; and the present attempt to disgrace her I regard as a cruel wrong. It will recoil, I trust, in a way not dreamed of."

"O Doctor, let me thank you for such words."

And Mrs. Floyd caught my arm with an eager movement.

"I speak soberly, madam, and from observation and reflection. And I trust to see Delia live and triumph over her enemies."

"Won't you talk with the Squire, Doctor?" She still grasped my arm. "He will not hear a word from me in favor of Delia. Mr. Dewey has completely blinded him."

"Wait patiently, Mrs. Floyd," said I, in a tone of encouragement. "Your daughter is not without friends. There are those upon her side, who have the will and the power to defend her; and they will defend her, I believe successfully."

A sigh fluttered through the room, causing us both to turn quickly towards the bed on which Mrs. Dewey was lying. Her lips were moving slightly; but no change appeared on her death-like face. I laid my fingers upon her wrist, and searched for her pulse. It was very low and thread-like; but with more vitality than on the occasion of my first visit to her in the morning.

"The signs are favorable."

Mrs. Floyd did not respond. She was looking at her daughter with an expression of unutterable grief upon her countenance.

I did not attempt to give medicine, but left unerring nature to do her own work.

Mrs. Dewey did not again look upon the faces of her dead children. They were buried ere her mind awoke to any knowledge of passing events. I was at the funeral, and closely observed her husband. He appeared very sober, and shed some tears at the grave, when the little coffins were lowered together into the earth.

It was a week before Mrs. Dewey was clearly conscious of external things. I visited her every day, watching, with deep interest, her slow convalescence. It was plain, as her mind began to recover its faculties, that the memory of a sad event had faded; and I was anxious for the effect, when this painful remembrance was restored.

One day I found her sitting up in her room. She smiled feebly as I came in, and said:

"Doctor, am I never going to get well? It seems like an age since I became sick."

T. S. Arthur

"You are getting on finely," I answered, in a cheerful way, sitting down by her and taking her hand, which was wasted and shadowy.

"I don't know about that, Doctor," she said.

"What makes me so weak? I've no more strength than a babe. And that reminds me of a frightful dream I had." And her countenance changed.

"A dream?" I queried.

"Yes; I thought Aggy and Lu were both dead! I saw them laid out, cold and white as statues, just as plainly as I see you now."

She stopped suddenly, an expression of fear going over her face - then looked at me in a strange, questioning way.

"Doctor" - she leaned towards me, with lips apart, and eyes full of a sudden, wild alarm. I laid my hand upon her, and said:

"You have been very ill for some time, Mrs. Dewey, and are too weak to bear excitement. Don't let mere dreams disturb you."

"Dreams?" Her eyes fell from mine. "Dreams?" she repeated. "I feel very weak, Doctor," was added, after a few moments. "Won't you assist me to lie down?"

And she made a movement to rise. I took her arm and supported her to the bed, where she quietly composed herself, and turned her face away, so as almost to hide it from my view. At this moment Mrs. Floyd came in, and I withdrew, leaving them together.

Memory had been restored. The accompanying shock was severe, but not heavy enough seriously to retard her recovery, which went on slowly. She still remained at the Allen House, rarely meeting her husband, who now spent a large part of his time in New York.

The period fixed for a trial of the case between them was fast approaching. He continued resolute, and she did not waver from her purpose to defend her good name. The deep interest I took in the case, led me to see Mr. Wallingford often, and make inquiry as to the evidence which could be produced in Mrs. Dewey's favor, and the probable chances of an honorable result. We both favored a settlement of the difficulty without a trial and its consequent exposure, if that were possible. But how to prevent this was the difficult question. Finally it was determined to make a copy of the letter found by Mrs. Dewey, and enclose it to her husband, giving him warning at the same time that the original would be produced at the trial.

Nothing was heard in response to this movement, until within a week of the day on which the case was expected to come up, when Mr. Dewey's lawyer called on Mr. Orton to know if it was still his intention to meet them in open court and resist their application for a divorce. On being assured that such was their purposes he expressed some regret at the consequent damage to the lady's reputation, as they had evidence against her of the most conclusive character. Finally he wished to know whether, in case a new ground were taken - one not touching the lady's good name - any opposition would be made. Mr. Orton said that he would consult his client, and answer the query with as little delay as practicable.

Mrs. Dewey expressed a willingness to remain passive, provided no allegations were made in the new bill that even remotely cast a shadow upon her virtue

But Mr. Wallingford, on taking the matter into further consideration, advised a different course altogether - no less than an application from the other side, on the ground of neglect, ill-treatment, and constructive conjugal infidelity, based on the important letter already referred to. Mrs. Dewey caught eagerly at this suggestion, as soon as it was presented to her. If a divorce were thus obtained, her vindication would be complete.

The ranks of the enemy were thrown into confusion by this diversion. Mr. Dewey was violent, and threatened most terrible consequences. But when the time set for the case to come up arrived, he failed to appear.

It was from the other side that the next movement came. A divorce was applied for on the part of Mrs. Dewey, in a bill carefully drawn up by Mr. Wallingford. It asked not only for a legal separation from her husband, but for alimony, and the possession of the two remaining children. An answer was filed; but it was of so feeble a character as to amount to scarcely anything in the way of opposition. The chief argument was directed against the claim for alimony. The result was as we had anticipated. In the following spring a divorce was granted, and Mrs. Dewey, with her two children, left the Allen House and returned to her father's. The maintenance allowed by the court, was one thousand dollars a year for herself, and five hundred a year for each of the children during their minority.

And so closed this exciting drama, begun in weakness, and ending in hopeless disaster. Oh, a few years! How many broken hearts do they close over? How many wrecks of goodly lives do they see scattered among the breakers!

The interposition of Mr. Wallingford, in this case, was so managed as to keep him entirely out of sight, and Mrs. Dewey was never made aware of the fact that he had rendered her a great service.

# CHAPTER XXIV.

We did not see a great deal of Mr. Dewey in S - for some months after this. I heard it casually remarked that he was traveling in the South and West, for a part of the time, on business. The large interests of his firm involved in the two mills, however, made his presence necessary among us, and late in the fall he came back, and remained through the winter residing at the Allen House.

In the spring a rumor got afloat that Mr. Dewey was soon to be married. A lady in New York was mentioned; the same, it was said, to whom the letter found by Mrs. Dewey was addressed. A few signs of renovation at the Allen House gave confirmation of this rumor, which at length assumed a more positive shape.

The intimacy between Mrs. Wallingford and Constance, had grown into a close interior friendship, and scarcely a week passed that an evening was not spent by them together, sometimes at our house, and sometimes at Ivy Cottage. Mr. Wallingford had developed into a man after my own heart; and so I shared, when professional engagements allowed, in the enjoyment of these pleasant seasons.

One evening Mr. and Mrs. Wallingford came round to

spend an hour with us. I was happily at leisure. Conversation naturally falls into the current of passing events, and on this occasion, the approaching marriage of Mr. Dewey came naturally into the field of topics. This led to a review of the many strange circumstances connected with Mrs. Wallingford's presence in S -, and naturally, to an inquiry from my wife as to the present position of the property left by Captain Allen.

"What about this young Garcia?" said Constance, addressing Mr. Wallingford. "I haven't heard of him for some time."

"He is at school yet, I believe," replied Mr. Wallingford, not showing much interest in the matter.

"He must be nearly of age," said I.

"About twenty, if his years were correctly given."

"He will come into the possession of a handsome property," I remarked.

"Yes, if it can be found by the time he is ready to receive it."

"Can be found! I don't comprehend you, Mr. Wallingford? Do you mean to question the integrity of the men who are executors to the estate?"

"No. But, they have embarked in the same vessel with an unscrupulous villain - so I regard Ralph Dewey - and have, as far as I can see, given the rudder into his hands. If he do not wreck them on some dangerous coast, or sunken rock, it will be more from good fortune than anything else."

"He is partner in a very wealthy firm," said I.

"The standing of Floyd, Lawson, Lee & Co., is, you know, undoubted. He can't wreck out friends Bigelow and Floyd, without ruining them also."

"I was in New York a few months ago, on business," Mr. Wallingford replied, "and it so happened, that I heard the firm of which Dewey is a partner spoken of. Among other remarks, was this: 'They are thought to be very much extended.'"

"What is the meaning of that?" asked Mrs. Wallingford.

"It is understood in business circles," replied her husband, "to mean, that a house is doing too much business for the amount of capital employed, and that it has issued, in consequence, a large amount of paper. Any very heavy losses to a firm in this condition might prove disastrous."

"Too much extended?" said I, thoughtfully, some new impressions forming themselves in my mind.

"Yes, that was the opinion held by the individual I refer to; and he was not one to speak carelessly on so grave a matter."

"If the house of Floyd, Lawson, Lee, & Co. should go down," I remarked, "there will be sad work in S -."

"There will, without any doubt," replied Mr. Wallingford.

"The executors to the Allen estate might find

themselves in a most unfortunate position," said I.

"Such a position as I would not be in, for all the world. Any thing but dishonor!"

"How dishonor?" asked Constance.

"The whole estate would be, I fear, involved."

"They gave security," said I.

"But the sureties are not worth a tenth part of the sum for which they stand responsible. The court acted with a singular want of discretion in appointing them."

"You don't mean to have us infer that Judge Bigelow and Squire Floyd have used the funds of this estate for their own purposes, to any great extent?"

"I would not care to say this out of doors, Doctor, but that is just my opinion of the matter as it now stands. Dewey is guardian to the heir, and would favor, rather than oppose, such a use of the funds."

"It might be just so much in favor of the heir," remarked Mrs. Wallingford, "if two-thirds of the property had disappeared by the time he reached his majority; for, from all that I have heard of him, he is not likely to become a man fitted to use large wealth either to his own or any body else's advantage. He was low born and low bred, in the worst sense of the words; and I fear that no education will change his original quality, or greatly modify his early bias. So while the wasting of his substance is a great wrong in the abstract, it may be a real blessing to him. Events in this life work out strangely to our human eyes, yet

T. S. Arthur

there is a Providence in them that ever educes good from evil."

"If we could always believe that," said I, "how tranquilly might we pass through life! How clearly would our eyes see through the darkest clouds, and rest upon the silver lining!"

"Is it not so? Does not God's providence follow us in the smallest things of our lives? Do we take a step that falls outside of his cognizance? We have only to look back, to be assured of this. We may walk on tranquilly, Doctor, for, as sure as we live, no evil can befall us that does not have its origin within our own spirits. All the machinations of our most bitter enemies will come to naught, if we keep our hearts free from guile. They may rob us of our earthly possessions; but even this God will turn to our greater gain."

Mrs. Wallingford spoke with a charming enthusiasm.

"With such a confidence," said my wife, "one is richer than if he had the wealth of an Astor."

"And with this great advantage," replied Mrs. Wallingford, "that he may enjoy the whole of his possessions. Moth and rust never corrupt them; and no man can take them away."

"I have a new book from which I want to read you a sentiment," said Constance, rising, and moving towards the secretary and book-case, which stood in the room.

Mrs. Wallingford rose and went with her.

"It is so beautifully accordant with many things I have heard you say," added my wife, as she took down the volume, and commenced turning over its pages.

After reading a few sentences, and commenting upon them, some remark directed the attention of Mrs. Wallingford to the antiquated secretary, which was the one I had purchased when the furniture of the Allen house was sold.

"I have reason to remember this old secretary," she said. "It was here that the will was found which cut off our interest in the estate of my uncle."

As she spoke in a pleasant way, she pulled out a drawer - the very one which had suggested concealment, when I first got possession of the piece of furniture - and said -

"This is where the will lay concealed."

And she pressed against the side firmly, when a portion of it yielded, and there sprung up another drawer, or receptacle, placed in vertically.

We were all very much interested in this curious arrangement. The drawer could not be pulled out much beyond half its depth; the secret portion lying within this limit.

As I stood looking at the drawer, a sudden thought flashed through my mind, and I pressed my hand against the other side. It began to yield! I pressed harder, and up sprung a corresponding secret recaptacle, from which a paper fell out. A hard substance rattled on the solid wood. It was a gold locket, tied

T. S. Arthur

with a piece of blue ribbon; and attached, with a seal, to the folded paper.

It was some moments before a hand reached forth to lift the document. It was at length taken up by Mr. Wallingford. As he did so, the locket swung free, and we saw that it contained a braid of dark hair. Unfolding the paper, and stepping back to the light, he read, in a low, firm voice, as follows:

"I, John Allen, being of sound mind, do make this as my last will and testament, revoking, at the same time, all other wills. I give and bequeath all my property, real and personal, to my sister Flora, if living; or, if dead, to her legal heirs - reserving only, for my wife, Theresa Garcia, in case she survive me, a legacy of five hundred dollars a year, to be continued during her natural life. And I name as my executors, to carry out the provisions of this will, Doctor Edward -and James Wilkinson, of the town of S -, State of Massachusetts."

Then followed the date, which was recent, compared with that of the other wills, and the signatures of the testator and witnesses, all in due form. The witnesses were men in our town, and well known to us all.

At the reading of her mother's name, Mrs. Wallingford sat down quickly, and, covering her face, leaned over upon the centre table. I saw that she was endeavoring to control a strong agitation.

I was the first to speak.

"The ways of Providence are past finding out," said I. "Let me congratulate you on this good fortune."

As I spoke, Mrs. Wallingford rose from the table, and, going to her husband, placed her hands upon his arms, and looking up into his face, fondly and tearfully, said:

"Dear Henry! For your sake, my heart is glad to-night."

He laid the will down, as if it were a thing of little value, and kissing her, said: -

"This cannot add to our happiness, Blanche, and may bring care and trouble."

"Not more trouble than blessing," she replied, "if rightfully used."

The locket attached to the will excited our curious interest. It was, we felt sure, the same that Captain Allen's mother had sent to him by the hands of Jacob Perkins. Doubtless, some memory of his mother, stirred by the sight of this locket, had caused him to revoke his former will, and execute this one in favor of his sister. There was no room to question, for a moment, its genuineness. It had all legal formality, and the men who witnessed the signature were living and well known to us all. I was named as one of the executors. So there was some perplexing business before me; for, in taking things as they were, it was not probable that the executors under the former will would be able, promptly, to give a satisfactory account of their trust, or to hand over the property in a shape acceptable to the right heirs.

But, of this, more anon. Our good friends went home early after this singular discovery, showing more bewilderment than elation of manner. I think that Constance and I were gladder in heart than they.

# CHAPTER XXV.

The first thing done was to place the will on record; the next to give proper legal notice of its existence to the executors under the previous will, Judge Bigelow and Squire Floyd. Mr. Dewey, on the announcement of this discovery, unhesitatingly declared the paper a forgery; but the witnesses to the signature of Captain Allen were living, and ready to attest its genuineness. They remembered, very distinctly, the time when their names were appended to the document. It was only a year before the Captain's death. They were walking past the Allen House, when the old man called them in, and asked them to witness the signing of a paper. Of its contents they had no knowledge, as he did not make any communication on the subject. But he signed it in their presence, and their signatures showed this will to be the paper then executed.

Notwithstanding this, it came to our ears, that Mr. Dewey persisted in alleging fraud, forgery, and the complicity of these witnesses. And from the manner of Judge Bigelow and Squire Floyd, in the first brief interview I had with them, it was plain that they were far from being satisfied that all was right. Their manner was that of men utterly confounded. If the property in question had been held by them as really their own, they could hardly have exhibited more feeling.

After the will was entered at the proper office, and thus made public, the following paragraph appeared in our "Weekly Star" -

*"Remarkable Discovery of a Will.* - A singular circumstance happened in our town last week, no less than the discovery of a new and more recent will of the late Captain Allen, by which all of his large property is devised to his sister and her heirs. It was found in a secret drawer, contained in an antiquated French Secretary, which Dr. - bought when the furniture of the Allen House was sold, previous to a renovation of the old mansion for the residence of Mr. Ralph Dewey. The late Mrs. Montgomery, who resided for a time at the Allen House, was sister to Captain Allen, and her daughter is now the wife of our townsman, Henry Wallingford, Esq. We congratulate the parties on the good fortune which has come to their door."

The marriage of Mr. Dewey took place within a month after the discovery of this will, and he brought his new wife to S -, installing her as mistress of the Allen House. She was a showy woman, past thirty, with a pair of brilliant black eyes, and a dark, rich complexion. Her long, thin nose, and delicate, but proudly arching lips, showed her to possess will and determination. It was the rumor in S -, that she brought her husband a considerable fortune. But she was not well received among us. The families of Judge Bigelow, and Joshua Kling, Cashier of the Clinton Bank, called immediately. Something later called the wives of two Directors in the Bank, and afterwards the wives of one or two citizens who had embarked some capital in the cotton mills. Beyond this, no advances were made towards an acquaintance with the new Mrs. Dewey.

T. S. Arthur

It shocked my sensibilities to see this woman dashing about through S - in the elegant equipage once the pride of the now humbled daughter of Squire Floyd, who, since the divorce granted on her application, had lived in strict retirement in her father's house. The only time when she was seen abroad, was on the Sabbath, at church, with her two children. The oldest, a daughter, in her thirteenth year; and the youngest, a boy, ten years of age. The terrible ordeal passed through by this unhappy woman, had told upon her severely. In a year, she seemed to have lived ten. All the fine roundness of her face and person had given way, and she presented the appearance of one who had come out of a long and exhausting illness.

Constance made it a point of duty to visit her often. She found her states of mind exceedingly variable. Sometimes she was in patient, tranquil states, and sometimes she manifested great bitterness of spirit, complaining of man's cruel selfishness, and God's injustice. The marriage of Mr. Dewey disturbed her considerably. One day, not long after this event, Constance called to see her. She was in one of her darker moods; and all the comforting suggestions which my good wife could make, seemed to go for nothing. They were sitting near a window, overlooking the street, when Delia suddenly turned pale, and caught her breath. A carriage went sweeping by at the moment, drawn by two spirited horses,

"Is that the woman?" she exclaimed, as soon as she recovered herself.

"That is the woman," Constance replied.

Delia clutched her hands so tightly that her arms

quivered, and grew rigid; while her pale face darkened with an expression so like revenge, that Constance felt a shudder of fear in her heart.

"If my prayers for her are answered," said the excited woman, speaking through her closing teeth, "she will find that day the darkest in the calendar of her life, when she stepped between me and my husband. I have only curses for her in my heart. Only curses!"

Constance, startled, and almost frightened by this wild burst of feeling, endeavored to soothe her; but the storm was too fierce to own the power of her gentle persuasions, and raged on for its brief season.

"I thought her mind had given way," said my wife, on relating what she had seen and heard. "It was fearful to look upon a human creature so terribly moved."

"The trial to her feelings must have been very

"But I thought the severe discipline through which she had passed, had chastened and subdued her," answered Constance. "I saw, or believed that I saw, the beginnings of a new and true life in her soul. But over all this, passion has swept with its besom of destruction."

"The better states," I replied, "may not have been destroyed in this evil whirlwind. Such states, when once formed, usually retire and hide themselves until the storm has spent its fury."

"I pray that it may be so in this case," said Constance. "But from what I saw to-day, my fears are on the other side."

T. S. Arthur

In the mean time we were taking such steps as the responsibility of our position required, towards getting possession of the property, which, under the will of Captain Allen, must come into our hands. My co-executor, Mr. James Wilkinson, a merchant of S -, was for adopting the most summary proceedings. He was annoyed at the questions, doubts, and delays which Judge Bigelow and Squire Floyd permitted to intervene; and more especially by the intermeddling of Dewey, towards whom, from some cause, he entertained hostile feeling.

As a matter of course, we were guided in all our movements by Mr. Wallingford. At the earliest term of court, we brought forward the claim of Mrs. Wallingford, under the last will and testament of her uncle. A feeble effort was made to throw doubt upon the genuineness of the document; but the oath of the witnesses to the signature of Captain Alien settled the question beyond the reach of cavil, and the executors under the first will were ordered to transfer, by a certain date, all property belonging to the estate into our hands.

I saw plainly enough, from the beginning, that the idea of giving an account of their stewardship was not an agreeable one to either of the executors under the old will. The direction which the property must take was one that would not admit of any holding back or covering up on their part. They would be required to exhibit clean hands.

The property clearly shown as having passed into their possession, was the old mansion and valuable grounds, which had been sold, under an order of the court, at a heavy sacrifice - bringing only thirty-five thousand dollars, instead of sixty thousand, its real value - and the proceeds re-invested. Then there was other town property worth twenty thousand dollars, and stocks valued at as much more: making seventy-five thousand dollars in all as the principal. Interest added, would swell the sum for which they must give account to over one hundred thousand dollars.

It was found, on looking into the business, that the whole of this immense sum was invested in the cotton mills. The search made into the legal condition of these mill properties was not satisfactory. There were several mortgages against them, one of which, for twenty-five thousand dollars, was held by the Clinton Bank as collateral security for loans.

After various delays and failures on the part of the old executors to meet us in a satisfactory manner, we all assembled, by appointment, in the office of Judge Bigelow. Mr. Dewey I was surprised to find present. But it was plain that he was there either by the consent or request of the Judge and Squire. The court had given a certain time for the executors under the first will to make up their accounts, and hand over the property in trust. That time had expired.

There was manifest embarrassment on the part of Judge Bigelow and his associate; while Dewey looked stern and dogged. We soon got into the centre of the business, and found it pretty earnest work. It was admitted by the executors that the greater portion of the estate was in the cotton mills. How to get it out was the question.

"I had always understood," said Mr. Wallingford, "that the mills were chiefly owned in New York."

T. S. Arthur

"The New York interest is large," replied Squire Floyd, in a husky voice.

"And can be increased, no doubt, to almost any extent, in order to enable you to withdraw the trust investments" resumed Mr. Wallingford.

"Why cannot you let it remain where it is for the present? The investment is safe and the interest sure," said Judge Bigelow.

"There isn't safer security in the state," spoke up Mr. Dewey, with animation.

"It isn't the kind of security we wish to hold," said Mr. Wilkinson firmly. "We have given heavy bonds, and prefer to get the property in a different shape."

Here followed a chilling silence, which was broken by Mr. Wallingford.

"There is one way in which this can be arranged," said he.

All eyes were turned upon him.

"If it is not convenient to transfer to new parties interests of such magnitude, we will take, at a fair valuation, the Allen House and grounds appertaining thereto, including the mill site."

Mr. Dewey was on his feet in a moment, and said -

"Never!" with considerable excitement of manner.

Judge Bigelow and Squire Floyd looked at each other

in a bewildered manner, and then at Mr. Dewey, who was walking the floor with many signs of disturbance.

"This is the family property," continued Mr. Wallingford, coolly -" and ought never to have been sold. It is but fair that it should come back."

"It can't go back," spoke up Mr. Dewey. "The present owners will not let it pass out of their hands."

"If that is the case," said Mr. Wallingford, "we shall have to look in another direction. It occurred to me that this might suit all parties, and lead to an easy arrangement. But if that cannot be - if the present owners, to use Mr. Dewey's words, will not let it go back - then my suggestion falls to the ground, and we must look to the investments as they stand. We do not press the matter."

I observed Mr. Dewey closely; the amount of feeling he displayed having drawn my attention upon him. Once or twice I saw him dart malignant glances towards Mr. Wallingford. And so, by degrees, I began to have a glimpse of what was passing in his mind. To go out from that elegant home, and let Wallingford succeed him as the owner, was something to which his proud heart could not submit - Wallingford, the once despised and contemned student of his uncle! That was too bitter a humiliation.

As nothing could then be decided, another meeting, to take place in three or four days, was agreed upon, and we separated.

# CHAPTER XXVI.

As my profession kept me going about all the while, I had opportunities for observing the movements of other people. The day following the meeting referred to in the last chapter, I saw Dewey, the Judge, and the Squire together several times, and always in earnest talk. As I came home, towards evening, I saw them all entering Mr. Dewey's residence. It was plain that there was trouble in the camp.

On the next day, Mr. Dewey left town. I noticed him going into a car at the depot. When the time came for our meeting, a postponement was asked for. I felt like demurring, but Mr. Wallingford readily consented.

"Give them a little more time," said he, as we walked away from Judge Bigelow's office. "It will come out as we desired. The easiest way for them to arrange with us, is to let us have the Allen House property, which is owned by the firm of which Dewey is a member; and it is with a view to this, I have no doubt, that he is now in New York."

So we waited a few days longer. The return of Mr. Dewey took place in the course of a week, when I received a note from Judge Bigelow, asking a private interview. I found him and his nephew alone. They received me in a pleasant, affable way; and the Judge said that he wished to have a little talk with me before another formal meeting of the executors. I answered that it would give me pleasure to confer with him; though I could neither accept nor propose any thing, standing alone.

"It is not with a view to that, Doctor," replied the Judge, his countenance putting on a shade of gravity that nearly obliterated the smiles with which he at first received me. "But I thought it might help to a better issue, if two of the parties representing the opposite interests in this case were to have a little informal conversation."

"I am ready to hear any thing you have to say, Judge, and shall be very happy if I can aid, in any thing, the satisfactory adjustment of these matters." My answer, I thought, appeared to give him confidence, and he said -

"Without doubt you can aid, Doctor. The position in which Squire Floyd and myself find ourselves placed, is one of some embarrassment. In making investments of the property which came into our hands, we had reference, of course, to its security and productiveness; at the same time looking to a period, still some years in advance, when our trust would cease, and the property pass in due course to the heir-at-law. To realize on these investments now, would be to damage the interests of others; and I cannot feel that it would be right for you to urge this. The discovery of a new will, bearing a later date, is a thing wholly unexpected. We had no warning to prepare for the summary action growing out of its appearance, and, as I have just intimated, cannot proceed without injury to others."

"I do not believe," said Mr. Dewey, "that the court, if

the case was fairly stated, would require this speedy settlement of the trust. And it is my advice, that the whole matter be referred back for a new award as to time. A year longer should be conceded to the executors under the old will."

"That would be equitable," said the Judge.

"I am afraid," I made answer to this, "that Mr. Wallingford will not consent to any postponement."

"He won't? The hound!" I was startled by the fierceness of Dewey's tone of voice, and, turning to look at him, saw on his countenance an expression of malignant hatred.

"Ralph!" said Judge Bigelow, in a warning voice.

"I can't repress my indignation," answered the nephew. "What demons from the nether hell have conspired to give *him* power over us? If it had been any other man in the world I could have borne it patiently."

"Ralph! Ralph!" interposed the Judge, in a deprecating voice.

"It is no use, uncle. I cannot keep down my feeling," was replied. "To see you hunted by this hound, who owes you everything."

"Pardon me, Mr. Dewey," said I, "but I cannot hear such language used towards a gentleman of irreproachable character. Mr. Wallingford is not entitled to the epithet you give; and I warn you, not to repeat that, or anything like it, in my presence."

"You warn me!"

A gleam shot towards me from his evil eyes.

"Ralph! silence!" The Judge spoke sternly.

"Yes, in all soberness, I warn you," said I, fixing my gaze upon him, and holding his eyes until they fell to the floor. "Mr. Wallingford is not the man to permit any one to use language about him, such as you have indulged in. If you make use of another opprobrious epithet, I will communicate the fact to him immediately. And let me say, that, unless a different temper is manifested, I must terminate this interview at once."

Judge Bigelow drew his nephew aside, and talked for some time with him, in a low, earnest tone; after which the latter apologized, though with an ill grace, for the intemperance of his manner - alleging that an old wound smarted whenever Wallingford crossed his path.

The result of this confidential talk was not as favorable on my mind as Judge Bigelow had hoped to make it. I pitied his embarrassment; but the conduct of Dewey confirmed my previous view of the case, which was to require a transfer of the property specified by Mr. Wallingford, or press for an immediate foreclosure of the mill investments. There was, I felt satisfied, hazard in delay.

When our next formal meeting took place, Dewey was again present. It was in my thought to suggest that he was not a party covered by the business to be considered, when Mr. Wallingford said, in his mild, grave way -

"I believe this is a meeting of the Executors under the two wills of Captain Allen."

The meaning of his remark could not be misunderstood, for he glanced towards Mr. Dewey as he spoke. That individual, however, did not choose to regard himself as referred to, and made no sign. But Mr. Wallingford was not the man to let a deliberate purpose fall to the ground. He had come with the intention of objecting to Dewey's presence at the conference, and to insist upon his retiring, as a preliminary to business.

No one replying to Mr. Wallingford's remark, he said, further -

"I do not mean to be uncourteous, but I must suggest the propriety of Mr. Dewey's withdrawal."

"I am an interested party," said Dewey, with ill-concealed anger.

"Ah! I was not before aware of this," replied Wallingford, and he looked inquiringly towards the Judge and Squire. They showed an uneasy perplexity of manner, but did not respond.

"In what way are you interested?" queried Mr. Wallingford.

"I am one of the guardians to the heir under an existing will."

"A will that the decision of our court has rendered null

and void," was promptly answered. "We have not met to consider questions in which Leon Garcia, or his representative, has any concern. Our business refers to other matters."

Dewey moved uneasily, and seemed struggling to keep down his rising displeasure. But he did not, manifest any intention to withdraw.

"Had we not better proceed to business?" suggested Squire Floyd.

"Not while Mr. Dewey remains," said I, firmly taking the side of Mr. Wallingford.

"Somebody will repent himself of this!" exclaimed the ill-governed man, passionately, starting to his feet, and striding from the office.

"I don't understand this individual's conduct," remarked Wallingford, in a serious way. "Why has he presumed to intermeddle in our business? It has a bad look."

He knit his brows closely, and put on a stern aspect, very unusual to him.

"You probably forget," said Judge Bigelow, "that you have proposed a change of ownership in property now occupied by him?"

"That was simply to give you more latitude in settling up the estate in your hands. I said we were willing to accept that property at a fair valuation, thinking it would offer a desirable mode of liquidation. It is for you to say yea or nay to us; not Ralph Dewey. If you

T. S. Arthur

cannot gain his consent to the transfer, there is an end of that proposal."

I really commiserated the embarrassment shown by the Judge and Squire. They seemed to be in a maze, without perceiving the right way of extrication. Dewey appeared to have over them some mysterious influence, above which they had not power to rise.

"If Ralph will not consent -"

"Ralph must consent!" exclaimed Squire Floyd, with a sudden energy of manner, and the exhibition of a degree of will not shown before. "Ralph *must* consent! The mode of adjustment proposed by Mr. Wallingford is the one easiest for us to accomplish, and I shall insist on Dewey's giving up his opposition. There is a vast deal more of pride than principle involved in his objection."

The Squire was breaking away from his fetters.

"It is plain," added Squire Floyd, "that his partners wish that property to go in preference to any other. And it must go."

This was a style of remark quite unexpected on our part; and only added firmness to our purpose. The interview was not prolonged in discussion. We merely reaffirmed our ultimatum, and gave one week for the two men to decide in what manner to close their trust.

# CHAPTER XXVII.

The decision was as I expected it to be; and the old property came back into the family. There were few hearts in S - , that did not beat with pleasure, when it was known that Mr. Wallingford and his lovely wife were to pass from Ivy Cottage to the stately Allen House.

I think the strife between Mr. Dewey and the old executors was severe, and that he yielded only when he saw that they were immovable. An open rupture with Squire Floyd was a consequence of his persistent determination to have the Allen property transferred; and after the settlement of this business, they held no personal communication with each other.

The change in Mr. Dewey's appearance, after it became a settled thing that he must remove from the splendid mansion he had occupied for years, was remarkable. He lost the impressive swagger that always said, "I am the first man in S -;" and presented the appearance of one who had suffered some great misfortune, without growing better under the discipline. He did not meet you with the free, open, better-than-you look that previously characterized him, but with a half sidelong falling of the eyes, in which there was, to me, something very sinister.

T. S. Arthur

As far as our observation went, Mr. Wallingford put on no new phase of character. There was about him the same quiet, thoughtful dignity of manner which had always commanded involuntary respect. He showed no unseemly haste in dispossessing Mr. Dewey of his elegant home. Two months after the title deeds had passed, I called in at Ivy Cottage, now one of the sweetest, little places in S -, for Constance, who had been passing the evening there. Not in any home, through all the region round, into which it was my privilege to enter, was there radiant, like a warm, enticing atmosphere that swelled your lungs with a new vitality, and gave all your pulses a freer beat, such pure love - maternal and conjugal - as pervaded this sanctuary of the heart. I say maternal, as well as conjugal, for two dear babes had brought into this home attendant angels from the higher heaven.

A soft astral lamp threw its mellow rays about the room. Mr. Wallingford had a book open in his hand, from which he had been reading aloud to his wife and Constance. He closed the volume as I entered, and rising, took my hand, saying, with even more than his usual cordiality -

"Now our circle is complete."

"Excuse me from rising, Doctor," said Mrs. Wallingford, a smile of welcome giving increased beauty to her countenance, as she offered the hand that was free - the other held her babe, just three months old, tenderly to her bosom.

"What have you been reading?" I asked, as I seated myself, and glanced towards the volume which Mr. Wallingford had closed and laid upon the table.

"A memorable relation of the Swedish Seer," he replied, smiling.

"Touching marriage in heaven," said I, smiling in return.

"Or, to speak more truly," he replied, "the union of two souls in heaven, into an eternal oneness. Yes, that was the subject, and it always interests me deeply. Our life here is but a span, and our brief union shadowed by care, pain, sickness, and the never-dying fear of parting. The sky of our being is not unclouded long. And therefore I cannot believe that the blessedness of married love dies forever at the end of this struggle to come into perfect form and beauty. No, Doctor; the end is not here. And so Blanche and I turn often with an eager delight to these relations, feeling, as we read, that they are not mere pictures of fancy, but heavenly verities. They teach us that if we would be united in the next world, we must become purified in this. That selfish love, which is of the person must give place to a love for spiritual qualities. That we must grow in the likeness and image of God, if we would make one angel in His heavenly kingdom."

His eyes rested upon Blanche, as he closed the sentence, with a look full of love; and she, as if she knew that the glance was coming, turned and received it into her heart.

I did not question the faith that carried them over the bounds of time, and gave them delicious foreshadow-wings of the blessedness beyond. As I looked at them, and marked how they seemed to grow daily into a oneness of spirit, could I doubt that there was for them an eternal union? No, no. Such doubts would have been false to the instincts of my own soul, and false to the instincts of every conscious being made to love and be loved.

"The laying aside of this earthly investiture," said Wallingford, resuming, "the passage from mortal to immortal life, cannot change our spirits, but only give to all their powers a freer and more perfect development. Love is not a quality of the body, but of the spirit, and will remain in full force, after the body is cast off like the shell of a chrysalis. Still existing, it will seek its object. And shall it seek forever and not find? God forbid! No! The love I bear my wife is not, I trust, all of the earth, earthy; but instinct with a heavenly perpetuity. And when we sleep the sleep of death, it will be in the confident assurance of a speedy and more perfect conjunction of our lives. On a subject of such deep concern, we are dissatisfied with the vague and conjectural; and this is why the record of things seen and heard in the spiritual world by Swedenborg - especially in what relates to marriages in heaven - has for us such an absorbing interest."

"Are you satisfied with the evidence?" I ventured to inquire, seeing him so confident.

"Yes."

He answered quietly, and with an assured manner.

"How do you reach a conclusion as to the truth of these things?"

"Something after the same way that you satisfy yourself that the sun shines."

"My eyes testify to me that fact. Seeing is believing," I answered.

"The spirit of a man has eyes as well as his body," said Wallingford. "And seeing is believing in another sense than you intimate. Now the bodily eyes see material objects, and the mind, receiving their testimony, is in no doubt as to the existence, quality, and relation of things in the outer world. The eyes of our spirits, on the other hand, see immaterial objects or truths; and presenting them to the rational and perceptive faculties, they are recognized as actual existences, and their quality as surely determined as the quality of a stone or metal. If you ask me how I know that this is quartz, or that iron; I answer, By the testimony of my eyes. And so, if you ask how I satisfy myself as to the truth of which I read in this book; I can only reply that I see it all so clearly that conviction is a necessity. There is no trouble in believing. To attempt disbelief, would be to illustrate the fable of Sisyphus."

He spoke calmly, like one whose mind had risen above doubt. I objected nothing further; for that would have been useless. And why attempt to throw questions into his mind? Was there anything evil in the faith which he had adopted as exhibited in his life? I could not say yes. On the contrary, taking his life as an illustration, good only was to be inferred. I remembered very well when his mind diverged into this new direction. Some years had intervened. I thought to see him grow visionary or enthusiastic. Not so, however. There was a change progressively visible; but it was in the direction of sound and rational views of life. A broader humanity showed itself in his words and actions. Then came the subtler vein of religious sentiments, running like pure gold through all that appertained to him.

If, therefore, he was progressing towards a higher life, why should I question as to the way being right for him? Why should I seek to turn him into another path when there was such a broad light for his eyes on the one he had chosen? "By their fruits ye shall know them." And by his fruits I knew him to be of that highest type of manhood, a Christian gentleman.

I noticed, while Mr. Wallingford spoke so confidently of their reunion in heaven, that his wife leaned towards, and looked at him, with eyes through which her soul seemed going forth into his.

As the conversation flowed on, it gradually involved other themes, and finally led to the question On my part, as to when they were going to leave Ivy Cottage.

"That is quite uncertain," replied Mr. Wallingford. "I shall not hurry the present occupant. We have been so happy here, that we feel more inclined to stay than to remove to a more ambitious home."

"I hear that Mr. Dewey is going to build," said I.

"Where?"

"He has been negotiating for the property on the elevation west of the Allen House."

"Ah!"

"Yes. The price of the ground, five acres, is ten thousand dollars."

"The site is commanding and beautiful. The finest in S -, for one who thinks mainly of attracting the attention of others," said Mr. Wallingford.

"If he builds, we shall see something on a grander scale than anything yet attempted in our neighborhood. He will overshadow you."

"The rivalry must be on his side alone," was Mr. Wallingford's reply. "No elegance or imposing grandeur that he may assume, can disturb me in the smallest degree. I shall only feel pity for the defect of happiness that all his blandishments must hide."

"A splendid Italian villa is talked of."

Mr. Wallingford shook his head.

"You doubt all this?" said I.

"Not the man's ambitious pride; but his ability to do what pride suggests. He and his compeers are poorer, by a hundred thousand dollars, than they deemed themselves a few short months ago."

"Have they met with heavy losses?" I asked, not understanding the drift of his remark.

"The estate in trust has been withdrawn."

"How should that make them poorer?"

"It makes them poorer, in the first place, as to the means for carrying on business. And it makes them poorer, in the second place, in the loss of an estate, which, I am sorry to believe, Mr. Dewey and a part of his New York associates regarded as virtually their own.

"But the heir was approaching his majority," said I.

"And growing up a weak, vicious, self-indulgent young man, who, in the hands of a shrewd, unscrupulous villain, might easily be robbed of his fortune. You may depend upon it, Doctor, that somebody has suffered a terrible disappointment, and one from which he is not likely soon to recover. No - no! We shall see nothing of this princely Italian villa."

"I cannot believe," I replied, "that the executors who had the estate in trust were influenced by dishonorable motives. I know the men too well."

"Nor do I, Doctor," he answered, promptly. "But, as I have before said, they were almost wholly under the influence of Dewey, and I think that he was leading them into mazes from which honorable extrication would have been impossible."

"Have you given Dewey any notice of removal?" I inquired.

"No - and shall not, for some time. I am in no hurry to leave this place, in which the happiest days of my life have passed. Any seeming eagerness to dispossess him, would only chafe a spirit in which I would not needlessly excite evil passions. His pride must, I think, lead him at a very early day to remove, and thus make a plain way before me."

"How long will you wait?" I asked.

"Almost any reasonable time."

"You and he might not take the same view of what was

reasonable," said I.

"Perhaps not. But, as I remarked just now, being in no hurry to leave our present home, I shall not disturb him for some months to come. No change will be made by us earlier than next spring. And if he wishes to spend the winter in his present abode, he is welcome to remain."

There was no assumed virtuous forbearance in all this; but a sincere regard for the feelings and comfort of Dewey. This was so apparent, that I did not question for a moment his generous consideration of a man who would not have hesitated, if the power were given, to crush him to the very earth.

Many thoughts passed in my mind, as I pondered the incidents and conversation of this evening. In looking back upon life, we see the sure progress of causes to effects; and in the effects, the quality of the causes. We no longer wonder at results - the only wonder is, that they were not foreseen. Wise maxims, some of the garnered grains of our fathers' experiences, are scattered through the books we read, and daily fall from the lips of teachers and friends; maxims which, if observed, would lead us to honor and happiness. But who gives them heed? Who makes them the rule of his conduct?

We might wonder less at the blind infatuation with which so many press onward in a course that all the wisdom of the past, as well as all the reason of the present, condemns, if it were possible to rub out our actions, as a child rubs from his slate a wrong sum, and begin the work of life over again. But this cannot be. We weave hourly the web that is to bind us in the future. Our to-days hold the fate of our to-morrows. What we do is done for ever, and in some degree will affect us throughout infinite ages.

"Poor Delia Floyd!" My thought had turned to her as I lay awake, long after the small hours of the morning, busy with incidents and reflections which had completely banished sleep from my eyes. In the strong pity of my heart, I spoke the words aloud.

"What of her?" said Constance, in a tone of surprise. And so intruding thought had kept her awake also!

"Nothing more than usual," I answered. "But I cannot sleep for thinking of her unhappy state, and what she might have been, if obeying her own heart's right impulses, and the reason God gave her, she had accepted a true man, instead of a specious villain for her husband. The scene in Ivy Cottage to-night stands in most remarkable contrast with some things I witnessed at the Allen House before she went out thence a wretched woman for life. She staked every-thing on a desperate venture, and has lost. God pity her! for there is no help in any human arm. To think of what she is, and what she might have been, is enough to veil her reason in midnight darkness."

"Amen! God pity her!" said Constance. "For truly there is no help for her in mortal arm."

# CHAPTER XXVIII.

The conduct of Mr. Wallingford, in regard to the estate which had fallen into his hands, rather puzzled Dewey. He had anticipated an early notification to remove, and, true to his character, had determined to annoy the new owner by vexatious delays. But after the passage of several weeks, in which came to him no intimation that he must give up the possession of his elegant home, he began to wonder what it could mean.

One day, not long after the conversation with Wallingford, mentioned in the last chapter, I met Mr. Dewey in the street. He stopped me and said, in half-sneering way,

"What of our honorable friend? Impatient, I suppose, to see the inside of the Allen House?"

"No," I replied, "he has no wish to disturb you for the present."

"Indeed! You expect me to believe all that, of course."

There was a rudeness in his manner that was offensive; but I did not care to let him see that I noticed it.

"Why should you not believe my remark?" said I. "Is it a new thing in your experience with men to find an

T. S. Arthur

individual considerate of another?"

"What do you mean by considerate of another?"

My form of speech touched his pride.

"Mr. Wallingford has manifested towards you a considerate spirit," said I, speaking slowly and distinctly. "It naturally occurs to him that, as you are so pleasantly situated at the Allen House, an early removal therefrom might be anything but desirable. And so he has rested quietly up to this time, leaving a decision as to the period with yourself."

"Humph! Very unselfish, truly!"

His lip curled in disdain.

"If you feel restive under this concession in your favor," said I, putting on a serious manner, "I would suggest independence as a remedy."

He looked at me curiously, yet with a scowling contraction of his brows.

"Independence! What am I to understand by your remark?"

"Simply this, Mr. Dewey. You are in the occupancy of property belonging to Mr. Wallingford, and by his favor. Now, if you cannot receive a kindness at his hands, in the name of all that is manly and independent, put yourself out of the range of obligation."

I was not able to repress a sudden feeling of indignation, and so spoke with warmth and plainness.

"Thank you for your plainness of speech, Doctor," he retorted, drawing himself up in a haughty manner.

"As to removing from the Allen House, I will do that just when it suits my pleasure."

"Mr. Wallingford, you may be assured," said I, will not show any unseemly impatience, if you do not find it convenient to make an early removal. He knows that it cannot be agreeable for you to give up the home of years, and he is too much of a Christian and a gentleman to do violence to another's feelings, if it can be in any way avoided."

"Pah! I hate cant!"

He threw his head aside in affected disgust.

"We judge men by their actions, not their words," said I. "If a man acts with considerate kindness, is it cant to speak of him in terms of praise? Pardon me, Mr. Dewey, but I think you are letting passion blind you to another's good qualities."

"The subject is disagreeable to me, Doctor. Let us waive it."

"It was introduced by yourself, remember," I replied; "and all that I have said has been in response to your own remarks. This much good has grown from it. You know just how Mr. Wallingford stands towards you, and you can govern yourself according to your own views in the case. And now let me volunteer this piece of advice. Never wantonly give offence to another, for you cannot tell how soon you may find yourself in need of his good services."

Dewey gave me a formal bow, and passed on his way.

About a week afterwards, Judge Bigelow inquired of Wallingford as to when he wished to get possession of the Allen House.

"Whenever Mr. Dewey finds it entirely convenient to remove," was the unhesitating reply.

"Suppose it should not be convenient this fall or winter?"

"Very well. The spring will suit me. I am in no hurry. We are too comfortable in Ivy Cottage to be in any wise impatient for change."

"Then it is your pleasure that Mr. Dewey remain until spring?"

"If such an arrangement is desirable on his part, Judge, it is altogether accordant with my feelings and convenience. Say to him that he has only to consult his own wishes in the case."

"You are kind and considerate, Mr. Wallingford," said the Judge, his manner softening considerably, for there had been a coldness of some years' standing on the part of Judge Bigelow, which more recent events had increased.

"And why should it be otherwise, Judge?" inquired his old student.

"Mr. Dewey has not given you cause for either kindness or consideration."

"It would hurt me more than it would him, were I to foster his unhappy spirit. It is always best, I find, Judge, to be right with myself."

"All men would find it better for themselves, were they to let so fine a sentiment govern their lives," remarked Judge Bigelow, struck by the language of Wallingford.

"It is the only true philosophy," was replied. "If a man is right with himself, he cannot be wrong towards others; though it is possible, as in my case, that other eyes, looking through a densely refracting medium, may see him out of his just position. But he would act very unwisely were he to change his position for all that. He will be seen right in the end."

Judge Bigelow reached out his hand and grasped that of Mr. Wallingford.

"Spoken like a man, Henry! Spoken like a man!" he said, warmly. "I only wish that Ralph had something of your spirit. I have seen you a little out of your right position, I believe; but a closer view is correcting the error."

Wallingford returned the pressure as warmly as it was given, saying, as he did so -

"I am aware, Judge, that you have suffered your mind to fall into a state of prejudice in regard to me. But I am not aware of any thing in my conduct towards you or others, to warrant the feeling. If in any thing I have been brought into opposition, faithfulness to the interests I represented has been the rule of my conduct. I have sought by no trick of law to gain an advantage. The right and the just I have endeavored to pursue,

T. S. Arthur

without fear and without favor. Can you give me a better rule for professional or private life?"

"I cannot, Henry," was the earnest reply. "And if all men would so pursue the right and the just, how different would be the result for each, as the sure adjustment of advancing years gave them their true places in the world's observation!"

The Judge spoke in a half - absent way, and with a shade of regret in his tones; Wallingford noted this with a feeling of concern.

"Let us be friends in the future," he added, again offering his hand to Wallingford.

"It will be your fault, not mine, if we are not fast fiends, Judge. I have never forgotten the obligations of my boyhood; and never ceased to regret the alienation you have shown. To have seemed in your eyes ungrateful, has been a source of pain whenever I saw or thought of you."

The two men parted, each feeling better for the interview. A day or two afterwards Wallingford received a note from Judge Bigelow asking him, as a particular favor, to call at his office that evening. He went, of course. The Judge was alone, and received him cordially. But, his countenance soon fell into an expression of more than usual gravity.

"Mr. Wallingford," he said, after the passage of a few casual observations, "I would like to consult you in strict confidence on some matters in which I have become involved. I can trust you, of course?"

"As fully as if the business were my own," was the unhesitating answer.

"So I have believed. The fact is, Henry, I have become so entangled in this cotton mill business with Squire Floyd, Dewey, and others, that I find myself in a maze of bewildering uncertainty. The Squire and Ralph are at loggerheads, and seem to me to be getting matters snarled up. There is no denying the fact that this summary footing of our accounts, as executors, has tended to cripple affairs. We were working up to the full extent of capital invested, and the absence of a hundred thousand dollars - or its representative security - has made financiering a thing of no easy consideration."

"I am afraid, Judge Bigelow," said Wallingford, as the old man paused, "that you are in the hands of one who, to gain his own ends, would sacrifice you without a moment's hesitation."

"Who?"

"You will permit me to speak plainly, Judge."

"Say on. The plain speech of a friend is better than the flatteries of an enemy."

"I have no faith in Ralph Dewey."

The two men looked steadily at each other for some moments.

"Over fifteen years' observation of the man has satisfied me that he possesses neither honor nor humanity. He is your nephew. But that does not signify. We must look at men as they are."

"His movements have not been to my satisfaction for some time," said the Judge; speaking as though conviction had to force itself upon his mind.

"You should canvass all he does with the closest care; and if your property lies in any degree at his mercy, change the relation as quickly as possible."

"Are you not prejudiced against him, Henry?" The Judge spoke in a deprecating tone.

"I believe, sir, that I estimate him at his real value; and I do most earnestly conjure you to set to work at once to disentangle your affairs if seriously involved with his. If you do not, he will beggar you in your old age, which God forbid!"

"I am far from sure that I can disentangle my affairs," said the Judge.

"There is nothing like trying, you know." Wallingford spoke in a tone of encouragement. "And everything may depend on beginning in time. In what way are you involved with him?"

It was some time before Judge Bigelow answered this direct question. He then replied,

"Heavily in the way of endorsements."

"Of his individual paper?"

"Yes. Also of the paper of his firm."

"To an extent beyond your ability to pay if there should be failure on their part?"

"Yes; to three times my ability to pay."

Wallingford dropped his eyes to the floor, and sat for some time. He then looked up into Judge Bigelow's face, and said,

"If that be so, I can see only one way for you."

"Say on."

"Let no more endorsements be given from this day forth."

"How can I suddenly refuse? The thing has been going on for years."

"You can refuse to do wrong on the plea of wrong. If your name gives no real value to a piece of paper, yet accredits it in the eyes of others, it is wrong for you to place your endorsement thereon. Is not this so?"

"I admit the proposition, Henry."

"Very well. The only way to get right, is to start right. And my dear, dear sir! let me implore you to take immediately the first step in a right direction. Standing outside of the charmed circle of temptation as I do, I can see the right way for your feet to walk in better than you can. Oh, sir! Let me be eyes, and hand, and feet for you if need be; and if it is not too late, I will save you from impending ruin."

Wallingford took the old man's hand, and grasped it

warmly as he spoke. The Judge was moved by this earnest appeal, coming upon him so unexpectedly; and not only moved, but startled and alarmed by the tenor of what was said.

"The first thing," he remarked, after taking time to get his thoughts clear, "if I accept of your friendly overtures, is for me to lay before you everything just as it is, so that you can see where I stand, and how I stand. Without this, your view of the case would be partial, and your conclusions might not be right."

"That is unquestionably so," Wallingford replied. "And now, Judge, if you wish my friendly aid, confide in me as you would a son or brother. You will find me as true as steel."

A revelation succeeded that filled Mr. Wallingford with painful astonishment. The endorsements of Judge Bigelow, on paper brought to him by Dewey, and of which he took no memorandums, covered, no doubt, from a hundred to a hundred and fifty thousand dollars! Then, as to the affairs of the Clinton Bank, of which Judge Bigelow was still the President, he felt a great deal of concern. The Cashier and Mr. Dewey knew far more about the business and condition of the institution than anybody else, and managed it pretty much in their own way. The directors, if not men of straw, might almost as well have been, for all the intelligent control they exercised. As for Judge, Bigelow, the principal duty required of him was to sign his name as President to great sheets of bank bills, the denomination running from one dollar to a thousand. Touching the extent to which these representatives of value were issued, he knew nothing certain. He was shown, at regular periods, a statement wherein the condition of the bank was set forth, and to which he appended his signature. But he had no certain knowledge that the figures were correct. Of the paper under discount over two-thirds was drawn or endorsed by Floyd, Lawson, Lee, & Co.

At the time Judge Bigelow began investing in mill property, he was worth, in productive stocks and real estate, from thirty to forty thousand dollars. He now estimated his wealth at from sixty to eighty thousand dollars; but it was all locked up in the mills.

The result of this first interview between the Judge and Mr. Wallingford was to set the former in a better position to see the character of his responsibilities, and the extreme danger in which he stood. The clear, honest, common sense way in which Wallingford looked at everything, and comprehended everything, surprised his old preceptor; and gave him so much confidence in his judgment and discretion, that he placed himself fully in his hands. And well for him was it that he did so in time.

# CHAPTER XXIX.

In accordance with the advice of Mr. Wallingford, the first reactionary movement on the part of Judge Bigelow, was his refusal to endorse any more paper for his nephew, or the firm of which he was a member, on the ground that such endorsements, on his part, were of no real value, considering the large amounts for which he was already responsible, and consequently little better than fraudulent engagements to pay.

A storm between the uncle and nephew was the consequence, and the latter undertook to drive the old gentleman back again into the traces, by threats of terrible disasters to him and all concerned. If Judge Bigelow had stood alone, the nephew would have been too strong for him. But he had a clear-seeing, honest mind to throw light upon his way, and a young and vigorous arm to lean upon in his hour of weakness and trial. And so Ralph Dewey, to his surprise and alarm, found it impossible to bend the Judge from his resolution.

Then followed several weeks, during which time Dewey was flying back and forth between New York and S -, trying to re-adjust the disturbed balance of things. The result was as Mr. Wallingford had anticipated. There was too much at stake for the house of Floyd, Lawson, Lee, & Co., to let matters fail for lack of Judge Bigelow's endorsements. Some other prop must be substituted for this one.

The four months that followed were months of anxious suspense on the part of Judge Bigelow and his true friend, who was standing beside him, though invisible in this thing to all other eyes, firm as a rocky pillar. No more endorsements were given, and the paper bearing his name was by this time nearly all paid.

"Right, so far," said Mr. Wallingford, at the expiration of the time in which most of the paper bearing Judge Bigelow's name reached its maturity. "And now for the next safe move in this difficult game, where the odds are still against us. You must get out of this Bank."

The Judge looked gravely opposed.

"It may awaken suspicion that something is wrong, and create a run upon the Bank, which would be ruin."

"Can you exercise a controlling influence in the position you hold? Can you be true, as President of the Clinton Bank, to the public interest you represent?"

"I cannot. They have made of me an automaton."

"Very well. That settles the question. You cannot honorably hold your place a single day. There is only one safe step, and that is to resign."

"But the loose way in which I held office will be exposed to my successor."

"That is not the question to consider, Judge - but the right. Still, so far as this fear is concerned, don't let it trouble you. The choice of successor will fall upon some one quite as facile to the wishes of Ralph Dewey & Company as you have been."

The good counsels of Mr. Wallingford prevailed. At the next meeting of the Board of Directors, the resignation of Judge Bigelow was presented. Dewey had been notified two days before of what was coming, and was prepared for it. He moved, promptly, that the resignation be accepted. As soon as the motion was carried, he offered the name of Joshua Kling, the present Cashier, for the consideration of the Board, and urged his remarkable fitness. Of course, Mr. Joshua Kling was elected; and his place filled by one of the tellers. To complete the work, strong complimentary resolutions, in which deep regret at the resignation of Judge Bigelow was expressed, were passed by the Board. In the next week's paper, the following notice of this change in the officers of the Bank appeared:

"*Resignation of Judge Bigelow.* - In consequence of the pressure of professional engagements, our highly esteemed citizen Judge Bigelow, has found it necessary to give up the office of President in the Clinton Bank, which he has held with so much honor to himself since the institution commenced business. He is succeeded by Joshua Kling, Esq., late Cashier; a gentleman peculiarly well-fitted for the position to which he has been elevated. Harvey Weems, the first Teller, takes the place of Cashier. A better selection, it would be impossible to make. From the beginning, the affairs of this Bank have been managed with great prudence, and it is justly regarded as one of the soundest in the State."

"My dear friend," said the grateful Judge, grasping the

hand of Wallingford, who called his attention to this notice, "what a world of responsibility you have helped me to cast from my shoulders! I am to-day a happier man than I have been for years. The new President is welcome to all the honor his higher position may reflect upon him."

"The next work in order," remarked the Judge's clear-headed, resolute friend, "is to withdraw your invest-ments from the cotton mills. That will be a slower and more difficult operation; but it must be done, even at a sacrifice. Better have fifty thousand dollars in solid real estate, than a hundred thousand in that concern."

And so this further disentanglement was commenced.

Winter having passed away, Mr. Dewey saw it expedient to retire from the Allen House. By this time nothing more was heard of his Italian Villa. He had something else to occupy his thoughts. As there was no house to be rented in S -, that in any way corresponded with his ideas, he stored his furniture, and took board at the new hotel which had lately been erected.

Mr. Wallingford now made preparations for removing to the old mansion, which was still the handsomest place, by all odds, in our town.

One day, early in the summer, I received a note from Mr. Wallingford, asking me to call around at Ivy Cottage in the evening. At the bottom of the note, was a pencilled line from his wife to Constance, asking the pleasure of seeing her also. We went after tea.

"Come with me to the library, Doctor!" said my excellent friend, soon after our arrival. "I want to have

T. S. Arthur

a little talk with you."

So we left the ladies and retired to the library.

"My business with you to-night," said he, as we seated ourselves, facing each other, on opposite sides of the library-table, "is to get at some adjustment of affairs between us, as touching your executorship of the Allen estate. I have asked two or three times for your bills against the estate, but you have always put me off. Mr. Wilkinson, on the contrary, rendered an account for services, which has been allowed and settled."

"The business required so little attention on my part," I replied to this, "that I have never felt that I could, in conscience, render an account. And besides, it was with me so much a labor of love, that I do not wish to mar the pleasure I felt by overlaying it with a compensation."

"No man could possibly feel more deeply your generous good will toward me and mine - manifested from the beginning until now - than I do, Doctor. But I cannot permit the obligation to rest all on one side."

He pulled out a drawer of the library-table, as he said this, and taking therefrom a broad parchment document, laid it down, and while his hand rested upon it continued -

"Anticipating that, as heretofore, I might not be able to get your figures, I have taken the matter into my own hands, and fixed the amount of compensation - subject, of course, to objections on your part, if I have made the award too low. These papers are the title deeds of Ivy Cottage, executed in your favor. There are memories and associations connected with this dear spot, which must for ever be sacred in the hearts of myself and wife; and it would be pain to us to see it desecrated by strangers. In equity and love, then, we pass it over to you and yours; and may God give you as much happiness beneath its roof as we have known."

Surprise kept me silent for some time. But as soon as my thoughts ran free, I answered -

"No - no, Mr. Wallingford. This is fixing the sum entirely beyond a fair estimate. I cannot for a moment -"

He stopped me before I could finish the sentence.

"Doctor!" He spoke with earnestness and deep feeling. "There is no living man to whom I am so heavily indebted as I am to you. Not until after my marriage was I aware that your favorable word, given without qualification, bore me into the confidence of Mrs. Montgomery, and thus opened the way for me to happiness and fortune. My good Blanche has often repeated to me the language you once used in my favor, and which awakened in her mind an interest which gradually deepened into love. My heart moves towards you, Doctor, and you must let its impulses have way in this small matter. Do not feel it as an obligation. That is all on our side. We cannot let Ivy Cottage go entirely out of the family. We wish to have as much property in it as the pilgrim has in Mecca. We must visit it sometimes, and feel always that its chambers are the abodes of peace and love. A kind Providence has given us of this world's goods an abundance. We did not even have to lift our hands to the ripe clusters. They fell into our laps. And now, if, from our plenty, we take a small portion and discharge

T. S. Arthur

a debt, will you push aside the offering, and say, No? Doctor, this must not be!"

Again I essayed objection; but all was in vain. Ivy Cottage was to be our pleasant home. When, on returning with Constance, I related to her what had passed between Mr. Wallingford and myself, she was affected to tears.

"If I have ever had a covetous thought," she said, "it has been when I looked at Ivy Cottage. And to think it is to be mine! The sweetest, dearest spot in S -!"

There was no putting aside this good fortune. It came in such a shape, that we could not refuse it without doing violence to the feelings of true-hearted friends. And so, when they removed to their new home, we passed to Ivy Cottage.

The two years that followed were marked by no events of striking interest. The affairs of Judge Bigelow continued to assume a better shape, under the persistent direction of Mr. Wallingford, until every dollar which he had invested in the cotton mills was withdrawn and placed in real estate or sound securities. Long before this there had come an open rupture between the old man and his nephew; but the Judge had seen his real character in so clear a light that friendship was no longer desirable.

# CHAPTER XXX.

And now we have come down to the memorable summer and fall of 1857. No gathering clouds, no far-distant, low-voiced thunder gave warning of an approaching storm. The sky was clear, and the sun of prosperity moving onward in his strength, when, suddenly, from the West came a quick flash and an ominous roll of thunder. Men paused, looked at each other, and asked what it meant. Here and there a note of warning was sounded; but, if heeded by any, it came too late. There followed a brief pause, in which people held their breaths. Then came another flash, and another rattling peal. Heavy clouds began to roll up from the horizon; and soon the whole sky was dark. Pale face looked into pale face, and tremulous voices asked as to what was coming. Fear and consternation were in all hearts. It was too late for any to seek refuge or shelter. Ere the startled multitudes had stirred from their first surprised position, the tempest came down in its fury, sweeping, tornado-like, from West to East, and then into one grand gyration circling the whole horizon. Men lost courage, confidence, and hope. They stood still while the storm beat down, and the fearful work of destruction went on.

No commercial disaster like this had ever before visited our country. Houses that stood unmoved through many fierce convulsions went down like brittle

T. S. Arthur

reeds, and old Corporations which were thought to be as immovable as the hills tottered and fell, crushing hundreds amid their gigantic ruins.

Among the first to yield was the greatly extended house of Floyd, Lawson, Lee, & Co. The news came up on the wires to S -, with orders to stop the mills and discharge all hands. This was the bursting of the tempest on our town. Mr. Dewey had gone to New York on the first sign of approaching trouble, and his return was looked for anxiously by all with whom he was deeply interested in business. But many days passed and none saw him, or heard from him. Failing to receive any communication, Squire Floyd, who had everything involved, went down to New York. I saw him on the morning of his return. He looked ten years older.

It was soon whispered about that the failure of Floyd, Lawson, Lee, & Co. was a bad one. Then came intimations that Mr. Dewey was not in New York, and that his partners, when questioned about him, gave very unsatisfactory replies.

"Have you any notes of the Clinton Bank, Doctor?" said a friend whom I met in the street. "Because, if you have, take my advice and get rid of them as quickly as possible. A run has commenced, and it's my opinion that the institution will not stand for forty-eight hours."

It stood just forty-eight hours from the date of this prophecy, and then closed its doors, leaving our neighborhood poorer by the disaster over two hundred thousand dollars. There was scarcely a struggle in dying, for the institution had suffered such an exhausting depletion that when its extremity came it passed from existence without a throe. A Receiver was immediately appointed, and the assets examined. These consisted, mainly, of bills receivable under discount, not probably worth now ten cents on the dollar. Three-fourths of this paper was drawn or endorsed by New York firms or individuals, most of whom had already failed. The personal account of Ralph Dewey showed him to be a debtor to the Bank in the sum of nearly a hundred thousand dollars. The President, Joshua Kling, had not been seen since the evening of the day on which the doors of the Clinton Bank were shut, never to be opened for business again. His accounts were all in confusion. The Cashier, who had succeeded him on his elevation to the Presidency of the institution; was a mere creature in his hands; and from his revelations it was plain that robbery had been progressing for some time on a grand scale.

As soon as these disastrous facts became known to the heaviest sufferers in S -, the proper affidavits were made out, and requisitions obtained for both Dewey and Kling, as defaulters and fugitives from justice. The Sheriff of our county, charged with the duty of arrest, proceeded forthwith to New York, and, engaging the services of detectives there, began the search for Dewey, who, it was believed, had not left that city. He was discovered, in a week, after having dexterously eluded pursuit, on the eve of departure for England, disguised, and under an assumed name. His next appearance in S - was as a prisoner in the hands of our Sheriff, who lodged him in jail. Very heavy bonds being required for his appearance at court, there was not found among us any one willing to take the risk, who was qualified to become his surety. And so the wretched man was compelled to lie in prison until the day of trial.

T. S. Arthur

Immediately on his incarceration, he sent for Mr. Wallingford, who visited him without delay. He found him a shrinking, cowed, and frightened culprit; not a man, conscious of rectitude, and therefore firm in bearing, though in a false and dangerous position.

"This is a bad business, Mr. Wallingford," he said, on meeting the lawyer - "a very bad business; and I have sent for you as a professional gentleman of standing and ability, in order to have a consultation in regard to my position - in fact, to place myself wholly in your hands. I must have the best counsel, and therefore take the earliest opportunity to secure your valuable services. Will you undertake my case?"

"That will depend, Mr. Dewey," was answered, "entirely upon how it stands. If you are falsely accused, and can demonstrate to me your innocence, I will defend you to the utmost of my ability, battling your accusers to the last. But if, on the contrary, you cannot show clean hands, I am not the one to undertake your case."

Dewey looked at Mr. Wallingford strangely. He scarcely comprehended him.

"I may have committed mistakes; all men are liable to error," he replied.

"Mistake is one thing, Mr. Dewey, and may be explained; fraud is another thing, and cannot be explained to mean any thing else. What I want you to understand, distinctly, is this: If your connection with the Clinton Bank has been, from the beginning, just and honorable, however much it may now seem to be otherwise, I will undertake your case, and conduct it, I care not through how great difficulties, to a favorable issue. But if it has not been - and you know how it stands - do not commit your fate to me, for I will abandon you the moment I discover that you have been guilty of deliberate wrong to others."

The countenance of Mr. Dewey fell, and he seemed to shudder back into himself. For some time he was silent.

"If there is a foregone conclusion in your mind, that settles the matter," he said, at length, in a disappointed tone.

"All I ask is clear evidence, Mr. Dewey. Foregone conclusions have nothing to do with the matter," replied Mr. Wallingford, "If you know yourself to be innocent, you may trust yourself in my hands; if not, I counsel you to look beyond me to some other man."

"All men are liable to do wrong, Mr. Wallingford; and religion teaches that the door of repentance is open to every one."

"True, but the just punishment of wrong is always needed for a salutary repentance. The contrition that springs from fear of consequences, is not genuine repentance. If you have done wrong, you must take the penalty in some shape, and I am not the man knowingly to stay the just progression of either moral or civil law."

"Will you accept a retaining fee, even if not active in my case?" asked Mr. Dewey.

"No," was the emphatic answer.

A dark, despairing shadow fell over the miserable man's face, and he turned himself away from the only being towards whom he had looked with any hope in this great extremity of his life.

Mr. Wallingford retired with pity in his heart. The spectacle was one of the most painful he had ever witnessed. How was the mighty fallen! - the proud brought low! As he walked from the prison, the Psalmist's striking words passed through his mind - "I have seen the wicked in great power, and spreading himself like a green bay tree; yet he passed away, and lo, he was not."

When the day of trial came, Mr. Wallingford appeared as counsel for the creditors of the Clinton Bank, on the side of the prosecution. He did not show any eagerness to gain his case against the prisoner; but the facts were so strong, and all the links in the chain of evidence so clear, that conviction was inevitable. A series of frauds and robberies was exposed, that filled the community with surprise and indignation; and when the jury, after a brief consultation, brought in a verdict of guilty, the expression of delight was general. Detestation of the man's crimes took away all pity from the common sentiment in regard to him. A sentence of five years' expiation in the State prison closed the career of Ralph Dewey in S -, and all men said: "The retribution is just."

Squire Floyd lost everything, and narrowly escaped the charge of complicity with Dewey. Nothing but the fact of their known antagonism for some two or three years, turned the public mind in his favor, and enabled him to show that what appeared collusion, was only, so far as he was concerned, fair business operations. With the wreck of his fortune he came very near making also a wreck of his good name. Even as it was, there were some in S - who thought the Squire had, in some things, gone far beyond the rule of strict integrity.

Judge Bigelow, thanks to the timely and resolute intervention of Mr. Wallingford, stood far away from the crashing wrecks, when the storm swept down in fearful devastation. It raged around, but did not touch him; for he was safely sheltered, and beyond its reach.

T. S. Arthur

# CHAPTER XXXI.

Two years have passed since these disastrous events; and twenty years since the opening of our story. The causes at work in the beginning, have wrought out their legitimate effects - the tree has ripened its fruits - the harvest has been gathered. The quiet of old times has fallen upon S -. It was only a week ago that steps were taken to set the long silent mills in motion. A company, formed in Boston, has purchased the lower mill, and rented from Mr. Wallingford the upper one, which was built on the Allen estate. Squire Floyd, I learn, is to be the manager here for the company. I am glad of this. Poor man! He was stripped of everything, and has been, for the past two years, in destitute circumstances. How he has contrived to live, is almost a mystery. The elegant house which he had built for himself was taken and sold by creditors, with the furniture, plate, and all things pertaining thereto, and, broken-spirited, he retired to a small tenement on the outskirts of the town, where he has since lived. His unhappy daughter, with her two children, are with him. Her son, old enough to be put to some business, she has placed in a store, where he is earning enough to pay his board; while she and her daughter take in what sewing they can obtain, in order to lessen, as far as possible, the burden of their maintenance. Alas for her that the father of those children should be a convicted felon!

I move about through S - on my round of duties, and daily there comes to me some reminder of the events and changes of twenty years. I see, here and there, a stranded wreck, and think how proudly the vessel spread her white sails in the wind a few short years gone by, freighted with golden hopes. But where are those treasures now? Lost, lost forever in the fathomless sea!

Twenty years ago, and now! As a man soweth, even so shall he reap. Spring time loses itself in luxuriant summer, and autumn follows with the sure result. If the seed has been good, the fruit will be good; but if a man have sown only tares in his fields, he must reap in sorrow and not in joy. There is no exception to the rule. A bramble bush can no more bear grapes, than a selfish and evil life can produce happiness. The one is a natural, and the other a spiritual, impossibility.

A few days ago, as I was riding along on a visit to one of my patients, I met Mr. and Mrs. Wallingford, with two of their children, driving out in their carriage. They stopped, and we were passing a few pleasant words, when there came by two persons, plainly, almost coarsely dressed - a mother and her daughter. Both had bundles in their hands. Over the mother's face a veil was drawn, and as she passed, with evidently quickening steps, she turned herself partly away. The daughter looked at us steadily from her calm blue eyes, in which you saw a shade of sadness, as though already many hopes had failed. Her face was pale and placid, but touched you with its expression of half-concealed suffering, as if, young as she was, some lessons of pain and endurance had already been learned.

T. S. Arthur

"Who are they?" asked Mrs. Wallingford.

"Delia Floyd and her daughter," said I.

No remark was made. If my ears did not deceive me, I heard a faint sigh pass the lips of Mr. Wallingford.

I spoke to my horse, and, bowing mutually, we passed on our ways.

"Twenty years ago, and now!" said I to myself, falling into a sober mood, as thought went back to the sweet, fragrant morning of Delia's life, and I saw it in contrast with this dreary autumn. "If the young would only take a lesson like this to heart!"

In the evening, Mr. Wallingford called to see me.

"I have not been able, all day," said he, "to get the image of that poor woman and her daughter out of my mind. What are their circumstances, Doctor?"

"They live with Squire Floyd," I answered, "and he is very poor. I think Delia and her daughter support themselves by their needles."

"What a fall!" he said, with pity in his tones.

"Yes, it was a sad fall - sad, but salutary, I trust."

"How was she after her separation from Mr. Dewey?"

"Very bitter and rebellious, for a time. His marriage seemed to arouse every evil passion of her nature. I almost shuddered to hear the maledictions she called down upon the head of his wife one day, when she rode by in the elegant equipage of which she had once been the proud owner. She fairly trembled with rage. Since then, the discipline of the inevitable in life has done its better work. She has grown subdued and patient, and is doing all a mother in such narrow circumstances can do for her children."

"What of Dewey's second wife?" asked Mr. Wallingford.

"She has applied for a divorce from him, on the ground that he is a convicted felon; and will get a decree in her favor, without doubt."

"What a history!" he exclaimed. Then, after a pause, he asked -

"Cannot something be done for Mr. Floyd?"

"I have understood," said I, "that the company about to start the mills again have engaged him as manager."

"Is that so? Just what I was thinking," he replied, with animation. "I must look after that matter, and see that it does not fall through."

And he was in this, as in all things, as good as his word. It needed only a favorable intimation from him to decide the company to place their works in the hands of Squire Floyd, who was a man of skill and experience in manufacturing, and one in whose integrity the fullest confidence might be reposed.

A month has passed; and Squire Floyd, engaged at a salary of two thousand dollars a year, is again at the mills, busy in superintending repairs, improvements, and additions. A few more weeks, and the rattle of industry will commence, and the old aspect of things show itself in S -. May the new mill owners be wiser than their predecessors!

Squire Floyd has removed from the poor tenement lately the home of his depressed family, and is back in the pleasant homestead he abandoned years ago, when pride and ambition impelled him to put on a grander exterior. It is understood that the company have bought the house, and rent it to him at a very moderate price. My own impression is, that Mr. Wallingford has more to do in the matter than people imagine. I am strengthened in this view, from the fact of having seen Mrs. Wallingford call at the Squire's twice during the past week. They are in good hands, and I see a better future in store for them.

And now, reader, you have the story I wished to tell. It is full of suggestion to all who are starting forth upon life's perilous journey. Let truth, honor, integrity, and humanity, govern all your actions. Do not make haste to be rich, lest you fall into divers temptations. Keep always close to the right; and always bear in mind that no wrong is ever done that does not, sooner or later, return upon the wrong-doer.

And above all, gentle maiden, be not dazzled by the condition or prospect of any who seek your hand.

Look away, down, deeply into the character, disposition, and quality; and if these are not of good seeming, shun the proffered alliance as you would death. Better, a thousand times, pass through life alone than wed yourself to inevitable misery. So heeding the moralist, you will not, in the harvest time which comes to all, look in despair over your barren fields, but find them golden with Autumn's treasures, that shall fill your granaries and crown your latter days with blessing.

T. S. Arthur